HER MONTANA COWBOY

JEANNIE WATT

MILLS & BOON

First Published in Great Britain 2018
by Mills & Boon, an imprint of HarperCollins*Publishers*
1 London Bridge Street, London, SE1 9GF

Her Montana Cowboy © 2018 Jeannie Steinman

ISBN: 978-0-263-26539-2

1018

MIX
Paper from
responsible sources
FSC™ C007454

This book is produced from independently certified FSC™ paper to ensure responsible forest management.

For more information visit: www.harpercollins.co.uk/green

Printed and bound in Spain
by CPI, Barcelona

This book is dedicated to my amazing niece, Hanna.
Thank you for carrying on the tradition.

CHAPTER ONE

FOR THE PAST several months, Lillie Jean Hardaway had had only two kinds of luck—amazingly good and crazy bad. The seesaw was starting to get to her. Now, as she braced her palms against the door of her car and let her head hang down in defeat, she wondered how she was going to get herself out of this latest instance of crazy bad.

After a couple deep breaths, she stepped back, surveyed her surroundings. The Montana sun had disappeared behind the mountains shortly after her last attempt to drive out of the deep muddy ruts that stubbornly held her car captive, and it was getting dark. Soon it would be seriously dark, so she had to make a decision—follow the road, which, according to the weathered sign she'd passed as she'd turned off the main road, led to the H/H Ranch, or stay with her car and walk in the morning.

Tough choice.

If she was going to walk tonight, she needed to start soon. Her phone was fully charged, so she could use its flashlight when it became too dark to see. And she had her protection dog, Henry—a Chihuahua-dachshund mix wearing a Christmas sweater because it was the only warm garment she could find on short notice. Who knew that Montana was so cold in the spring?

Lillie wrapped her arms around herself as she stared down the long road. What kinds of predators lurked out there, waiting for the cover of darkness? She shuddered at the thought. She knew nothing about fighting off wolves. Should she carry a tire iron or something?

On the other hand, while she had a coat, she had no blanket and it was already getting cold.

Cold? Or wolves in the night?

Lillie went with cold. She and Henry could huddle together for warmth.

Letting out a long sigh, she walked around to the driver's side to pop the truck latch. It took a little searching by the dim light that shone down into the packed trunk, but finally she found the tire iron under one of her three suitcases. She took it with her as she situated herself in the front seat of the car, reclining the seat back as far as it would go before settling in for what was no doubt going to be a long miserable night.

Yet another tick mark in the "this sucks" column of life. Lillie Jean's mouth drooped. Until the beginning of this calendar year, she hadn't had all that many bad experiences. Her childhood had been pleasant and uneventful. She deeply missed her mom, who'd succumbed to breast cancer two years ago, just before Lillie Jean's twenty-fourth birthday, but after that devastating loss, life had once again shifted back into its normal path. She'd started her small business with her boyfriend, Andrew, who eventually became her fiancé, Andrew. Then, six months before the wedding, he'd become ex-fiancé/business-stealer Andrew.

Lillie Jean rubbed her forehead.

Naive, naive, naive.

Oh, did I mention the part about being naive?

Yeah. I got it. Never again.

She was starting from scratch—financially and emotionally. She was going to watch her back from here on out. If the past several months had taught her anything, it was that there were no excuses for being caught unaware. A little due diligence on her part, and she'd probably still be an owner of A Thread in Time, and she would have cut loose Andrew a long time ago, instead of being caught off guard and humiliated.

A howl in the distance brought Lillie Jean's head up and made her heart beat a little faster. Cold was definitely better than wolves. Henry snuggled up against her as if to say, "Don't worry. I'll fight those wild beasts for you," because her little dog had yet to figure out that he wasn't ten feet tall. Lillie Jean stroked his ears, then reached out to touch the cool metal of the tire iron leaning against the gearshift and told herself to be thankful it was March and not January. Although, obviously, March in Montana could be brutal, too.

Maybe that was why her grandfather had left the state for the warmth of central Texas all those years ago.

She'd only know if Thaddeus Hawkins, his business partner, had answers to share. The lawyer hadn't been able to tell her anything after her grandfather's unexpected death three weeks ago, except that, in addition to inheriting his personal effects, she would soon be half owner of a Montana ranch. She could truthfully say she still wasn't over the shock of that meeting. Her grandfather had rented a small house in a modest neighborhood. Driven a twenty-year-old car, which she was driving now. Rarely splurged and had next to no savings. Yet he'd owned half interest in a ranch—eight hundred acres according to the documents. Small by Texas standards, but still, a ranch. Which she hadn't known about. She and her grandfather had been close, the last of the Hardaway line, and she was still trying to figure out if she felt more mystified or betrayed at being kept in the dark.

A secret ranch. Why?

She hoped the answer lay at the end of the long road she was on…if she ever got there. She wanted to see the place and introduce herself to Thaddeus Hawkins, her grandfather's former business partner. She had no intentions of lying about who she was or why she was there, but she didn't think it would hurt to do a little anonymous reconnaissance first. Her experience with Andrew had left her feeling cautious, nowhere close to trusting people blindly as she'd once done. Learning about the ranch had only reinforced the fact that there were just too many secrets in this world, too much double-dealing to take anything at face value.

No matter what, she was never going to be caught off guard again.

Gus Hawkins yawned as he turned onto the ranch road. His last official shift at the Shamrock Pub, which he owned with his Uncle Thad, had been something. Even though he would still fill in as needed, the patrons of the popular Gavin, Montana, bar had treated the event as a wake. Some brought food. Others brought gag gifts, which was why he now had a temporary tattoo of an anchor on the back of his neck and a lip print on his forehead. One of the college girls had offered him a particularly personal going away present, but he'd gently turned her down. He wouldn't miss the nightly headaches of the pub, but he would miss the people. The majority of them, anyway.

He slowed as he rounded a series of corners, watching the edge of road as his headlights cut through the darkness. The snow was mostly melted—for now, anyway. Late spring snow and ice storms were a regular occurrence, and since the H/H Ranch still had a number of cows to calve out, there was certain to be one last nasty storm, which would probably coincide with a particularly difficult birth. But for the time being, the new grass was growing and the deer were active as they moved from the valleys to the foothills, following the melt and new growth. He'd had a close call the night before with a large doe and wasn't all that keen to have another one.

As he topped the hill, he could just see the ranch yard lights in the distance. The place that had been his home since he was fifteen would now be his sole place of employment. He'd essentially worked full-time on the ranch for the past several months, as Salvatore, the H/H's aging ranch manager, came to terms with the fact that he couldn't do as much as he once could. Then, after the ranch work was done for the day, Gus put in full shifts at the pub four or five nights a week. The schedule had been grueling—especially during calving season—but Thad had needed the help and Sal needed time. Now Sal was living with his brother in Dillon, and Gus was done double shifting. It'd been easier to hire a good bartender than a good ranch manager, and he had no doubt that Ginny Monroe was more than up to the task of running the bar with Thad. And Thad liked her... maybe more than he wanted to let on.

Go, Ginny. Thad had been single for too darned long.

Gus was smiling at the thought of Ginny easing Thad out of his long bachelorhood as he started back down the hill, driving on the wrong side of the dirt road to avoid the hellacious mud puddle that had formed at the bottom, just around the blind corner. The smile abruptly disappeared as he rounded the corner and found the back end of a giant car directly in front of him. He swung hard to the left, then pulled back onto the road and eased to a stop after barely missing the vehicle. Mystified, he grabbed his flashlight out of the door-panel pocket and got out of his truck, walked back to the car and shined the light on the license plate.

Texas?

What was a gas-guzzling vehicle from Texas doing stuck in the mud on the ranch driveway? No one, save parcel delivery rigs and seasonal hunters, ventured onto this road. Gus pushed back his hat, then stilled as he caught a movement inside the car.

It looked like he was about to get an answer to his question…or so he thought before the head in the car ducked out of sight.

Huh.

He moved closer and bent forward in an attempt to see through the darkly tinted windows into the interior of the car, wondering if someone had left their dog inside to guard the car while they went for help. No…that was definitely a person in there, hunched down in the seat. Probably scared.

"Hi," he called. "I live on this road. Do you need some help?"

Obviously they needed help, since their car was axle-deep in the mud.

For a moment there was no movement, and then the person leaned across the seat and turned the key, then rolled the window down about an inch.

"I'm Gus Hawkins. I live about five miles down the road. Can I call someone or give you a lift?"

"You live on the H/H Ranch?"

The voice was feminine. Husky. Nervous.

"I do."

"Oh."

Gus waited for more. He didn't get it. "Is that where you were going?"

"Yes. I…uh…thought that Thaddeus Hawkins lived there. Is he a relative?"

His insides went cold when the woman mentioned Thad's name. Oh, please, not again.

"He's my uncle."

A shiver went through her as she stared up at him through three-inch opening in the window. He had no idea who she was, or what her intentions were toward his uncle, but he couldn't leave her there to spend the night in her car.

"Look—it's cold out here. Do you want a lift?"

"I…uh…yes. Thank you." She scooched back across the seat and got out of the passenger side, a small dog under her arm and what looked a whole lot like a tire iron in one hand.

"You aren't going to conk me with that and steal my truck, are you?" he asked, starting to rethink his offer of a lift. "Because if you are, you should know that there isn't enough fuel to get back to town."

In the reflected lights of the headlamps, it looked as if the woman was blushing. "I have no designs on your truck."

"Good to know." He smiled, trying to look friendly, while still wondering if he wanted a woman carrying a tire iron riding with him. "These are unusual circumstances and we can sort things out when we get to the ranch, but right now I gotta tell you it makes me nervous having you armed like that."

"I don't understand."

"I don't know you," he explained. *You might be crazy.*

"I don't know you," she pointed out as the little dog lifted his lip to show his teeth in a ridiculous display of bravado.

"I'm not carrying a big chunk of metal to hit you with.

Besides—you know my name. I don't know yours. Or why you're here."

"My name is… Lillie Jean. The rest I'll discuss with Thaddeus."

Gus closed his eyes, then quickly opened them again. She was carrying a tire iron, after all. "How do you suggest we come to a compromise, Lillie Jean?"

It took her less than a second to say, "Pull me out?"

Just what he wanted to do at 2:00 a.m. He jerked his head toward his warm truck. "Grab your tire iron and let's go."

"To the ranch."

"Yes." Now that he knew she was there to see Thad, he wanted to keep an eye on her. The last incident might have been online, but Thad coming so close to losing so much money had Gus on alert. For all he knew Thad may have met this woman online, and she was here for… He hated to think.

She didn't move, so he added, "You can either come with me, or stay with your car. There is no option *c*."

It might have been the swirl of icy wind sweeping by them that decided her, but whatever the reason, she gave a nod, hugging her dog a little closer as she did so.

"Let me get my bag."

Instead of following instinct and offering to help, Gus stood back as she awkwardly balanced dog and tire iron while dragging a zippered gym bag out of the backseat. Finally she shut the door with her hip, then headed toward the passenger side of the truck. When she got inside, he had his first good look at her face in the light and found that he had to take a second. Dark hair waved around her face and fell down her back, but it was her eyes that had made him look again. Maybe it was a trick of the light, but the blue-green color reminded him of his favorite alpine fishing lake—a place he hadn't had time to visit in well over a year.

She placed the gym bag on the console between them, forming an impressive barrier, then settled in her seat, fastening her seat belt as Gus shut his door. He had no idea what she'd done with her weapon, and as he started back down the road, he tried to put himself in her position, assuming that she wasn't there for a nefarious purpose. A lone female in the middle of nowhere with no cell signal and only a dog in a reindeer sweater for protection. Of course she was nervous.

But why was she traveling to the ranch, and how did she know Thaddeus?

Why would she come to the ranch without calling first?

Gus hoped that he really was rescuing the woman rather than giving trouble a ride to the ranch, but his gut told him that a woman who gave her name reluctantly was not a woman he wanted staying at his place.

LILLIE JEAN KEPT her eyes forward as the truck bounced over ruts and skirted vehicle-eating puddles. This situation was surreal. She was no longer in control—of anything, it seemed—but she did her best to appear unconcerned about her lack of power.

"How long were you stuck?"

Lillie Jean gave her rescuer a quick sideways look. He had a strong profile, high cheekbones. A chin that kind of said, "Don't mess with me." Dark brown scruff covered his jaw, but it looked as if it was the result of forgetting to shave, rather than an affectation, as was often the case where she came from. She thought his hair might be dark blond, but too much of it was hidden by the battered cowboy hat to be sure. He did not look like someone who would hurt her, but she was in the middle of nowhere and he was a stranger, so she was taking no chances. Henry also kept an eye on the guy while pressing his warm body against her chest. Her little dog was taking no chances, either.

"Since around four o'clock." She'd arrived in the small town of Gavin around three o'clock and decided to drive to the ranch, take a look at her inheritance, meet her grandfather's partner, then head back to town and stay in a motel for the night. She should have gone with her *other* plan of heading out to the ranch first thing in the morning, but she had a feeling she would have still gotten stuck.

"Long time."

"I never expected a mud puddle to be on the other side of the corner."

"Always expect the unexpected on a country road."

And in life. Lillie Jean sat a little straighter in her seat as the lights of the ranch came into view and stayed there instead of disappearing as they crested small hills. What now? She'd meet Thaddeus Hawkins late at night. Probably get him out of bed. He and his nephew might offer her a bed. And she would accept, because what was her other option?

This was not the position she'd hoped to be in when she arrived.

She should have called ahead. Should have set up an appointment via her grandfather's lawyer. There were a ton of things she should have done. Maybe it was grief, maybe it was the need to simply get away from her old life, but climbing into the boat of a car that her grandfather had kept for "old time's sake" and driving to Montana to see the ranch and ferret out some answers from Grandpa's partner before seeing if he wanted to buy her share had seemed like a good idea. No—it had seemed like a way to take control of a life that seemed to be barreling out of control. And, indeed, as she'd driven north, she'd started to feel almost intrepid, following a course that was so out of the ordinary for her. She was in control, and, darn it, she was going to get answers. She'd played over many scenarios in her head as she'd driven—and not one of them had ended like this.

The cowboy—Gus—slowed as he drove under a weathered wooden arch into the ranch proper, which was nothing like Lillie Jean had envisioned. A light on a tall pole illuminated two small run-down houses and another light shone on a cluster of weathered buildings—a barn and several sheds. There was movement in the shadows behind the fence next to the barn. Henry's hackles lifted and he let out a low growl.

"Better keep hold of him until we get into the house. You don't want him disappearing out into the pasture."

"Are those horses?" she asked as Gus pulled to a stop next to a picket fence.

"Cows." He shut off the engine and the headlights faded.

Cows. Of course. It was a ranch.

They opened their doors at the same time. Lillie Jean scooped up Henry and held him against her chest with one hand as she pulled her tote bag out of the truck with the other. The tire iron stayed where it was, lying on the floorboards. She felt a little foolish about her self-protective measures, but if she had it to do again, she'd do the exact same thing. A wooden sign attached to the gatepost welcomed her to the H/H Ranch. Lillie Jean's mouth tightened. The H/H didn't feel very welcoming…but it was half hers. The land was worth something even if all the buildings looked as if they were about to fall down.

Once the gate was closed behind her, she put Henry on

the ground and followed Gus up the uneven walkway to the back door. Henry quickly did his business, then hurried back to Lillie Jean. Gus opened the door, and they walked directly into a mudroom with boots lining the wall and a broad assortment of coats and hats hanging on hooks above them. The room was freshly swept and baskets of folded clothing sat atop the washer and dryer next to the door leading into the house.

Gus crossed to the door, snapped on a light and stood back so that she could enter first. The big kitchen was as neat as the mudroom. The oak table in the center of the room was an antique and the simple white appliances were close to being antique.

"You can sleep in Thad's room. Give me a sec and I'll get you some sheets."

"Where will Thad sleep?" she asked, horrified at the idea of rousting the old man out of bed and sending him to sleep who knew where.

"Where he's probably sleeping right now. In the apartment over the bar."

"What bar?"

"The Shamrock Pub. His bar. Our bar."

"I don't understand."

"Thad doesn't live on the ranch. He hasn't lived here for years. He only stays here when he needs to pitch in around the place."

Lillie Jean's mouth fell open. "You're saying…"

"It's just you and me here tonight." He folded his arms over his chest and his expression wasn't at all amused as he said, "Do you want to go back to the truck for your weapon?"

CHAPTER TWO

TWENTY MINUTES LATER, Lillie Jean was lying in a twin bed, staring at the ceiling, too keyed up to go to sleep even though it was almost 3:00 a.m. Gus had handed her sheets for the stripped bed, pointed her in the direction of the bathroom, then disappeared down the hall to a room at the end.

None of this is going according to plan.

Not one thing. Thaddeus had been in the town she'd driven through on her way to the ranch, and, as things stood now, she was dependent on a guy who was probably going to be none too happy when he discovered the reason she was at the ranch in the first place.

A guy who didn't know her last name, because she hadn't wanted to tip her hand.

A guy with lip prints on his forehead

That had been startling. It had taken a moment for her to realize that the prints weren't lipstick. She didn't want to think about what the prints *were* made of or how they got there. None of her business, but seeing them had been enough to make her flip the lock on the bedroom door. She knew nothing about this guy, except that he was extremely good-looking and walked with just a hint of a limp.

Lillie Jean rolled over, pulling the sheet with her. Her insurance covered towing, so tomorrow she'd call her company and have them get her car out of the mud—

if they would travel out this far to rescue her. She truly was isolated out here in the middle of Nowhere, Montana. There were other ranches in the vicinity—she'd seen lights in the distance as she'd followed Gus into the house—but for all intents and purposes, she was stranded in a place with no close neighbors, no easy access.

Again…nothing going according to plan.

Kind of the theme in her life over the past months.

Suck it up. The one thing she would not succumb to was self-pity. Her mom would have her hide for that…or rather, she would have had it. Lillie Jean had grown up knowing that even if she was a touch shy, and even if she wasn't confrontational, she was expected to be strong and roll with the punches. She'd done a crazy thing coming here to Montana on impulse, and now she was suffering consequences. A natural part of life.

She squeezed her eyes shut, felt a touch of moisture at the corners at the thought of her mother. Drew in a deep breath and did her best to come to terms with the situation at hand.

I'm rolling, Mom.

I'm rolling so hard that I get dizzy sometimes.

GUS SCRUBBED AWAY at the lip print on his forehead, then gave up in disgust. If he didn't stop scrubbing, he'd have no skin left. No wonder the woman had looked at him so strangely the night before when he'd come back with the sheets. She'd stared at his forehead, then looked down with a few mumbled words of thanks before disappearing into the bedroom. As expected, he'd heard the lock click shut.

Thank you, Mimi, for the "temporary" tattoo and the strategic placement.

The door to Thad's room was closed as he went by on

his way to the kitchen. He started the coffee, then went to the mudroom, slid his feet into his chore boots and shrugged into his heavy canvas coat before heading out to start the tractor. After feeding, he'd roust the woman and before they took the tractor down to pull her car out of the mud, he was going to get some answers. Like who was she and what did she want with his uncle? He wasn't a big fan of mysteries and secrets. He'd let her hedge the night before, but now that they'd gotten a few hours of sleep, he wanted to know what was what before dragging Thad into it.

There was just enough frozen moisture in the air to feel sharp as he drew it into his lungs, and to coat the gravel with a thin skiff of frost. He unplugged the tractor's block heater, started the big machine and left it to idle while he fed the barn cats and then tossed hay over the fence to the horses.

He crossed the driveway with a scoop of food for Clancy, the cat who lived under the front porch of the empty manager's house. Clancy popped his head out, then disappeared back under the porch when Gus set down the bowl, pushing it far enough under the floorboards to allow the cat to feel safe while eating. He then snagged the empty bowl from yesterday and carried it back to the barn with him. The cat had never warmed up to anyone other than Sal, but was too wild for the old guy to take him with him when he retired to Dillon.

When Gus returned to the barn forty-five minutes later, after feeding two pastures of hungry cows, he left the tractor running. If his guest was out of bed, he was ready to yank her car out of the mud—after she answered a few questions.

He heard water running in the bathroom when he walked into the kitchen, so he poured a cup of coffee from the full carafe and sipped it while leaning against the counter. The house felt different with someone else in it. Strange how vibes or energy levels or something like that changed. And the house didn't feel the same way it did when his uncle spent the night.

Finally footsteps went to the bedroom, then a few seconds later he heard Lillie Jean coming down the hall to the kitchen. Last night he'd come to the conclusion that his guest reminded him of the Disney princesses on the T-shirt Callie, his fill-in bartender, regularly wore. She was small with a lot of dark hair falling down her back and framing her face. Nice mouth, wide eyes. Suspicious wide eyes. She wet her lips as their gazes met and her back went just a little straighter.

"Good morning."

It was almost but not quite a question. She moved past him to check to see if the yard gate was closed, then opened the back door and let her dog outside.

"Good morning. Coffee?"

"Please."

She hovered near the doorway as he poured her coffee, and then he set the cup on the table and took the chair at the other end. A few seconds later she opened the door and the little dog raced in, his nails clacking on the mudroom floor.

"Nice sweater," Gus said drily.

"Henry doesn't have a lot of hair. Can't have him freezing to death."

"No. I guess not."

"This was the only sweater I could find in a gas station when I realized how cold it was up here."

Lillie Jean pulled out the chair and sat, taking hold of the coffee cup with both hands, but making no move to drink.

"Things look different in the light of day?"

She gave him a startled look. "What does that mean?"

Gus regarded the table between them, a frown pulling his eyebrows together. Play the game or cut to the chase?

He looked up, met those blue-green eyes and made his decision. Cut to the chase. How many people had this woman twisted around her finger with that innocent expression and those startling eyes? However many, he wasn't going to be one of them.

"Who are you and why are you here?"

Her eyes went wide at the blunt question, then narrowed as she pressed her lips together, her gaze never leaving his face. At least she didn't play coy. Gus had no patience with eye batting and mock shyness, having dealt with that particular come-on about a zillion times during his shifts at the pub.

"I told you my name and I'll discuss the rest with Thaddeus when I get back to town."

"Why do you want to see him?"

"Are you his keeper?" she responded coolly.

Lillie Jean looked like a waif in the storm, but she had some backbone. "No. I'm his nephew and I watch his back."

"I will not come at him from behind."

Was she messing with him? Three years of tending bar at the pub had given him a pretty good feel for people, but now he suspected his first read on Ms. Jean was off base. Maybe he wouldn't be able to intimidate her into telling him her mission. But he was going to give it another shot.

"Why are you here?" he asked softly.

"I need to talk to Thaddeus. It's…personal."

Her continued use of his proper name threw him. "How do you know him?"

"I don't. But we have mutual acquaintances."

"Who sent you here?"

She put her palms on the table on either side of her coffee cup. "I don't know you, so pardon me if I don't unburden myself to you upon request."

Now Gus's eyes narrowed as he regarded the woman across the table. He'd definitely read her wrong. Her delicate appearance and the fact that she'd been rattled the night before had thrown him off track. This woman was a straight-talker. Now it was up to him to discover if that was good or bad.

"Tell you what… I'll call Thad, tell him you're here, and he can decide whether he wants to see you."

It took her less than a second to say, "Very well."

He pushed his chair back and went to the old-fashioned wall phone hanging near the fridge. He hoped Thad wasn't going to kill him for getting him out of bed early, but this matter needed to be dealt with. His uncle's voice was thick with sleep when he answered on the fifth ring, and then he cleared his throat and said hello once again.

"It's me," Gus said. He glanced over at Lillie Jean who sat watching him, an impassive look on her face. "There's a person here at the ranch who wants to talk to you."

"Who?"

"Her name is Lillie Jean."

"I don't know a Lillie Jean." Thad sounded bemused. Gus knew the feeling. From behind him Lillie cleared her throat.

"Hardaway," she said. He gave her a confused look. "Lillie Jean Hardaway."

Gus gave his head a shake and repeated what she'd said. "Hardaway. Lillie Jean Hardaway."

There was a silence on the other end of the phone, and then Thad said, "I'll be right out."

Gus frowned at the change in Thad's voice. "Wait. Explain what's going on."

"I will." He exhaled loudly. "When I get there. Just… make sure she doesn't leave."

"I don't think that will be an issue," Gus said. "Her car is axle-deep in the mud on the blind corner. Watch yourself coming around it."

"I will." Was it his imagination, or did his uncle suddenly sound older? "I'll be there in forty minutes."

Which meant he was pretty much going to put on his clothes and walk out the door. Which in turn meant that he was in some way familiar with Lillie Jean Hardaway and that seeing her was important enough that he wasn't going to burn any daylight before doing so.

"I'm curious," Gus said, folding his arms over his chest. "Why you didn't give me your last name? Why did you let me assume that Jean was your last name?"

"I'm cautious," she said matter-of-factly.

"That's not an explanation."

"I told you…"

"I know. You don't know me. You don't know Thad, either."

"That doesn't really matter."

He was about to ask why when she frowned at him.

"I have to ask," she said in a way that made him think she was purposely changing the subject, "what happened to your forehead?"

"I'm *not* overly cautious," he said darkly. Which was a lie. He was always careful in his dealings, which was why Lillie Jean's appearance on the ranch was sending up so many red flags.

"Is that a tattoo?"

Gus ran his hand over his forehead. The skin was still tender from the scrubbing, but the mark was just as dark as when Mimi had put it on him the night before. That was the last time he let a roll of the bar dice decide his future.

"It's supposed to be temporary."

"Not the result of a drunken trip to the ink parlor?"

He didn't have to ask why she assumed it would be a drunken trip. What kind of sober person would do this to themselves? "It was part of a going-away party gag gift."

"Are you going somewhere?" she asked politely, although he also read a hopeful note in her voice.

"I worked my last shift at the bar last night. Now I'm full-time manager here."

An odd expression flickered across her face, there, then gone. "On the ranch."

"Yes."

She finally lifted her cup to take a drink. Seconds ticked by and Gus found himself gripping the edge of the counter.

"Where are you from?"

"A smallish town not far from Austin, Texas."

"That's quite a distance. How long did it take you to get here?"

"Several days. I took it slow." She looked out the window at the bare branched trees edging the yard. "Do you mind if I step outside?"

"Not at all." At least he couldn't think of a reason to object. He didn't trust her, though. Not even a little bit. This whole "air of mystery" thing was getting old, but Thad would be there in less than half an hour and maybe then he'd have some answers. In the meanwhile, he'd shut off the tractor, have another cup of coffee and wonder what the hell Lillie Jean Hardaway was up to.

MONTANA SMELLED GOOD. Lillie Jean would give it that. There was a cold snap to the air that made her feel like shivering as she drew in the scent of evergreens and moist earth. Wrapping her coat more tightly around herself, she walked down the concrete steps leading from the back door to the broken sidewalk. The front entrance was slightly grander, sporting an actual porch and wooden stairs, but the newels were leaning a little and as she walked further into the yard, she could see that the porch roof needed replacing.

Fine. She wasn't there for the house.

She made her way to the driveway and walked toward the big green tractor parked there. When she was midway between the house and barn, she turned back toward the house, fairly certain she'd catch Gus Hawkins watching her through the window. Sure enough, there he was. He made no effort to step back or to appear as if he wasn't keeping an eye on her. He didn't trust her, and, truly, she couldn't blame him. If positions were reversed, she wouldn't trust her, either, but she wasn't going to let anything slip until she met Thaddeus Hawkins. If there was bad blood between Thaddeus and her grandfather, why hadn't one of them sold his part of the ranch to the other and walked away? Or sold it to someone else? There had to be a reason for that.

There also had to be a reason that her grandfather never once mentioned the ranch to her. Considering the fact that she was his lone surviving relative, that was borderline amazing. And hurtful.

Her nerves jumped when she saw a truck come over the hill in the distance. The problem with her current situation, as opposed to yesterday when she'd tried to drive to the ranch, was that she had no means of escape. Right now, escape sounded good.

Sucking in a breath of crisp air, she turned and walked back to the house, pushing her hands deep into her pockets as she walked and trying very hard to remember just why she thought this might be a good idea.

Answers. She wanted to know why she hadn't known about this place. Who Thaddeus Hawkins was and why she'd never heard about him. And she wanted to know if Thaddeus would buy her half of the ranch. She needed the money to start a new life, a new business, a new everything. It'd be a lot easier and faster to unload it to the man who already owned the other half.

CHAPTER THREE

GUS HAD HAD no idea what to expect after Thad parked his pride and joy—a '72 Ford F250 that guzzled gas as if it had a hole in the tank—next to the tractor and made his way to the house. He came in the back door as usual, then stopped dead when he caught sight of the woman sitting at the table, still wearing her coat.

"Lillie Jean Hardaway?" he asked, as if there might be another woman in the house he didn't know.

"Yes." She got to her feet, squared her shoulders, then crossed the room to hold out a small hand. Thad swallowed, looking as if he was half-afraid to have Lillie Jean touch him. They shook hands, and then Lillie Jean clasped her hands in front of her and Thad stuck his deep in his pockets. For a long moment he stared at her, as if trying to convince himself that she was real.

"I wouldn't mind some coffee," he finally said in a low voice.

Thad looked like he needed more than coffee, but without waiting for Gus to acknowledge his coffee request, he pulled out a chair and sat, motioning Lillie Jean to sit opposite him. Once she was seated, he said, "How is your grandfather?"

"He passed away three weeks ago."

Thad's forehead crumpled. "Sorry to hear that." The comment was perfunctory, but Gus could see that the news impacted his uncle deeply. He set a cup of coffee in front of Thad, then moved back to his vantage point on the other side of the kitchen. He'd give them some space, but he wasn't leaving his uncle alone with this woman. Not unless he received a direct order.

"Yes. It was peaceful. He'd been having health issues, but we didn't expect him to go so soon." Lillie Jean glanced down, pursed her lips as if gearing herself up for some big announcement. "There was some trouble finding the will. Lawyers' offices moving." She waved a hand. "When it did surface…he left me his half of the ranch. I found out about it last week."

"I hadn't heard anything," Thad said in a low voice. "No one's been in contact."

"They will be."

Gus's back jerked straight as the meaning of the conversation became clear. "Wait a minute. Half of *this* ranch?"

"Yeah." Thad met his gaze, his expression solemn. "Lyle and I started this ranch as partners."

Thad had a partner? With the exception of the time he'd spent bull riding, Gus had lived on the ranch since he was fifteen, and he and his uncle had always been close—so why the hell was this the first he'd ever heard about the ranch having dual ownership. "So he's like what? A silent partner?"

"I guess you could call it that." Thad turned back to Lillie Jean, leaving Gus to stare at him. "I have a little money in the ranch account that will be yours, too." Thad smiled grimly. "The accountant sent Lyle a yearly check. It was never that much, but we only went in the red a couple of times over the past few decades."

"Decades." Gus realized that his mouth had fallen open and quickly shut it. Funny how you could get out of bed one morning and everything was fine and a little more than twenty-four hours later, you find out that the truth as you know it, isn't the truth at all.

"How do we know that Lyle Hardaway is really your grandfather?"

Both Thad and Lillie Jean looked his way, but before either could speak, he said to Thad, "Doesn't it seem kind of unusual for you to get no word of your partner's death and then she shows up out of the blue, saying that she's your new partner?"

"I have identification." Lillie Jean spoke coldly.

"In this day and age, that doesn't mean a lot." Maybe he was being rude, but from the moment he'd set eyes on this woman, she'd been secretive. Maybe he'd tended bar for too long, but her story just didn't smell right. "Why hasn't Thad heard from the executor?"

"I told you they just found the will." She glanced over at Thad. "You'll get your copy soon. Everything except his car was designated transfer-at-death."

"Did you bring a copy?" he asked.

"I did."

"Tell you what," Thad said to Lillie Jean. "Why don't you let my nephew and me have a few minutes and then I can take a look at the document?"

"Sure." Lillie Jean pushed her chair back and stood, leaving her barely touched coffee sitting on the table. "I'll take a walk."

"It's cold out there."

"I don't mind."

The little dog looked like he minded. When Lillie Jean pulled her coat off the chair, he gave her a startled "Again?" look, but trotted after her when she headed for the mudroom. Gus waited until she stepped outside and pulled the door shut behind her before turning to Thad and saying, "I had no idea you had a partner." He sounded harsh, but then he was feeling harsh. All the times they'd talked about Gus taking over the operation of the ranch and never a mention of a partner. And now that partner was dead and who knew what his heir was about to do?

"Not something I talk about."

"Obviously, but if I'm the manager of the place, don't you think it would have been good for me to know there's someone else involved?"

"It's only been on paper."

"Kind of more than paper now." He turned to the window, watched Lillie Jean pace near the trucks, giving them the privacy he needed to process this gut-wrenching turn of events. "What kind of agreement did you and Lyle make?"

"A thorough one."

"Can she sell?"

"Yeah." The answer came out on a short definitive note. "If her claim is legitimate, she can sell."

Gus let out a breath, pushed his hands over his forehead. Cursed under his breath. So much for the business plan he'd drawn up. And the comfortable feeling of knowing his future.

"I don't blame you for being mad," Thad said.

"I'm not mad." He had no right to be mad. He didn't own any part of the ranch. He'd lived there, worked the land, managed the animals since he was a teen. It *felt* like his place...but it wasn't.

"Yeah. You are."

Yeah, he was. But more than that he was stunned that Thad had never told him any of this—and hurt. Mad felt a whole lot better than hurt.

Thad was studying him with a tight look on his face, waiting for a response of some kind. Gus did his best to focus on the main issue in front of them.

"This woman showing up out of nowhere concerns me. She could be anyone."

"I'm pretty sure she's Lyle's granddaughter."

"Why?"

"Well, for one thing, his name was Lyle Gene. Her name is Lillie Jean."

Gus stared at his uncle. "I hope you have more than that."

"There's a resemblance," Thad said in a low voice.

"How long's it been since you've seen this guy?" When Thad gave him a questioning look, he added, "Memories fade."

"Some don't." There was a tone in his uncle's voice that brought a frown to his face. "She doesn't look like Lyle…she looks like her grandmother."

"You know her well?"

Thad gave a small snort. "You could say that…we were married for three years."

That was the point where Gus felt the need to sit down. "You were married to Lillie Jean's grandmother?" It was no secret that Thad had divorced long ago, before Gus had been born.

"Yeah. Married Nita and started the ranch the same year. Three years later, Lyle and Nita left for Texas, and I had the ranch all to myself."

"Son of a…" Gus blew out a breath. Shook his head as if to clear it. "But you guys remained partners."

"We communicated through accountants and lawyers. I couldn't afford to buy Lyle out."

"In all these years."

Thad turned his coffee cup in his hands. "It was something I'd always meant to address…but never did. I let the days slip by. Sent him a check every year." He raised his gaze in a quick jerk. "I never had enough to buy him out, okay?"

But he'd managed to buy the pub they now owed together. That was telling.

Gus tilted his head toward the window where Lillie Jean was walking near the barn. "Even if she is a carbon copy of your ex-wife, you still don't know she's who she says she is. Maybe she's a niece or something. Someone who doesn't have claim."

"You're right."

The words didn't ring true. Thad was already convinced of Lillie Jean's identity.

"Get some ID and take a long hard look at that will. Better yet, let your lawyer take a long hard look."

Thad nodded, but his gaze was still fixed on the table. "Lyle never asked anything of me...he felt guilty because he and Nita fell in love."

"Must have been a hell of a guilt to have let that much money lay fallow for so many years when he had the right to sell."

That seemed highly unlikely. Yeah. There was a lot to be ironed out, checked out and generally dealt with. Although...maybe this did solve one mystery.

"Is this why you moved to town?"

"I never liked it here after Nita left. The place felt empty. Sad."

"But you kept it." He could have sold for a major profit in recent years, but hadn't. Instead he'd bought the bar, poured his time and energy into it, building it from nothing while Salvatore ran the ranch.

Thad gave him a fierce look. "I worked like hell to keep my head above water for years. Just to show Lyle and Nita that I could do it without them. I was angry. Bitter. Buried myself on the place. Went a little nuts I think.

I didn't realize just how bitter I was until I had that accident. Didn't know if I was going to make it back to the
ranch." He gave a laugh. "I had a lot of time to think as
I dragged myself back to the trail."

The accident had happened right around the time Gus
had been born. Thad's horse had lost footing on a steep
trail, rolled down the mountain, landed on Thad and
broke his leg. Tough old Thad pulling himself back up
onto the trail was part of the family lore.

"I realized that I had to get off the ranch, find a new
purpose. I hired Salvatore, bought the bar and moved
to town."

Thad and Sal had continued to do the seasonal work—
haying, branding, moving cattle—together, but he spent
most of his time making the Shamrock Pub the most
popular bar in Gavin. And because he didn't care about
the ranch, it had slowly gone to seed.

Gus drummed his fingers on the table, then abruptly
stopped. He needed time to work this out. Needed to
know if Lillie Jean was legit and if she planned to re-
main a partner or sell. From the way she shivered every
time she hit the Montana air, he was guessing she wasn't
planning to take up residence. He met his uncle's gaze.
"I don't know what to say."

"Nothing much to say. This is the way things have
been since long before you were on this planet."

"Still kind of a shock."

"Yeah."

"Tread lightly," Gus advised, not liking the way Thad
was watching Lillie Jean through the window, looking
as if he was staring into his past. Judging from his expression, the bitterness he might still feel toward his ex-
wife, Lillie Jean's grandmother, was tempered by another,
softer, emotion. Thad was only a month shy of turning

eighty, and while he was mentally as sharp as ever, Gus couldn't help but wonder how the old guy was doing emotionally. Was he at a point where sentiment might overshadow logic?

"I'm not about to lose my head, if that's what you're thinking." Thad ground the words out in a gruff tone. "I'm just...processing."

So was Gus.

"I'll do some digging while you pull her rig out of that muck hole."

Gus raised his eyebrows.

"I'm old. I've had a shock. But I'm not stupid. I'll get hold of the lawyer that we sent the checks to—I just gotta find his address. Usually Betts takes care of that."

"Maybe call Betts."

"If I can get her. She tends to turn off her phone during tax season."

Gus let out a breath as he watched Lillie Jean pull her coat around her and duck her chin inside. "Do what you can. I'll take my time pulling out the car."

LILLIE JEAN HADN'T had a clear picture of what a Montana ranch looked like when she'd left Texas. Born and raised in a suburban environment, her limited knowledge of ranching came from watching television, reading novels and visiting a friend's ten-acre ranchette in high school. None of those experiences had prepared her for the reality of her inheritance.

She didn't know a lot about ranches, but she knew a run-down property when she saw one. The outbuildings were old and weathered. The house hadn't seen a new coat of paint in many years. The yard was wild and fences that weren't made of wire were made of long poles instead of flat planks. Any fanciful thoughts she'd had of keeping her part of the ranch and moving to Montana, thus putting a lot of miles between her and Andrew and all reminders of her failed engagement and stolen business, evaporated early that morning when the sun had risen and she'd gotten a good look at the H/H in the light of day. This was not a place she wanted to live.

The sound of the door opening brought her head up. A second later, Gus Hawkins emerged from the house, heading toward her like a man on a mission. And that mission was to get her off the ranch. Great. They had the same objective.

"Thad needs some time to work through things," he said as he drew closer. "In the meanwhile, we'll get your car out of the mud."

She leaned down and scooped up Henry, who was pressing against her legs while keeping an eye on Gus. "All right."

There wasn't much else she could say. She lifted her chin to meet Gus's less than friendly gaze, hugging her dog a little closer. *Do not show weakness.* Bullies thrived on weakness. She didn't think that Gus was a bully, per se, but he was protective of his uncle and his ranch and had made it clear that he didn't trust her one bit.

Fine. She didn't trust him, either. He was tall and good-looking and probably used to getting his way. He thought he'd be able to run her off the property, get her away from his uncle—and she *was* leaving, but not because of anything he'd done. She'd wanted to meet Thaddeus Hawkins, learn her grandfather's secrets, before putting her part of the ranch up for sale.

She started toward the truck they'd traveled in the night before, but Gus called her name and she stopped, looked at him over her shoulder. He jerked his head toward the tractor. "We'll take that."

"Why?"

"Because it's better at pulling things out of the mud. You might want to leave your little dog with Thad." He started toward the tractor without another word and, after a brief hesitation, Lillie Jean crossed the driveway to the house. The kitchen was empty, so she set Henry on the floor and promised him she'd be back shortly.

Gus was waiting in the idling tractor when she returned. She started to the passenger door, but he motioned her to the other side of the machine. Cautiously she climbed the steps, finding a small jump seat beside the operator's chair.

Once the door was closed, Gus pulled a few levers, raised the bucket, and the tractor started down the driveway, shaking and rumbling as he shifted to a higher gear.

Lillie Jean simply held on and focused on the road ahead of her, doing her best to tamp down the feelings that (a) she didn't belong in a tractor, and (b) the cab of the tractor was too small for two people who didn't trust one another.

"Do you have the keys?" he asked as they drove through the log archway that marked the entrance of the ranch proper.

"Yes," she said shortly, glad that she did indeed have the keys sitting deep in her coat pocket. She could have left them in the car, stuck as it was, but old habits died hard. One didn't leave keys in the car for even a little while where she lived. The place wasn't crime ridden, but enough things happened, even in the suburbs, to leave one erring on the side of caution.

Lillie Jean held herself so stiffly in the small seat, trying not to let any part of her body come in contact with Gus in the small confines of the tractor cab, that by the time they reached her car, her muscles were starting to cramp. For his part, Gus ignored her. No small talk. No questions about who she really was, or dire warnings about taking advantage of his uncle—both of which she'd fully expected. Instead he'd focused straight ahead, his eyebrows drawn together in a frown of concentration. Plotting how to get rid of her, probably.

Lillie Jean refused to let it bother her. Instead she thought about next steps. The trip back to Texas. Going through the last of her grandfather's personal belongings which were stacked in her friend Kate's basement and attic. Her grandfather hadn't left much. He'd lived comfortably, but hadn't possessed a lot of material things. Lillie Jean had always assumed his frugal habits had been born of necessity, only to find out that he'd owned half of an eight-hundred-acre spread. It still boggled her.

Lillie Jean had questions about her grandfather and his secret past, and before she left, she hoped that Thaddeus Hawkins would give her answers. He wasn't suspicious of her, like his nephew was, but he was unsettled by her sudden arrival, and she sensed that it went beyond the surprise element. What on earth had gone on between him and her grandfather?

LILLIE JEAN SMELLED like lilacs, a scent Gus knew well, due to the thick hedge near the ranch house that burst into blossom each spring, filling the air with perfume and sending old Sal's allergies into high gear.

He hated that he noticed that Lillie Jean smelled good. Hated the way the delicate floral scent made him feel like leaning closer and taking a deeper breath. In fact, it was really annoying to find himself feeling that way, so he was very glad to finally arrive at the car.

Lillie Jean put her hand on the door handle before he'd rolled to a stop, and he automatically reached past her to keep her from opening the door. She shot him a startled look, which he met with a frown, once again doing his best to ignore the lilacs and the incredible color of her eyes.

"Never open the door until the tractor is out of gear." He made a show of moving the gear lever. "Big tires," he said in a clipped voice. "Very unforgiving."

"Is it okay now?" Lillie Jean asked as she eyed the giant rear wheels.

"Yeah." He put on the hand brake and set a hand on the back of her seat to maneuver himself out of the cab. Lillie Jean took the hint and climbed down the stairs and jumped to the ground, quickly moving out of range of those big tires. Gus followed her and then reached up to drag the chain off the floorboards under the seat.

The mud was deep and water soaked into his jeans as he crouched down to attach the chain to the frame of the big car. Once done, he motioned for Lillie Jean to get into the driver's seat.

"What do I do?"

"You start the engine and steer. Do not step on the gas."

"Why?"

"Because it'll annoy me if you ram that big car into the tractor."

"Oh." She moistened her lips—a mistake in the cool weather—and then said, "You don't have much faith in my driving ability."

All he did was point a finger at the car in the mud then turn and walk back to the tractor. "Just put it in Neutral," he said, "and let me do the rest."

"Why even start it?"

"So that the steering wheel works."

From the way her jaw muscles tightened, Gus deduced that she was starting to hate him a little.

"I knew that." She abruptly turned and headed toward the car, mincing her way across the lumpy half-frozen mud next to the door.

Gus climbed into the cab and, once Lillie Jean was situated behind the wheel, he gently eased the tractor back until the chain was taut. He continued inching backward until the car jerked, then moved forward. Lillie Jean kept the wheels straight until finally the car was free, and he swore he could see her biting her full bottom lip as she concentrated, even though they were separated by twenty feet and two windshields. Once he was certain Lillie Jean wasn't going to throw the car in gear or anything unexpected, he moved the tractor forward so that the chain sagged.

"There are no more puddles between here and the ranch house, so you should be okay," he said as he unhooked the chain. "You should be equally okay when you leave, which will be in short order, right?"

Lillie Jean propped a hand on her hip and stuck her chin out. "Enough, okay?"

He stowed the chain back in the cab of the tractor and then turned to her. "Enough what?"

"Enough passive-aggressive crap. And enough insinuating that I'm not who I say I am, and that I'm here to try to take advantage of your uncle. I'm not."

"I have no way of knowing that."

"And you have nothing to do with this situation. It's between me and Thaddeus."

"Thaddeus is getting up there in years. I'm his nephew, his ranch manager and half owner of his bar."

"Meaning?"

He gave her a small, not particularly friendly smile. "Meaning that, until Thad tells me otherwise, it'll be you and Thaddeus and me."

CHAPTER FOUR

LILLIE JEAN WAS hot, in the angry sense, and maybe she had reason. Gus rubbed his forehead, then dropped his hand back to his side. Her eyes were pretty much spitting blue fire, but there was something else there besides outrage. Hurt, maybe? She gave the impression of being a woman who expected to be trusted. A woman not accustomed to having her honesty questioned. She was either truly insulted, or she was a very good actress—as an effective scam artist would be.

He needed more information.

He met her angry gaze and said, "Try to see my side of things. You show up out of nowhere, claim to be related to a man I didn't know existed and twist my uncle into a knot."

"I twisted nothing. Not your uncle. Not the truth."

"Sometimes," he said, fully aware that he was about to insult her again, "people have been known to do deep research and pretend to be people they are not, for personal gain."

Anger shifted to ice. "I'm not one of them and you have a lot of nerve insinuating that I am."

"Lillie Jean." Her name felt odd on his tongue, as if saying it somehow made their relationship more intimate, which was nuts. "Until we have all this ironed out, I'm going to have my suspicions. I'd be stupid not to."

She pushed her hands deep into her coat pockets and

shivered. These were not temperatures she was used to. Her cheeks and the tip of her nose were red, while the rest of her face was pale, making the blue-green color of her eyes more intense. She wore no makeup and a smattering of light freckles showed over her nose. Maybe that was part of her act. The sweet down-home girl without artifice.

Or maybe it wasn't an act at all.

The one thing he was certain of was that, whether she was legit or not, she'd thrown a monkey wrench into his plans.

He jerked his head in the direction of the ranch. "Let's get back to where it's warmer."

"Yes. Let's." There was a faint note of sarcasm in her voice, and maybe he couldn't blame her, if she was legit.

Big *if*.

Gigantic *if*.

He got into the tractor and waited until she pulled past him in the giant boat of a car with the Texas plates. Was it really her grandfather's car? A prop? His head was starting to ache.

Life had been so freaking simple only twenty-four hours ago, when he'd thought he was beginning a new chapter in his life. One he'd planned for so carefully. Those plans had not included Lillie Jean Hardaway.

If that was her real name.

THAD LOOKED GRIM when Gus followed Lillie Jean into the house after the car rescue. She excused herself and headed down the hall, an overjoyed Henry prancing close behind her. Thad waited until they heard the door shut before saying, "I called Lyle's accountant—the one Betts sends the checks to and she gave me the lawyer's name. The lawyer's assistant is calling me back within the hour." Thad looked past Gus toward the hall where Lillie Jean had disappeared. "I need more time."

"When he calls, maybe you can nail down the reason they didn't contact you the minute the will surfaced?"

The bedroom door opened again and he and Thad exchanged looks.

"I think she should stay here until we know more." Thad shifted his weight in the chair. "If she's who she says she is, we need to talk. If she's not, we need to know. I want all the facts before we make any kind of decision."

"I agree." The door closed, and footsteps sounded on the old wooden floorboards. "In fact, I have some work to do."

"Guess you could use some company," Thad murmured in a low voice as Henry danced into the kitchen without his reindeer sweater. "Maybe show our guest some country."

"Uh-huh." There were heavy cows to check, a hole in the fence line between the H/H and Carson Craig's ranch, which the King of Montana demanded be fixed, even though it was a joint boundary and they were both responsible for upkeep and repair. As near as he could tell, Carson's idea of joint maintenance was for him to order Thad to fix the damned fence. Now.

An uncomfortable silence settled over the room as Lillie Jean entered, and then Thad said to Gus in an overly casual voice, "You better get going before Craig has kittens."

Gus gave a nod and glanced over at Lillie Jean. "You want to ride along?"

Instant suspicion. "Where?"

"I have to fix a hole in the fence. You've come this far, you may as well see some of the ranch before it snows."

"Snow?" She looked shocked.

"Supposed to have snow tomorrow."

She glanced over at Thad who nodded. "But the forecast changes hourly. May not be any snow at all. But if you want to go, I'll babysit your little dog," he said in a reassuring tone. "And when you get back we'll have a sit-down."

"Or the dog can come with us," Gus said. Dumb sweater and all.

Lillie Jean's jaw shifted sideways, as if she was well aware that she was being played. "All right. Yes. I'd like to see some of the property." She glanced down at her dog, who was giving her a beseeching "don't abandon me" stare. "I'll leave Henry here where it's warm."

"I'll enjoy the company," Thad said, making Gus wonder if maybe his uncle needed a dog of his own.

Henry didn't look all that pleased with the decision, but when Thad reached down and scooped him up with one big hand, the little dog settled on his lap, watching Lillie Jean closely as she gestured toward the coats hanging on hooks next to the back door in the mudroom. "Maybe I could borrow a warmer coat?"

"Sure, but I promise it'll be plenty warm in the truck."

"Unless you break down," Thad said, idly scratching Henry's ear.

Was that a hint?

"Good point," Gus said. He headed into the mudroom where he pulled his spare coat off a hook and handed it to Lillie Jean. She slipped into it, put her hands in the pockets and then grimaced. No matter how many times a guy turned his pockets inside out and beat on them, there was always bits of itchy hay there. He reached for a new pair of gloves and handed them to her.

"No hay," he said. "You might want to grab one of those fleece hats in the basket."

"Thanks." She lifted a hat out of the wicker basket that sat on the floor beneath the coats while he wrapped his wild rag around his neck. If he'd had a clean scarf, he would have given it to her, but he didn't, so she'd simply have to turn up the collar of his coat. But like he'd said, it'd be plenty warm in the truck. It wasn't that far below freezing, but according to the weather station on the kitchen windowsill, the windchill had knocked the temperatures down below twenty degrees.

He put on his cowboy hat, then pulled open the door and stepped back to let Lillie Jean precede him outside. Before following her into the crisp air, he once again met his uncle's gaze. Thad gave him a grim nod. The dog on his uncle's lap looked as if he were about to implode from anxiety, but he stayed put as Lillie Jean stepped out of the house. Gus just hoped Thad had some answers when he got back. He looked determined. The one benefit of almost being scammed last year was that his uncle had no intentions of being played again.

THE HEAVY COAT Lillie Jean wore smelled of hay and earth and Gus. The warm scents teased her nostrils as she followed the man across the frosty driveway, making her feel as if she was encroaching on intimate territory instead of simply wearing a borrowed coat to keep the wind from cutting through her. She should have simply believed Gus when he said the truck heater would keep her warm enough, and worn her own less than adequate coat.

The wind was blowing stronger than it had been when Gus had pulled her car out of the bottomless pit. Clouds were moving in from the north, a solid bank, grayish at the top, dark charcoal at the bottom, pushing the wind ahead of it. She pulled the coat around her more tightly, the gloves still in her hand. She didn't want to put them on yet. They were huge but preferable to putting her hands in the prickly pockets of the coat if she needed to warm her fingers. She sincerely hoped she wouldn't.

Her grandfather's old car looked ridiculous parked next to the barn—like a time machine. It did not belong on this ranch, and she couldn't picture her grandfather on the ranch, either. He'd never seemed all that rural to her. He and her grandmother had lived quietly on a one-acre rented lot near the edge of town. They hadn't kept livestock, or even much of a garden, except for her grandmother's flowers and tomatoes. He'd worked for nearly three decades at first as a welder, then a shop foreman. For relaxation, he tinkered with motorcycles.

Had he ever been on this ranch? Had he invested with Thad? Were he and Thad friends? Enemies? What?

She was going to get answers before she left.

She hoped. Gus's grim profile wasn't making her feel particularly optimistic, but since arriving at the ranch, her mission had crystallized. She'd left Texas to get away from Andrew and the stress of losing her business, losing her grandfather, but the answers she thought she'd *like* to have, had become answers she *needed* to have.

Gus led the way to an old truck loaded with posts, wire and tools that looked as if it would fall apart if she breathed on it. But it sounded solid enough when he wrestled open the passenger door and motioned for her to get inside. Everything he needed must have been in the mechanical beast, because after closing her door with a clang that reverberated through the mostly metal interior, he walked around to his side, got in and started the engine. It chugged a few times, then fired to life with a blast of exhaust. The entire cab vibrated.

Lillie Jean couldn't help frowning over at Gus, who ignored her as he put the vehicle in gear and started down the driveway, stopping at a gate. He got out and opened it, drove through, then got out and closed it again. They drove across the pasture to another gate. This time Lillie Jean said, "Would you like me to open it?" It only seemed polite.

"This one is kind of tricky."

"I can probably handle it. We do have gates in Texas." She'd spent time on her best friend's tiny ranchette during high school. They had wire gates very similar to the one in front of them.

"Have at it."

She got out and went to the latch, where she realized she'd never seen anything like it before. There was a lever and a loop and, feeling a little foolish at having to take her time to study the contraption, she finally managed to pop the loop off the top of the wire gate and drag it open so that Gus could drive through.

"That lever is kind of counterintuitive," she said as she got back into the truck.

"I'm not a fan," he agreed.

Common ground. She brushed the thought aside. What did she care if he agreed with her or not? Especially when it was patently obvious that she was with him because he hadn't wanted to leave her alone with Thad. What did he think she would do? Weave some kind of a hypnotic spell over his uncle?

No. He thought she might listen in on phone calls. A phone had been sitting on the table when she and Gus had returned to the house, as if Thad had been making or waiting for calls. She didn't blame him. She would have done the same. She could have helped him *do* the same, but that was neither here nor there. They didn't trust her, and she couldn't force them to. Let Thad get his answers—then perhaps he'd give her some.

Gus drove across the grassy pasture to the tree line and then followed the narrow road through the deciduous trees that were just leafing out. They came to another field and then a fence. Gus turned to the truck to follow the wire along what was more of a trail than a road. The grass was short and slick with frost in the high area between the two ruts that the tires were following.

"Is it always this cold in March?"

"Pretty much. The weather changes fast here. It might be balmy in a few days."

"Define *balmy*," Lillie Jean muttered.

"Not freezing."

"Kind of what I thought." She glanced over at him, but he kept his eyes on the fence. She had a sense of him wanting to say something, but holding back. Okay. He could talk when he was ready. She was certain he wasn't going to say anything she wanted to hear, anyway. She'd gone with him for two reasons—to get a look at her inheritance, and to give Thad time to check her out. She hoped he did a lot of research while she was gone. Once he understood that she was on the up-and-up, then they could move forward.

The truck lurched and it hit a deeper rut, knocking her against the door, then shooting her sideways to bump shoulders with Gus, causing the seat belt to cut into her.

"Road gets rough sometimes."

This isn't a road. It wasn't. It was a rutted track, working its way through a pasture, over and around rocks, through boggy spots. Gus was now driving so that the tires were next to the ruts, rather than in them, but every now and again, the truck slid into one of the deep Vs.

He pulled to a stop, put the truck in neutral and set the parking brake. "I'll leave the heater on. You'll be fine."

"I'll get out for a while."

He gave her a "suit yourself" shrug and opened his door. While Lillie Jean stepped down into the crunchy frozen grass, he went to the rear of the truck and pulled out a bucket and an odd contraption. He walked to the fence, set them down and then went back for a roll of wire. For some contrary reason, Lillie Jean did not want to get back into the truck. Maybe it was because he thought she was too wimpy to stand out in the cold— and it *was* at least ten degrees colder here than it had been at the ranch. Altitude, maybe. Her lips twitched grimly. They didn't have much altitude where she came from. Rolling hills, but no big changes that would drop temperatures ten degrees or so.

Gus set about connecting new wire to old, stretching it tight with the metal contraption, then crimping it off with a small tube and pliers. He did it for all five strands in a surprisingly short period of time, then loaded his tools back into the truck, which was still chugging away, sending up an exhaust cloud near the rear wheels. There was something satisfying about watching a guy do something he did well, or maybe there was something satisfying about watching a guy as good-looking as Gus do something he did well. And maybe it was just a little irritating that, due to circumstances, he was probably always going to view her through a veil of suspicion.

So be it. Some things were simply out of her control. Like the fact that she felt this crazy tug toward the man. Despite everything, he kind of fascinated her. Well, he was a Montana cowboy—the stuff of which legends were made. She wasn't going to think about the fact that legends were made about Texas cowboys, too, and so far she hadn't met a man from Texas who'd fascinated her like this guy was doing.

Time to get her mind back on the here and now. "Do

you have deer on the ranch?" Mentally she rolled her eyes. Of course, they had deer. She'd seen them last night.

"Deer and elk and antelope. Moose."

"Bears?"

"Yes."

She wasn't a big fan of bears. She'd never seen one in person and she didn't want to.

Gus headed for his door, leaving Lillie Jean to wrestle with hers. Finally she got the thumb latch pushed in and pulled the heavy door open on protesting hinges. "You should put some grease to this thing."

"I'll see to it," he said in a tone which indicated a lack of appreciation for her helpfulness.

"Just a suggestion." *Not trying to tell you your business or take over the ranch.*

Nope. She had no intentions in that direction. She'd seen enough of the ranch to satisfy her curiosity, and now she was going to settle matters with Thaddeus, get her answers and drive back home. Once there, she'd find a job and a more permanent place to live than her friend Kate's tiny house. And maybe, because of this quest and her time away from Serenity, Texas, she'd be better equipped to deal with the fallout of her broken engagement and the fact that A Thread in Time was no longer hers. Maybe some new scandal had rocked her community and she wouldn't be on the receiving end of pitying glances and less than helpful reassurances that this had all happened for a reason.

But no matter what, it was going to sting to drive past her storefront, and it was going to suck to run into Andrew and her other ex-partner, Taia. The business stealers.

How had she not seen any of this coming?

The fact that she hadn't, that she'd assumed that Andrew's vague withdrawal had something to do with prewedding jitters, left her shaken. Half-afraid to trust her own judgment. And worse than that, it had affected her creativity. She hadn't sewn or picked up her sketch pad in six weeks. And the way things were going, it didn't look like she was going to reclaim her creativity anytime soon.

She let out an audible sigh, and then her eyes flashed open as she realized what she'd done. *Audience. You have an audience.*

But when she gave Gus Hawkins a furtive sideways glance, he appeared as lost in thought as she'd been, eyes fixed on the track in front of them.

LILLIE JEAN HUDDLED in the oversize coat, even though the heater was blowing full blast and Gus was starting to sweat, almost as if she was trying to disappear inside of it. Every now and again he'd hit a rut wrong or the tire would bump up over a rock and it would throw her sideways, but she always righted herself without a word. It was obvious that she didn't have a lot of experience driving over rough terrain, because she didn't have a clue how to anchor herself in place with strategic handholds. The truck was old and had lap belts instead of shoulder harnesses, and he couldn't help but note that Lillie Jean needed a shoulder harness.

"You might want to grab the handle above the door," he said after a big bump that almost brought her out of her belt. "It'll keep you from bouncing around so much."

"Thank you." The words came out stiffly, but she took hold of the plastic handle.

"Not a problem." His words were equally clipped.

The rest of the boundary fence in this pasture was intact, which would keep Carson off his back for a day or two. The man understood next to nothing about ranching, but that didn't keep him from giving directives. Gus had felt sorry for the guy Carson hired to manage his place a few months ago, but the man quickly came to his senses and quit two weeks in. Now Carson ran the place himself and let everyone know it when they met at various public events.

"Do *you* own an interest in the ranch?"

Gus shot Lillie Jean a frowning look. He'd been so deep in his head that she'd startled him by speaking.

"I manage the place."

"Are you Thad's heir?"

He didn't want to answer that question, but couldn't come up with a reason not to. "The last I heard."

"Does he have a will?"

"He does."

"So this isn't only about you watching out for your uncle. You're watching out for you, too."

He shot her a cool look. "Something wrong with that?"

"No." She spoke lightly. "But maybe being in that position will help you to understand that I'm in the same boat."

He didn't have a lot to say to that. Did he resent her showing up out of nowhere? Oh yeah. But facts were facts, and if she was the silent partner's heir, then he had to adapt. In twenty-four short hours his life had essentially been turned upside down by something that Thad had been aware of all along. Who would have thought quiet Thad would have been embroiled in such a soap opera?

But it did explain why he wouldn't live on the ranch. It might even explain why he'd clung to his bachelorhood so tightly. He was afraid not to. And that kind of broke Gus's heart. Decades of loneliness and now Lillie

Jean shows up as a flesh-and-blood reminder of every-thing that had gone down. He hated that his uncle had to deal with this.

"Did it occur to you before you arrived that showing up as you did would upset Thad?" He tried not to sound judgmental, but failed.

"I wanted answers." There was a tightness to her voice. "I wanted to see the ranch."

"So, no." Gus glanced sideways at his passenger, then let out a curse as the truck lurched sideways, yanking the steering wheel out of his hands. The frame of the truck hit rock as the front wheel slipped deep into a rut. Lillie Jean's head snapped forward on impact, her forehead making solid contact with the dash.

"Lillie Jean—"

She pulled herself upright, one hand pressed against her forehead just over her right eyebrow, her eyes wide with shock. He gave another silent curse as he saw blood oozing from between her fingers.

"Keep your hand there."

She instantly pulled it away, took a look at her bloody fingers, gasped, then quickly put her fingers back where they'd been, smearing blood across her forehead. Gus had caught a quick look at the wound, which was bleed-ing freely as head wounds tended to do. It was short and gaping. Deep, dark red.

"Hold on." He fished around under the seat and pulled out a first aid kit sealed in a zipper bag. It contained only rudimentary supplies, but had saved his butt a time or two when he'd injured himself while working alone. He pulled out a box of gauze pads and peeled one off the top and handed it to her, she pressed it to the wound for a few seconds, then turned and pulled down the visor.

"No mirror," she muttered.

"Old truck." If it had been newer, she probably wouldn't have an injury, but the dash was sunbaked and hard as a rock.

She peeled the gauze off and tilted her head toward him, obviously wanting an opinion.

Gus shook his head and handed her another gauze pad. "Quick, before it drips."

Lillie Jean slapped the new gauze in place, and Gus said, "We can go to the urgent care clinic and they can put a butterfly on it and close it up."

"Or…?"

Or? What did she mean "or"?

"I can do the same?"

She reached for another gauze pad. "Take me to the ranch. We can do it there."

"You're sure?" Because he didn't want her coming back at him later.

"Yes." She gave him a conflicted look. "I don't want to pay for urgent care at this point in my life."

That gave him something to chew on as he very carefully drove back to the house. He stopped at the first gate and Lillie Jean started to open the door, as if she was going to open the stubborn gate latch with one hand, and hold the gauze to her forehead with the other. Gus stopped her with a quick, "I'll do it."

"Afraid of getting blood on your coat?"

Gus almost smiled. Almost. "Yeah."

"Whatever." She reached for the first aid bag as he got out of the truck. When he got back in she had another pad in place. The bleeding had slowed and he hoped by the time they got back to the ranch they'd be able to work on the cut.

Thad was still at the kitchen table, talking into the landline when Lillie Jean walked into the kitchen ahead of Gus. He nearly dropped the phone when he caught sight of bloody Lillie Jean. "Excuse me," he said into the receiver. "What happened?" His gaze went straight to Gus.

"I hit a rock, slid into a rut. Lillie Jean's forehead slammed into the dash. I'm going to render first aid."

Thad bounced a frowning look between the two of them. "You want to go to the clinic?"

"No," Lillie Jean and Gus said in unison.

She glanced up at Gus. "I'll clean it up and then call you when I need help with the butterfly."

He nodded and then shrugged out of his coat as Thad went back to his phone call. Henry followed Lillie Jean down the hall, the bathroom door closed, and Gus went to pour a cup of coffee. What a morning.

As near as he could tell, Thad was talking to his attorney, so he wandered into the mudroom and threw a bunch of dirty jeans into the wash to give his uncle some privacy. When he heard the bathroom door open again, he poked his head into the kitchen and Lille Jean beckoned him from the hallway.

"Prognosis?" she asked. She removed the folded tissue she had over the wound to show him a half-inch-long cut that would be a cinch to butterfly closed.

"I think we can do this without leaving a scar."

She narrowed her eyes at him. "Are you some kind of an EMT or something?"

"Bull rider." One corner of her mouth quirked up as he corrected himself. "Former bull rider. I know about scars." And regardless of how he felt about her being there, he'd hate to leave one on her beautiful brow.

"In that case, carry on."

He was kind of surprised that she placed herself so totally in his hands, but if she didn't have money for urgent care, then that could be a big influencer in her decision. He stepped closer and opened the medicine cabinet and pulled a box of adhesive stitches off the shelf. Lillie Jean swung the mirror closed again and he dug in the box for the size he wanted.

"Why don't you take a seat." He gestured at the commode and she sat, lifting her chin. Gus brushed the hair away from her forehead as he surveyed the cut, trying not to notice how the silky strands teased his fingertips. He opened the suture package. "Dab the blood away. Press hard, then lift the tissue."

Lillie Jean pushed hard against her forehead and when she lifted the tissue, he quickly applied the butterfly, expertly pulling the edges of the cut together so they touched. He dropped his hands and sat back on his heels. It looked good. She looked good. He was losing it.

Lillie Jean got to her feet and moved past him to look in the mirror, tilting her chin sideways to get a better angle. "You did well."

"Like I said, practice."

Lillie Jean lightly touched the wound as if testing for pain. "Remind me not to ride with you again."

"I should have kept my eyes on the road." *Instead of on you*. The crazy thing was that once again he was having a hard time keeping his eyes off her. Something about her tugged at him, made him want to study her.

Okay. She kind of fascinated him.

Suddenly the bathroom was about half the size it usually was, and he felt a deep need to escape. "I'll, uh… let you…yeah."

CHAPTER FIVE

WHEN WAS THE last time he'd been at a loss for words? Pub keepers had to have their wits about them and he was kind of known for snappy comebacks. But not today. He felt like a tongue-tied junior high kid as he escaped the overly small bathroom.

Thad was in the mudroom putting on his coat.

"Going somewhere?"

"Sal's place." Thad jerked his head toward the hallway. "Is Lillie Jean okay?"

"Seems to be doing all right. She's tougher than she looks." He half muttered the second part, coming to terms with the fact that maybe Lillie Jean was a fish out of water, and maybe she resembled a Disney princess in some regards, but that didn't mean she was overly delicate.

Thad shot him an accusing look as they went out the door. "I told you to buy me some time, not bring her home all bloody."

"It was an accident."

"Yeah. I know. But I want to keep on her good side."

"She is who she says she is?"

"Appears so. I had a long talk with the lawyer kid, who said the will was straightforward. The deed automatically transferred to Lillie Jean at Lyle's death. There's just a little paperwork to clear up."

Gus rolled his eyes at the word *kid*. To Thad, anyone

under the age of forty was a kid, even if he was a lawyer or a bull rider or whatever. "Why weren't you notified of your partner's death?"

"They're behind. They just moved offices and his father retired." Thad's mouth twisted. "I gave him a little guff, but, bottom line, Lillie Jean is who she says she is."

Even though he'd expected something along those lines, Gus felt his stomach twist. His carefully planned future was now null and void.

"I stored some papers in Sal's house. I want to take a look at them." Thad gestured toward the manager's house with his gray head. "You may as well come."

He may as well. They crossed the short distance to the house without speaking. Thad pushed the stubborn door open and it scraped its way across the worn carpet. The interior of the house felt colder than the outside air, even though Gus knew the furnace was set to come on at fifty degrees and thus keep the pipes from freezing.

Sal had left some time ago, and a layer of dust had settled over the carpet and the few pieces of furniture the former manager had left behind. Furniture that had probably been in the house when he'd first moved in twenty-five years ago.

Thad went to the hall and pulled the cord that lowered the attic steps. The attic was cramped, so Gus waited near the kitchen door while Thad thumped around upstairs, then came back down carrying a metal box.

Gus asked the obvious question once Thad placed the strongbox on the wobbly kitchen table. "Why do you keep things here?" It wasn't like there wasn't a lot of room in the main house. It, too, was sparsely furnished.

"I burned most of it. Didn't want the rest anywhere near me."

Thad pulled a key out of his pocket, turned the lock

and opened the lid. There wasn't much inside—a couple of envelopes, a small box and a set of keys. Safety-deposit box keys. Thad pulled out an envelope, spread the yellowed paper it contained on the table. It was a handwritten agreement, signed by Thad and his partner.

"The official agreement is exactly the same."

"You're sure?"

"Called Ned." His current lawyer, who happened to be his original lawyer's son. Another lawyer kid. "He found a copy of the agreement and answered some questions for me. It's something called Tenant in Common. I kind of remember Ned's dad talking us into it, saying that this way, we were both protected. Neither of us could force the other to sell. We could just sell our interest to someone else."

"Is it transferable?"

"This one is." Thad gave a rueful cough. "You see, Nita and I were thinking about kids and we wanted to protect their interests, too."

Nita eventually did have kids. But Thad hadn't—even though he had been like a father to Gus, after Gus had lost his own dad in his early teens.

"You're saying she can sell."

"That's what I'm saying."

Gus tried to tamp down the rising swell of disappointment and anger. This was Thad's ranch. Not his. He'd lived here for almost fifteen years, had worked the land, felt like he was part of the place, but it wasn't his. The subject of Gus buying into the ranch had come up a couple times when they'd had slow times at the pub. Gus wanted to trade his part of the pub to Thad for a down payment, and then work from there. Thad had seemed interested, but even then, Gus had had the sense that there was something going on that he wasn't aware of.

Something holding Thad back. At the time he'd assumed that Thad wasn't yet ready to part with the place—and it wasn't as if he would have had to do that. Gus never intended for anything to change, except for the names on the deed.

Come to find out, there were more names on the deed than he'd been aware of.

"How long had you known this Hardaway guy before you partnered up?"

Thad raised his eyebrows as if surprised at the question. "We grew up next door to one another. Knew each other since we were in diapers. Lyle was the best friend I ever had."

Gus dropped his gaze to the table. Rough topic. Not one he wanted to pursue. His uncle had lost his wife, his partner, his lifelong best friend in one fell swoop.

"He couldn't have been that much of a friend."

"You didn't know Nita."

"No," Gus said softly. "I didn't."

"She was special. Real special. And—" Thad dropped his chin before going on "—I might have missed the mark as a husband." His throat moved as he swallowed. "Too blasted busy trying to build the place up...and maybe I partied a little too hard when I wasn't working on the ranch." He gave his head a shake as if trying to dispel an unsettling image. He met Gus's eyes and made a mighty effort to look as if all were good, then ran a gnarled hand over the yellowed paper. "I wanted to see the words myself—the words Lyle and I had written."

Gus didn't know what to say, so he erred on the side of caution and didn't say anything.

"Sorry to burden you with this, but it affects you. I should have told you sooner. I knew Lyle was getting up there, just like I am, knew this would have to be dealt with." He gave a small snort. "Tomorrow always seemed like a good day to do that."

"Pretty natural under the circumstances." Gus spoke in a way that he hoped sounded understanding.

There was a folder in the bottom of the strongbox. Thad's hand hovered for a split second before he pulled it out, then opened it up and laid it in front of Gus. Lillie Jean—or rather her double—stared back at him. The woman's hair was shorter, waving around her shoulders, and she had short bangs, but there was no getting around the similarity between Lillie Jean and her grandmother.

"I wanted you to see the picture before Lillie Jean left. In case you still had doubts. I don't know who her dad was, but he didn't pass along a lot of his genes. Or a last name."

"Doesn't look like it." Gus picked up the photo, studied first Nita, then a much younger version of his uncle. Thad looked solemn, proud. His hand rested lightly on his wife's hip. She wore a corsage on a fancy short white dress. Thad was dressed in a dark suit.

"Wedding day. We went to the courthouse. Nita didn't want to waste money we could pour into the ranch. She was practical that way." Thad met Gus's gaze. "She was a good woman."

"I believe you," Gus said quietly. He'd never seen his uncle like this, on the edge of breaking. Thad had always been the picture of quiet control. He hated seeing his uncle confronting his past—something he might never have had to do if he'd died before Lyle. Then Gus would have been left sorting out the pieces of a secret puzzle.

Isn't that what Lillie Jean is dealing with? Because Gus had a strong feeling that she had been in the dark about a lot of this herself. She'd said she wanted answers. People in the know didn't need answers.

He was about to let out a heavy breath when Thad beat him to it. His uncle gave his head a weary shake before packing the photo back into the strongbox along with the handwritten contract. The keys he dropped in his vest pocket.

"Do you want to keep that out? Compare it to the one in the safe-deposit box?"

Thad shook his head. "It's the same. I just wanted to see the words." After the strongbox was stowed back in the attic, Thad started for the door only to stop short. He turned back to Gus, his expression both stubborn and sincere.

"I know this messes with your life, but once the legalities are settled, Lillie Jean has the right to sell. I hope she doesn't, but I can't see her letting this place lie fallow. She won't make enough to live on after we pay taxes and production costs."

"Does she have any profit waiting for her anywhere?"

"Betts sent Lyle a check every year, so only last quarter's take, which isn't much. I can show you the books."

"No need." Gus just hoped they were good books, because there was a decent chance they'd be gone over thoroughly as they cleared up this situation.

"I imagine she'll be leaving soon."

"Probably." But the crazy thing was that she had more of a right to be there than he did. She was half owner. He was simply the manager, which was beyond frustrating. What had she put into the place? What had her grandfather put into the place in the past twenty-some years? Nothing. Yet she was an equal partner.

Thad opened the door and they stepped out into the blustery March weather. "Never meant to do this to you."

Yeah. But he had. It took him a couple of seconds to

say, "What did you think was going to happen, with Lyle out there somewhere?"

"I don't know. Like I said, I was always going to take care of things tomorrow."

Tomorrow was officially here.

LILLIE JEAN TOOK a couple aspirin for the headache beating at her temples. The laceration on her forehead didn't hurt as much as the goose egg she'd got from smacking her head on the rock-solid dashboard. She lightly touched the area around the butterfly strip. It was tender and probably in the process of turning blue. Who would have thought such an injury could occur going less than ten miles per hour?

Things like this didn't happen in Serenity, Texas. At least not in the suburban part. Nope. In Serenity, people got shut out of the business they'd built. That hurt worse than her forehead and was going to leave more of a scar.

She'd been in Montana for a little over twenty-four hours and she was already convinced that she wasn't cut out for ranch life. Bouncing around in a truck on a road that wasn't a road, or stepping out into weather that chilled her to the bone wasn't her thing. Nor was spending time with a guy who was easy on the eyes, but openly suspicious of her and her motivations.

She had a right to be there, and she had a right to sell her half of the ranch. All she wanted was some answers before she did so. Then maybe she'd be able to settle, in an emotional, rather than a physical sense. Get her creativity back, and make her living doing what she did best—creating designs that people loved to wear.

The hard truth was that she may not be able to do that for a long, long while—at least not full-time. It could take years to sell her interest in the ranch, which meant she'd be back to working a day job and building a business on the side. Competing with Andrew and Taia. Or maybe moving to a different part of the country for a fresh start. There was nothing tying her to Serenity, except her friendship with Kate Tanner.

Kate and her mom had had as bad a run of luck as Lillie Jean recently. When Kate's husband had abruptly left her for another woman, Lillie Jean had talked Andrew and Taia into hiring her to do the books so that she could work closer to home and not have to commute to her office job in Austin. She'd done an amazing job, but, rat that he was, Andrew had fired Kate the same day he'd forced Lillie Jean out of the business. Lillie Jean could understand him not wanting to have her around after they'd broken up, but there was no excuse for him cutting Kate loose when she had two little kids to care for.

Lillie Jean's head came up at the sound of boots on the old porch boards. She closed her eyes again, trying to will the headache away as she listened to the men enter the house and clunk around in the kitchen.

Time for answers. Thad seemed like a nice enough guy, plainspoken and a little gruff, just like her grandfather. She could totally see Lyle being friends with Thad. But if they'd been friends, if they'd partnered in this ranch, why had she never heard of Thad? And why hadn't Gus heard of her grandfather?

Something had happened to drive a wedge between the older men. A substantial wedge.

A woman or money?

Lillie Jean found herself hoping it was money, but as she considered that matter, and judging from the way Thad had looked at her last night, as if she was someone he knew well and had never expected to see again, she had a feeling it was a woman. Her grandmother, to be exact.

Had Lyle and Thad fallen for the same woman?

If so, then why hadn't her grandfather sold his interest in the ranch? Cut himself free from it?

If she'd known about the ranch only a few months ago, she could have demanded answers and she wouldn't now be feeling her way along in the dark. She wouldn't need to ask personal questions of Thad.

Maybe she shouldn't ask questions.

She could leave without her answers—without upsetting an old man, as Gus had said she was doing. Maybe if she was careful with her money, she could drive to the coast, look for a new place to land before returning to Serenity. A place that was warm and sunny and where people liked to shop for funky clothing. A place Kate and her mom might like. She didn't want much—just a tiny storefront. A start. A new life.

And no partner.

There were low voices and sounds of movement in the kitchen. The back door opened and closed, and then a single set of footsteps started down the hall, stopping just outside her door. For no reason she could think of, Lillie Jean's heart started to beat faster. When the knock sounded, she jumped, just as if she was guilty of something. And that was ridiculous.

She pulled open the door, found herself facing Gus. There was something about this guy that put her on edge. His gaze went almost instantly to the adhesive on her forehead and she had to fight to keep her hand from touching the spot.

"It's sore, but I'm sure it'll heal just fine," she said without waiting for the question. Her lips curved into an ironic half smile as her gaze shifted to his forehead.

"My mark might be gone before yours is." The lip print was fading, but she couldn't resist the dig.

"You said you came here for answers."

The stark statement begged for a stark response. "Yes."

"Are you sure?" His voice was low, as if he was afraid of being overheard.

Lillie Jean felt heat rise in her cheeks. "What do you mean?"

"Sometimes the truth can be unsettling."

"Oh. Like discovering your closest male relative had a huge secret he never told you? Even though he knew it had to come out eventually?"

"Yeah." There was a sardonic note to his voice. "Something like that."

All right. He was going through the same thing. But the difference was that he'd probably already gotten an explanation. She had not.

"I want to know why I never knew about this place."

"My guess is because your grandfather was trying to protect someone."

"Or the memory of someone?" Lillie Jean asked softly. Gus's eyes narrowed and she pushed on. "I know I look like my grandmother and Thad was shocked to see me this morning. I didn't understand why at the time, but now I think I do." She saw Gus's throat move, but he gave no answer. "Did something happen between Thad and my grandmother?"

"If I tell you what I know, will you refrain from questioning Thad about it?"

It was obvious from the taut edge to his voice that his main interest was to protect his uncle, and she couldn't fault him for that.

"That bad?"

"My uncle is old, and he's just been slapped in the face by something he wants to forget."

"Me?"

Gus gave his head a slow shake. "Your grandma. Is it a deal?"

"Deal." Lillie Jean spoke in an equally low voice, and once again her heart was beating harder.

Gus glanced down the hall, then brought his gaze back to Lillie Jean. "You're sure."

"I want to know."

Gus pulled in a breath. "Thad and your grandmother were once married."

Lillie Jean felt as if a blow to her midsection had pushed all the air from her lungs. "No. She and my grandfather were married forever."

"Except for the three years your grandmother was married to Thad. I've seen the photo of their wedding day. You look just like her."

Lillie Jean realized her mouth was open and abruptly shut it. "How...?"

"They started the ranch together, your grandfather and Thad. An *H* for Hawkins, an *H* for Hardaway."

"I guessed that much."

"Long story short, your grandfather and Thad's wife fell in love and ran away to Texas, leaving Thad on the ranch."

"No." The low exclamation escaped her lips before she was even aware of speaking.

"Yeah. Thad and Lyle remained partners with all matters handled through lawyers and accountants." Gus cleared his throat. "I'm giving your grandfather the benefit of the doubt and assuming he didn't sell his part of the ranch because he felt bad about what he'd done. Thad couldn't afford to buy him out, so he hung on. Penance or something."

Lillie Jean pushed a palm to her brow, then grimaced as pain shot through the injured part of her forehead. She dropped her hand. "This is hard to believe."

"There's documentation." Gus leaned a hand on the door frame and brought his face a few inches closer to hers. "Did you stop to think for even a moment about the possible consequences of a surprise visit? To you? To my uncle?"

Lillie Jean gave a soft sigh. "It was kind of crazy coming up here like this. But I never meant to upset him."

"What did you think was going to happen when you showed up out of the blue?"

"He knew he had a partner, so I didn't think it would hurt to introduce myself as his *new* partner." She hadn't realized she was a secret partner and that he had a secret past.

"Without warning."

That was tougher to address, but she gave it a shot. "I was afraid that if Thad knew I was coming…somehow it would change things."

"How?"

A valid question. "I don't know," she said honestly. "I've had a few recent experiences that have left me a little suspicious, I guess." She met Gus's eyes, held his gaze.

"What kind of experiences?"

"I trusted people. I shouldn't have."

He pushed back from the door frame, dropping his hand to his thigh. His fingers were long and strong, beat up from work and weather, but attractive all the same. "Are you running from something?"

She felt her cheeks start to grow warm, even though

she hadn't begun to mutter a denial. She'd never been good at untruths. "No."

"Then what happened?"

"It's none of your business, Gus."

Flat-out truth. She wasn't pouring out her guts. Not to a virtual stranger—even if he was her business partner's nephew and she had this nagging feeling that she could trust him. That she *should* trust him. The back door rattled and Gus gave Lillie Jean a grim look.

"Do not upset my uncle."

"I won't ask questions." Now that she knew the facts, the last thing she wanted to do was to discuss the matter with Thad. She'd research it later, after she was off this ranch. "But he and I need to talk business before I leave."

"And when will that be?"

"Today." She wanted to put some miles between her and this ranch. And mull over the depressing fact that her grandparents were not the people she thought they were.

"What are you going to do with the ranch, Lillie Jean?"

Another blunt question, but this time she didn't have a blunt answer. "I don't know."

Somehow, she managed to lie without blushing. She knew exactly what she was going to do with the ranch, but she didn't want to argue matters with Gus before discussing them with Thad. She was going to sell and use the money to invest in a new business, a new life.

Gus had asked earlier if she was running from something. The answer was, of course, yes. She was running from an uncomfortable situation, and in a way running from herself. Her grandfather had done the same. Now it was time to stop being impulsive, stop running and fix her broken situation. Selling the ranch would give her an opportunity to do that.

"Thad's putting out lunch." Gus moved his head toward the kitchen. "We'll eat. You can talk to Thad."

"You're going to sit in?" Because he really had no right to do that unless Thad wanted him to be there—which he would, so it was a moot point. Judging from the expression on Gus's face, he was aware.

Two against one? Just as it had been when Andrew and Taia had ousted her from the business.

Fine. Bring it on. Gus was going to find that she wasn't one to roll over quickly and easily.

THE MICROWAVE WAS humming when Lillie Jean and Gus walked into the kitchen.

"You hungry?" Thad asked as she crossed to the table where Thad had a legal pad and phone near his chair. He'd scribbled a lot of notes on the pad.

No. "A little." She needed to eat, even if her stomach said that it wasn't one bit interested in food, and wouldn't be until she'd processed the information Gus had passed along. Had she known her grandparents at all? Did one big lie by omission mean that she couldn't trust any of her memories?

"Have a seat, then."

Thad gestured toward a chair with a serving spoon and Lillie sat down. Henry pressed his body against her leg as Gus started pulling dishes out of the cupboard. "I've got this," he told Thad. "Go sit down."

Thad made a low grumbling noise, but put the serving spoon on the counter and headed for the table. Henry met him at his chair. Apparently Henry had a new friend.

"How are you feeling?" Thad asked Lillie Jean as soon as he was seated.

"I'm doing okay."

"Your head?"

"Probably looks worse than it feels."

The microwave dinged, and Gus used an oven mitt to pull out a tray of lasagna. The scent of bubbling tomato sauce filled the kitchen, reminding Lillie Jean of her own kitchen back home, and of all the prefab dinners she'd eaten while working late into the night creating her designs. Lasagna had been her go-to favorite. Only, this lasagna didn't smell prefab and when Gus set it on the table, she could see that it had not come from the freezer section of the local grocery store. It was homemade.

"Who cooks?" she asked, looking at first Gus, then Thad.

"Gus likes to relax by cooking." Thad looked at his nephew as if such a thing was beyond his understanding.

"Beats starving," Gus said, setting a stack of three plates and a fistful of flatware next to the lasagna. "Let it cool a bit," he said to no one in particular.

"What do you do in Texas?" Thad asked in an obvious bid to break the tension that settled over the table as soon as Gus had taken his seat on Lillie Jean's right-hand side.

"I'm between jobs right now," she said. "I just sold my share of a business to my partners." Almost true. "So I'm looking at starting something new." She made starting over sound like an easy thing to do. Like she hadn't been emotionally invested in the business she'd just lost and like her creativity hadn't dried up.

"What kind of business?"

"Clothing." And so much more. She didn't want to get into it. She wanted to eat her meal, have an uncomfortable conversation with Thad, then head south—where she probably should be right now.

"Ah," Thad said. Gus said nothing, and Lillie Jean focused on her plate. She was hungry, but she didn't feel like eating. Her stomach was in a knot and the sudden buzzing of her phone in her pocket didn't help matters. How sad was it that she instantly assumed that a text was bad news?

She forced herself to eat a couple of bites before asking Thad about his pub.

The old man smiled politely, but the pained look in his eyes told her that she had turned his life upside down. "Maybe you should stop by before you leave. I'll give you a tour." He raised his eyes to Gus. "Speaking of the Shamrock, I have to head back pretty soon. Ben called in sick and I have to open."

Gus nodded. "You want me to come in?"

"No. I'll be fine. Ginny said she'd be in early to help with the heavy lifting."

Lillie Jean's phone buzzed again and she reached into her pocket to turn it off.

"You can look, you know," Gus said. "We're not big on phone etiquette here."

She pulled the phone out, looked at the screen and did her best to keep her expression from changing as she read the short message. Andrew wanted to talk.

What little appetite she'd had evaporated.

"Bad news?" Thad asked.

She gave her head a quick shake as she hit the power button, darkening the screen. "Just the regular kind." Where Andrew was involved, anyway.

What on earth could he want to talk about?

It couldn't be anything good.

"You okay?" Gus asked, ignoring her assertion that all was well.

"Yes." Her tone sounded strained and she made an effort to lighten her voice as she added, "I'm fine." She turned to Thad. "I'm sure you want to know what my plans are."

"Yeah. I do."

"How much income did my grandfather get from the ranch?" Because maybe, if this place produced income, she wouldn't have to instantly sell.

"Not a lot," Thad said. "The place kind of went to he…heck over the past few years. Sal was getting old and Gus was on the bull riding circuit. And I… I didn't spend a lot of time here. I was busy with the pub." He reached for the glass of water at his elbow. Took a drink. "Gus has plans to build the place back up. We'll see an increase in income if the cow and hay markets and the weather cooperate, but it's a slow process."

"I see." Not exactly the words she'd wanted to hear, but the old man spoke so earnestly it kind of broke her heart. She pushed the lasagna around her plate, then set down her fork. "I need to sell. It's the only way I can get back on my feet relatively rapidly after losing my business."

"I thought you sold your business."

Lillie Jean met Gus's gaze dead on. "I got forced out by my two business partners, and thanks to my trusting nature, I didn't get all that much in return. I don't have nearly enough money to start again without getting a day job. Or two." The thought of going through the agony of starting over was enough to give her an instant bellyache. But start over she would.

"Or selling your part of ranch," Gus supplied.

"Yes."

"I'd hate to see this ranch broken up," Thad said.

The phone buzzed again in Lillie Jean's pocket. Stress upon stress. Gus not only heard it, he exchanged a glanced with his uncle. Lillie Jean reached in her pocket to hold down the power button, completely turning off the phone—which she should have done the last time it vibrated.

"I understand," she said as if nothing had happened. "I'll give you first refusal."

"Doesn't mean a lot if I have nothing to pay you with," Thad muttered.

Lillie Jean let out a breath that made her shoulders droop. "I'm sorry things are what they are, but, Thad... I need the money. And I want to apologize for dropping in out of the blue. I wanted to find out why I didn't know about this place."

"And your grandfather just died." Thad's voice was soft and understanding, despite her having just told him that she was going to mess up his ranch.

"Yes." She pressed her lips together. "That, too."

"How's the rest of your family holding up?" The old man spoke the words stiffly, in an awkward tone that would have had her frowning if Gus hadn't clued her in as to the startling truth about her family.

"The rest of my family is me," she said simply. "Both grandparents have passed away. My mother died of breast cancer. I never knew my father."

Another exchange of glances between Gus and Thad, and then Lillie Jean decided it was time to go. Coming here had been a mistake. She wasn't certain whether learning the truth about her grandparents was a good thing or bad. It was, after all, the truth and had always been the truth, but her memories of them were altered in a way that she wouldn't be able to change.

Yes, it was definitely time to go.

CHAPTER SIX

THAD WAITED UNTIL Lillie Jean retreated to the bedroom to gather her belongings before asking Gus, "What do you think's going on?"

Gus knew exactly what his uncle was getting at. Lillie Jean had gone pale after reading the phone text, like she'd received unwelcome news.

"Not a clue."

"I think we should let her stay awhile if she needs to."

Gus's jaw dropped. "What?"

"You heard me."

"What makes you think she needs to stay?"

"She's got no family and just lost her business."

Gus glanced toward the hallway before saying in a very low voice, "Maybe she's hard to work with, Thad. Maybe she deserved to lose her business."

"I don't believe that."

Gus blew out a breath. "Are you sure this is a good road to take?"

Thad motioned Gus into the mudroom. "I think it might be the thing to do. She wouldn't have shown up here out of nowhere if everything was going well. She said she has no family, and you saw how she jumped whenever her phone went off."

"Maybe she's a nutcase." He didn't think she was, but he tossed the idea out anyway.

"The lawyer kid didn't think so."

"I don't know, Thad…"

"She's in our lives one way or another."

Gus pressed his mouth in a flat line. "This is Lillie Jean. Not Nita."

Thad's face went red. "I haven't lost my marbles yet."

"That's not what I meant." He rubbed a hand over his neck. "But they look alike, and it would be natural to kind of…" His words trailed off as he met Thad's challenging gaze.

"What?" his uncle demanded.

"Making up your shortcomings with Nita by helping the granddaughter."

"And maybe," Thad said, gritting out the words in a low voice, "we'd have a better chance of bringing Lillie Jean around to our way of thinking if she got to know us." He gave another quick look over Gus's shoulder. "Maybe," he said, his voice even lower than before, "she won't automatically sell if she stays for a while."

"And maybe that's a freaking long shot." But he had to admit that Thad had a point. If Lillie Jean was in Texas, dealing through lawyers, they'd have no idea what was going on.

"I'm not saying that she won't sell, but maybe if she sees how things are, she might hold out for someone we can work with."

"Or maybe she'll fall in love with the place and decide to stay?" Gus asked darkly. He had a feeling that was another possible outcome on his uncle's short list of happy endings.

"I don't see that happening," Thad said. "Have you seen how cold she gets every time she steps outside?" He snorted. "And kind of hard to fall in love with a place when you get a head injury your first time out."

"I messed up," Gus said. One minute all'd been well,

and the next minute, the truck had bottomed out in the rut. Kind of like his life over the past couple days.

Thad looked at his watch as the bedroom door opened. "Let's talk to her right now."

Gus sucked in a breath and followed.

Henry danced across the room and sat at Thad's feet. The old man's face softened as he crouched down to stroke the little dog's ears, and then he stood again as Lillie Jean walked into the room, her gym bag in one hand.

"Thank you for letting me stay."

"You could stay longer, you know."

Lillie Jean's mouth fell open, very much as Gus's had a few minutes ago. She shot him a startled look, then transferred her gaze back to Thad. "I... Why?"

"Just throwing it out there as an option," Thad said.

Gus could see another *"Why?"* hovering on Lillie Jean's lips before a faint frown creased her brow and she pressed her mouth flat. "Maybe it would be best to wait until everything is ironed out legally."

"Maybe," Thad agreed. "But if you wanted to stay a day or two, rest up for the trip home, you're more than welcome. Really, you are."

Lillie Jean glanced down at the floor, her shoulders dropping as if the weight of the gym bag was getting to her, although Gus had a feeling it was a weight of a different kind that was affecting her.

"You're welcome to stay," he said in a low voice. Her eyes came up and Gus was fairly certain he saw a measure of relief in her gaze. She didn't want to go back home. Not yet, anyway. "Thad has to head to town to open the pub, so it'd just be you and me."

"Is that a warning?" she asked.

"Maybe."

A faint smile curved her mouth, lifting the corners just

enough to let him know that she didn't find the prospect of sharing the ranch with him all that intimidating—not compared to the prospect of going home, anyway.

"I don't know what to say."

Henry scratched at Thad's pant leg with one stubby paw and Thad bent down to pet the little dog again. "You just do whatever you want, but this place is here and it isn't like you'll take up a lot of room that's needed for someone else."

"You can see the operation," Gus added. It was obvious that Lillie Jean was not used to being on the receiving end of hospitality.

"That's a good point." She pressed her lips together and Gus could see that she was wavering. She wanted to stay. Or, perhaps more accurately, she didn't want to go home.

Lillie Jean validated his assumption by saying, "I wouldn't mind a day or two before heading back."

"Then maybe you should put your suitcase back in the bedroom," Thad said gruffly. Gus had the feeling his uncle was looking back through the years, but even if he was, he was also looking toward the future, which was why Gus had to agree that having Lillie Jean stay on the ranch wasn't a bad idea.

"WHAT ARE YOU going to do?" Kate Tanner, Lillie Jean's best friend, sounded worried. Lillie Jean understood the concern. A lot had happened in twenty-four hours and as she'd filled in Kate, it sounded kind of sketchy to her, too.

"I'm going to stay for a day or two. It'll give me a chance to see the ranch. Settle a few things in my head."

"The better to sell?"

"Exactly." She told herself that was the only reason. That staying had nothing to do with learning more about

Gus Hawkins, who seemed to have taken up permanent residence in her head. There was something about the guy, beyond the good looks and rugged cowboy appeal, that made her want to know more, which felt kind of dangerous, but she couldn't help herself. Maybe it was the way he was so protective of his uncle. Or the way he'd become flustered in the bathroom after applying the adhesive suture to her forehead.

Or maybe it wasn't so much about learning more about the guy as it was showing him that she wasn't the person he seemed to think she was. She hated having the guy believe she was some kind of an opportunistic gold digger. That was so not her modus operandi.

"Maybe your partner can buy you out."

"Maybe." But she wasn't getting that feeling. "If not, there are people—rich people—who invest in ranches. Unfortunately, this ranch is kind of run-down."

"How run-down?"

"You know what the Howe place looked like?" The Howe place was a neighborhood landmark back in Serenity, with a house that had never been painted and deteriorating sheds in the backyard surrounded by old car parts and tires.

Kate let out a low breath. "Really?"

"A couple notches up from that, but there's work to be done. Thad's nephew plans to revamp the place."

"Do you sell before or after the revamp?"

"I'm going to sell just as soon as I am legally able. The land is still worth quite a bit."

"All I can say is that you deserve a little good luck after everything else that has happened."

Good luck for her. Bad luck for Gus.

Lillie Jean felt guilty getting a windfall when Kate and her mother were struggling to get by on their part time jobs, but when she'd mentioned helping out, Kate would hear none of it. "It's bad enough that Mom insists on paying rent," she'd said. "I won't be taking a handout from you, too." Like it wasn't Lillie Jean's fault that Kate had quit her corporate job to go to work for A Thread In Time's.

Lillie Jean would try later, when she actually had something to offer.

Which may not happen for a long, long time.

Her inner voice made an excellent point.

"I got a text from Andrew. He wants to talk."

Kate gave an audible snort. "Why haven't you blocked him?"

"Because I never thought he'd contact me."

"Block him now. The last thing you need is that slime puppy trying to wheedle his way back into your good graces."

"Like that could happen." But having him contact her was unsettling. "I hate unfinished business, and his text makes our relationship unfinished—on his end."

"Maybe staying up north for a while isn't that bad of an idea."

Lillie Jean paced to the window and looked out over the fields on the south side of the house. "If I don't mind running from my problems." Which was pretty much what she'd been doing when she left Texas. Yes, she'd wanted answers, but she hadn't minded quitting the state one bit. The highway had been freeing, and then she'd come to a splashing halt in a mud hole and suddenly trouble started catching up with her again.

"Sometimes a short run isn't a bad thing," Kate pointed out. "Like you said, you can use the time to get your thoughts in order. Decide your next move. What's your partner like?"

"He's Grandpa's age." *Once married to my grandmother.* She wasn't ready to talk about that yet. "He runs a bar in town. His nephew runs the ranch."

"So why didn't you know about him?"

There was no easy way to answer that question. "As I understand it, Grandpa and Thad started the ranch together, then they split and Grandpa went to Texas."

"The guy ain't talking," Kate guessed.

"Mr. Hawkins hasn't exactly been a well of information." Unlike his nephew. She was grateful to know the truth. It helped her as she figured out how to handle things.

There was a silence on the other end of the phone, and then Kate said, "The thing that worries me about you staying is that you know nothing about these people."

"They have no records of arrest." She'd researched Thaddeus Hawkins before leaving Texas, and she'd researched his nephew the night before. Montanan through and through. Former bull rider. Part owner of the Shamrock Pub. "There's nothing to set off red flags, and honestly? I'll probably just stay a day or two, then come home." Face the music. And Andrew, who wanted to talk to her.

She forced a smile into her voice. "How are the kids and your mom doing? How are *you* doing?"

"You aren't fooling me with the change of subject. Just so you know."

"Yeah, yeah, yeah. I miss you guys."

"We miss you, too. And even though Mom is moving in, you know we can find room for you."

Lillie Jean couldn't help the laugh that escaped her lips. As if there were an inch of spare space in her friend's house. "Thank you, Kate. I appreciate that, but I'm going to pack my stuff and get out of your hair as soon as I get back. That way your mom won't have to sleep in the bathtub."

"I'm serious. We'll find room."

"I know." And that was why she loved her best friend.

GUS HAD A LOT on his to-do list that day. The tractor needed servicing, and he wanted to ride the northern border fence, which was only accessible by horse or four-wheeler. Lillie Jean's presence put a halt to all work that day, but the more he thought about it, the more Thad's strategy made sense. Why alienate the woman, or send her off to Texas? Why not keep her close, so they had a fighting chance of being in the loop as she made decisions? If she turned out to be trouble, better to know now than later.

And, as Thad had reminded him more than once, she had a right to stay. She could demand to stay. Gus propped his elbows on the table and massaged his forehead with his fingertips. Yes. Communication was key, as was developing a friendly working relationship. Too bad he'd started off their relationship by insinuating that she wasn't on the up-and-up. Injuring her forehead hadn't earned him any points, either.

Time for damage control.

He wasn't good at damage control. In the bar, he simply kicked out patrons who became rowdy or uncoop-erative. He didn't try to talk them into seeing things his way. Not for long, anyway. Arguing with someone who'd drank too much was like arguing with a dog—only you had a better chance of coming to an understanding with a dog.

The coffeepot gave its last gurgling gasp as Lillie Jean opened the bedroom door and started down the hall to the kitchen. She'd made a phone call—he'd heard the muffled rise and fall of her voice through the walls—and he figured he'd discover the effect it'd had on her decision to stay within the next few minutes. Henry trotted over to him and sat, staring up at him with his shiny eyes. It was like he had some kind of magnetic power, because every time he was near, Gus felt like crouching down and petting him.

Lillie Jean stopped just inside the door, looking first at the coffeepot and then at Gus.

"You guys drink a lot of coffee."

"Habit. It kept me awake when I worked the ranch during the day, then pulled the second shift at the pub." He raised his eyebrows politely. "Want some?"

"Sure. I probably won't be sleeping tonight anyway."

Gus let the remark pass as he got up to pour coffee into a fresh mug for Lillie Jean and refilled his own.

Once he was seated, he lightly cupped one fist in the other. Where to begin?

"Maybe we should give each other some background?" he asked. "Learn a little about one another?" Awkward, but a beginning.

"Kind of like speed dating?" Lillie Jean asked blandly.

"I wouldn't know." He hadn't had time for dating, speed or otherwise.

"You go first."

The ball had landed in his court faster than he'd expected. "I…uh…" *Hate this.*

Lillie Jean frowned at him. "I thought bartenders were good conversationalists."

"No. We're good listeners." Gus blew out a breath and gripped his fist more tightly as he addressed the table instead of Lillie Jean. "I was born in southwest Oregon. I was a holy terror and my dad got custody when my parents divorced. My mom remarried and kind of disappeared from my life. My dad got killed in a logging accident when I was fifteen and I came to live with Thad here in Montana. Thad didn't put up with any of my angry teenager crap, so I turned out to be a fairly decent human being."

When he finished he raised his gaze and found Lillie Jean staring at him. She cleared her throat. "Succinct."

Gus gas a small shrug. "Like I said. I'm a listener, not a talker."

"What did you do after becoming a decent human being? College?"

"I went to college at the University of Nevada, Las Vegas, so that I could rodeo on the college team. I quit after two years, went pro bull riding. Had a decent, if undistinguished, career and now I'm back home." It kind of hurt to say *home*. "I used my earnings to buy into the Shamrock and became Thad's partner. I planned to trade my half of the Shamrock to Thad as a down payment on half interest in the ranch after Sal retired, but now that is all up in the air."

Lillie Jean's lips parted, and then she pressed them shut again.

"Your turn." He released his cupped fist and reached for his mug.

She cocked her head. "It's kind of amazing how that all just fell out of your mouth."

Gus gave another shrug. He liked to get things over with. Hated unfinished business, which was yet another reason having the ranch in limbo ate at him. How did one move toward the future when the present was messed up?

"I won't be so smooth." Lillie Jean took her first sip of coffee, then set the cup back down. "I was born and raised in suburbia. Unlike you, my dad was never in the picture. My mom never made that an issue. I had a super supportive and excellent childhood. Grandpa…" She hesitated, then pushed on. "Grandpa did all the male role model stuff and he was good. Grandma was there for me when Mom wasn't. They're all gone now."

"What do you do for a living?"

"I'm a clothing designer."

"You work for a company?"

"I started out working for a clothing company, then I branched out on my own. My ex-fiancé, another…friend, I guess…and I started a vintage clothing store and online business. High-end stuff. He searched out the clothing. I did repairs, and eventually started designing and sewing retro-inspired pieces. One-of-a-kinds. They sold well, especially with the music people from Austin, and eventually became the mainstay of our business."

"You could support yourself doing that?"

"Yes. Business was good. The sewing got to be more than I could handle, so we hired a lady to do the repairs and I did the designs. Taia—our partner—and I sewed the pieces."

"You said ex-fiancé." Which might explain why Lillie Jean had showed up out of the blue.

"Yes." She met his eyes in a way that told him she wasn't comfortable with the subject, but she wasn't going to avoid it either.

"And you mentioned earlier that your business partners forced you out."

"My ex wasn't keen on working with me after he dumped me."

Bluntly spoken, but he could see that it cost her. She was still dealing with the aftermath of what had happened to her.

"I'm guessing," he said slowly, "that you're not going back to much in Texas."

"That pretty much sums it up."

"You have a right to stay here, you know. For as long as you like."

"So you can keep an eye on me?"

Gus's eyes narrowed as she hit the bull's-eye first guess. She was sharp, and he saw no reason to hedge. "Maybe."

One corner of her full mouth tightened, making a faint dimple appear in one cheek, totally at odds with her humorless expression. "Keep your friends close and your enemies closer?"

"You're not exactly an enemy."

"I'm not a friend, either."

"You could be."

She shook her head as if that was totally impossible. Had he been that much of a jerk to her earlier? Maybe. That was where damage control came in.

He watched as she thought over his proposal, a faint frown drawing her dark eyebrows together. She had a delicate appearance, and may not know crap about ranching, but she was tough. She'd been ready to take him out with a tire iron the night before if he tried anything and she'd never said a word about the wound on her forehead after they'd finished doctoring it.

"If you stayed here, you'd have to pull your weight, of course."

Her gaze snapped up. He wasn't certain why he'd said what he just said, but it seemed to have a positive effect.

"Yes. I will," she answered in a cold voice.

Lillie Jean was motivated by challenge. Good to know.

"After you learn what to do?" Gus asked softly.

"There may be a learning curve."

He leaned back in his chair, stretching his legs out under the table. Waited. Lillie Jean wrapped her hands around the coffee mug. "Maybe we should just get everything out into the open. Do you plan to sell your interest in the ranch?"

"I need the money. A lump sum, not a trickle."

Gus gave a silent nod. She wasn't telling him anything he hadn't already suspected.

She raised her blue eyes to meet his, her expression sincere as she said, "I'd give you first refusal."

He snorted before he could catch himself. "That's not in the cards unless I qualify for a big loan." And if he could sell his half of the Shamrock for enough money to make the kind of down payment a lending institution might require.

Her eyes flashed. "I didn't create this situation."

"I'm aware." He wasn't going to make things better by putting her back up. "It could take years to sell," he said quietly. Or days. His gut tightened. All it took was the right buyer to come along on the right day.

"I would like to learn about the ranch. Educate myself. As you say, it may be mine for years." She spoke grimly, making him believe that she did indeed need the money.

"Which means we'd be partners for years."

"Which means we should develop a business relationship."

"Agreed."

Lillie Jean unclasped her hands and laid her palms flat on the table. "I'm starting over, Gus. I got squeezed out of my business and, other than the original investment price, I came out with next to nothing. I want to start a new business. It's what I *need* to do."

"So you'll sell the ranch to finance."

"I'm not going into partnership again…except for this one, of course. In the future, it's just me."

From the way she spoke, he had a feeling that she was

talking more than business. Gus pushed his untouched coffee aside. "Because your ex-fiancé squeezed you out of the business you started together."

Lillie Jean gave a silent nod.

"Heck of a guy."

Her lips tightened, but she made no response. He couldn't really blame her. His gaze strayed up to the bruise that had formed beneath the butterfly adhesive on her forehead. She started to lift her hand, as if to touch the spot, then stopped herself. Lillie Jean did not like to show weakness.

"I guess I told you all this so that you would understand why I might behave cautiously in a partnership. I've been burned. I don't want to get burned again."

"We'll be fair, Lillie Jean. All we ask is that you be fair with us."

She glanced down at the table, the corners of her mouth tightening, once again bringing out the dimple. "Then I guess we want the same things." She raised her gaze, met his dead on.

"Guess so."

She pulled in a breath and once again fixed those incredible blue-green eyes on him. "I hope you understand why the relationship between us will be business only."

"As opposed to…?"

"Becoming friends, Gus. I'm not falling into that trap with a business partner again."

CHAPTER SEVEN

AFTER LILLIE JEAN drew her no-friendship line in the sand, Gus's expression shifted in a way that made her want to know what he was thinking. Probably something along the lines of "like we'd ever become friends." Good. Even though her stomach was tight, as it always was after confrontation, she didn't regret her flat statement. There was an advantage to a civil, yet distant relationship— decisions would be based on facts, not swayed by emotions. And while she might study her cowboy partner, and catalog details, make discoveries and assumptions about him, she wouldn't be getting any closer. How could she, and keep her pride, after laying things out so definitively?

"Is that house next door habitable?"

Gus's eyebrows drew together. "Sal moved out six weeks ago."

"Could I live there? While I'm here?" Because, while there were advantages to staying on the ranch for the time being, the intimacy of sharing a house with this cowboy made her feel uncomfortable. The prospect of bumping into him on the way to the bathroom, sharing a kitchen table…yeah…not something she wanted to contend with on a daily basis. Not when being around him made her nerves tingle in a way that made it hard to relax.

"I'd have to see how much propane is in the tank, but if we have the ability to heat the place better than its being heated right now, I can't think of a reason why you couldn't stay there." In fact, he looked kind of re-lieved at the idea, as if he'd been considering the inti-macy issue himself. "I have some business to attend to," he said abruptly, pushing the chair back and getting to his feet. "Feel free to eat whatever you find in the freezer."

"The freezer?"

"The lasagna was the last of the real food. All I have left are frozen dinners."

"I'll pay you back."

He gave her a bemused look. "If you want. Or you can work it off."

Was he making fun of her? Or maybe she was a touch oversensitive after hanging herself out there, letting go with her secrets. "Got peanut butter?"

"In the cupboard next to the fridge."

"I'll make a sandwich." There was a loaf of bread on the counter.

"Suit yourself. I won't be gone long." He headed to-ward the mudroom, grabbed his coat, pulled keys off the rack and let himself out of the house. Lillie Jean watched through the kitchen window as he went to his truck and got inside. The sun had just disappeared be-hind the mountains, and she couldn't help but wonder what chore took him out so close to dark.

Lillie Jean let herself out of the house via the mud-room to walk the short distance to the house next door. The yard light lit the driveway as she made her way down the walk and out the gate. A gray cat blinked at her from under the porch as she approached the house, making her glad she'd left a mournful Henry in Gus's kitchen. Henry fancied himself a cat hunter, but the two times he'd ac-tually cornered a gnarly neighborhood kitty, he'd come out on the bottom and her grandfather had spent days putting salve on the scratches on his nose.

The old house looked just this side of haunted as she climbed the three creaky steps. Were there ghosts on the property? Lillie Jean did not believe in ghosts, but she did believe that houses held energy generated from the feelings within. Love and laughter made even the humblest house feel good, while more negative emotions could turn a mansion into a mausoleum. It worked both ways, of course. She flicked on the light and stepped into the empty living room, shutting the door behind her, and then she stood, soaking in the atmosphere. Nope. Not haunted. Not sad. Just…waiting.

And cold. She could almost see her breath. Hopefully there was propane in the tank. She took a couple more steps into the living room, hugging her arms around her and wrinkling her nose as the musty smell became stronger. Her footsteps echoed as she slowly explored the tiny house. The kitchen was small, with next to no counter space, but the midcentury appliances gave it a funky retro look. Right up her alley.

She traveled on to the bathroom with its black and white tile. Someone had painted the room a white so white that it kind of hurt the eyes. On to the bedroom. There was no bed. Sal must have taken it with him. Lillie Jean wondered if Gus had a bed stowed somewhere? Did he expect her to come up with one? If so, she'd sleep on the floor—after a good scrubbing, of course. In the hall between the rooms was a pull cord for attic steps, but Lillie Jean didn't pull it. That was private space. The final room was small with a north facing window. If she'd been a painter, it would have made a cute little studio. As it was, it would make a nice place to sew.

If she could bring herself to sew. She hadn't touched her machine, except to finish two contracted jobs, since Andrew had dropped his bombshell. It was as if her creativity had withered after Andrew destroyed her trust. She hadn't so much as taken out her sketchbook, hadn't searched eBay for vintage pattern inspiration.

A small part of herself had died that day.

Headlights shone through the curtainless front windows, giving her a guilty start. Gus returning from wherever. Lillie Jean snapped off the light and headed out the door just as he pulled the truck to a stop. They met at the gate, and Gus stood back after unlatching it, allowing her through. He carried a bundle of mail in one hand, thus answering the question of where he'd gone just before dark.

"I thought I'd take a look at the house before committing myself."

"And?"

"I can make it work. But I'll have to come up with a bed," she said as they walked to the backdoor.

"I'll take care of it."

And that was it. Discussion over. He opened the screen door and Lillie Jean opened the interior door, stepping into the mudroom. She took off her coat and folded it over her arm.

"You can hang it on the hooks if you want."

"I'll keep it with me," she said. She preferred all her stuff together. Who knew, maybe she would have cause to suddenly bolt. But looking up into Gus's face, she didn't think so.

He was ridiculously handsome with that shadow of brownish-blond scruff over his cheeks, ending just below his high cheekbones. He was Kate's type of guy. She'd always gone for the Nordic types, while Lillie Jean had been more of a tall, dark and handsome girl. But now, as she studied Gus's face, she had a strong feeling she'd been limiting herself.

Gus was studying her as intently as she was studying him. They both became aware of the fact at the same moment and Lillie Jean felt color rising from her collar. This awareness between them was not something she'd banked on, and it was something she wanted to tamp down. No...something she *needed* to tamp down. There was a difference between wants and needs, especially in a business relationship.

She wondered if Gus was thinking something along the same lines as he shifted his weight and jerked his head toward the hallway.

"I've got some work to do in the office. There's a TV in the living room."

"I'll make my sandwich, then read in my room."

"Fine. We feed at six."

The statement drew her up short. Six? It would be dark. Why feed in the dark?

"In the morning?"

His expression didn't change. "Coffee's on at five."

Five? She was so not a morning person. Lillie Jean gave a quick nod. "I'll be ready at six."

LILLIE JEAN'S ROOM was dark and quiet when Gus passed it on his way down the hall the next morning. He'd showered the night before, and shaved. The lip prints were starting to fade, but not fast enough for his liking. He owed Mimi some payback.

The coffeepot was on a timer and the coffee had just finished brewing when he snapped on the kitchen light. He poured a cup and leaned back against the sink as he took his first sip of the nerve-jolting brew. He was a morning person, which had made tending bar a challenge at times, and coffee gave him that extra bit of energy he needed to tackle the day. He loved the stuff.

He also loved this part of the day. The quiet before the

storm. A chance to sit at the table and gather his thoughts while the possibilities of the day stretched out before him. There was no sign of movement in Lillie Jean's room. He didn't know what time she'd gone to bed, but when he'd emerged from his office the night before, and stopped by the kitchen for a glass of water before calling it a night, light had shone from under her door.

The one thing he *didn't* need help with was feeding, but he figured that if Lillie Jean experienced life on the ranch, understood what he did and why, saw the connection between the work and the land, that perhaps she'd work with him when it came time for her to sell. It was just a theory, but his gut was telling him to keep her close—but not too close. Sal's house was perfect. He was glad she'd come up with the idea.

If none of the pregnant cows looked like they were going to calve that morning, he'd head to town and get his twin bed from the apartment over the pub. He rarely used it, and if, for some reason, he needed to spend the night in town, he'd use the blow-up thing that he'd had in college. It still held air—for most of the night, anyway.

At quarter to six, the bedroom door opened, and Lillie Jean headed down the hall to the bathroom, Henry's paws clicking on the floor behind her. The sound of her footsteps made his body tense, but he reminded himself that this was his reality. He had a partner. And when she sold, he'd have a different partner. All he was doing now was buying time, but maybe, *with* time, he could come up with a way out of this mess.

Gus set down his coffee and went to the mudroom to shrug into his coat. The air wasn't quite as cold as it had been the past few mornings, but it still nipped at him. He unplugged the tractor and started it, leaving it to idle as he went back to the house. Lillie Jean was in the kitchen, her loosely braided hair falling over one shoulder as she dressed Henry in his sweater. She looked tired and the butterfly suture covering the bruise over her eyebrow gave him a twinge of guilt.

"Do I have time for a cup of coffee after I walk Henry?" she asked.

He pulled a cup out of the cupboard and filled it before handing it to her, handle out. She took it with a grateful expression on her face, which made him wonder if she'd gotten much sleep the night before. She closed her eyes as she sipped her coffee, then drew in a breath, as if steeling herself for what lay ahead.

"Maybe you could let Henry tour the front yard on his own. I closed the gate when I came in."

"Yes. That's a good idea." She let the little dog outside. When she came back, Gus topped off both their cups. Lillie Jean finished her second cup of coffee in record time and set down the cup. "I'm ready for…whatever."

He jerked his head toward the mudroom. "Let's go."

After she was once again bundled into his jacket, he reached for his wool cap with earflaps.

"Really?" she asked as she gingerly took the hat from him.

"You may as well learn to dress like a rancher, since technically you are one." Or will be one. "Those fleece hats don't cut it when the wind blows."

"I thought ranchers wore cool cowboy hats."

"Not on a cold morning when they're feeding the cows."

Lillie Jean gave him a dubious look as he reached for a cowboy hat. "Where's your Elmer Fudd hat?"

"In your hand." He opened the door and Henry dashed in. Lillie Jean took off the dog's sweater, told him to be a good boy, then followed as Gus led the way out the door and across the driveway to where the tractor idled. This time Lillie Jean knew the drill. She waited for him to climb the stairs into the cab before following. Once inside she shut the door. The cab felt just as claustrophobic as it had the previous morning. Maybe a little more so, because it seemed like he was even more aware of Lillie Jean—which he would have said was utterly impossible the day before.

"What exactly is my job?"

"You open gates and watch."

He lifted the bucket high enough to allow him a field of vision beneath it and headed for the haystack, wondering how it was, that despite the chilly air that made the diesel fumes hang low, all he could smell was the faint scent of lilacs.

LILLIE JEAN KNEW enough to wait until Gus had put the tractor in neutral before she opened the door and climbed down the steps at the first metal gate, which fastened with a wraparound chain—no levers and loops to confound her. She opened the gate and waited as the big tractor rolled by.

Kate would be impressed—not by the gate opening, but by the fact that Lillie Jean was up at dawn and out in the cold. She scrambled back up the steps into the warm cab and pulled the door shut. Gus's arm brushed hers as he put the machine in a forward gear, and she did her best to ignore the fact that they bumped shoulders every time the tractor lurched. She was out of her element, but that was good for personal growth. Right?

She closed her eyes as the tractor swayed. She was tired. She hadn't had enough caffeine. She was riding in a tractor with a guy she hadn't known existed a few days ago, but who was now a part of her life—until she sold the ranch, anyway.

Sold the ranch. It was crazy that such an option even existed. It was so far out of what she would have considered the realm of possibility less than a month ago that it still kind of boggled her mind. But here she was. And she was staying for a while.

After her grandfather passed away, Lillie Jean had lost her last anchor, other than Kate, who had a full-to-the-brim life and didn't need to add Lillie Jean's issues to her load. Late last night, as she'd stared at the ceiling, willing herself to sleep, she'd concluded that staying at the ranch was an anchor of sorts. Temporary or not, it provided a base, a place where she could get her footing as she waited for life to smack her with the next unexpected blow. Because at this point, she was fully expecting another bad surprise.

Was all the stuff happening to her payback for the charmed life she'd led prior to losing her mother? Because until then, everything had gone her way. She'd gotten a design school scholarship, a coveted internship. Andrew proposed. A Thread in Time had taken off almost as soon as they'd hung out the shingle. Isabella, an up-and-coming Austin musician, had essentially become a patron of the business. Lots of good things, one after the other.

And now one bad thing after another, the latest being the discovery that her grandparents had shared a big secret. They'd been runaway lovers.

She gave a slightly choked laugh, felt Gus glance her way, but kept her eyes front and center. She didn't need to see the quizzical expression in his eyes. Didn't need to feel that jolt of connection she knew would follow. He slowed as they approached a haystack.

A week or two in Montana and she'd see things more clearly, have an idea of where she wanted to go and what kind of new business she wanted to build. She'd keep her hands busy and her mind would settle. And maybe she'd start to feel some sparks of creativity.

Maybe she'd get lucky and sell the ranch immediately. One could hope.

Gus edged the tractor to the haystack. The stack swayed as the bucket made contact, then he pulled a lever and the big claw above the bucket came down, impaling the giant bale and tipping it back into the bucket.

Gus put the tractor in reverse, lowered the bucket and started toward another gate, which Lillie Jean opened. He motioned for her to stay put, then drove into a smaller pasture and set the bale on the ground next to a large metal feeder. He climbed down from the cab, pulled knife from his pocket and cut the strings, expertly folding them into a single coil as he circled the huge bale. A few seconds later, he was back in the cab, lifting sections of hay and setting them in the feeder.

He made two trips between the haystack and the feeders, Lillie Jean waiting at the gate, watching, shivering despite being wrapped in the big coat.

Cows and calves were pressing against the gate on the opposite side of the field and after the last feeder was filled, Gus crossed to open it. After the cattle had poured through and were pushing and shoving at the feeders, he got back in the tractor and headed for Lillie Jean, who was all but hopping up and down with cold.

When she got into the warm cab, she gave an uncontrollable shiver.

"The cold came up through my feet," she muttered.

Gus frowned as he glanced down at her running shoes. "Yeah. It does that. I wasn't thinking."

"Maybe I can play a more active role in the future. Then my feet won't freeze to the ground."

"Now that you've seen the routine, we'll keep you moving."

"What now?" Lillie Jean asked as they approached the barn.

"We feed the cats, throw some hay to the horses, check the heavy bunch." She frowned at him and he clarified. "The pregnant cows."

"And that's it?"

"If I wasn't going to town, I'd start working on the fences. They sag in the winter and need to be fixed every spring. And I have to service the tractor."

"What else do you do to fill your days?"

He gave a humorless laugh. "There's always something. The sheds need repairs," he said drily.

That was an understatement, but she'd noticed stacks of siding and roofing beside some of the most decrepit buildings.

"Later in the spring the fields need to be attended to. Weeds need to be chopped, the roads need to be graded." He pulled the tractor back into its parking place and turned off the engine before reaching across her to open the door, making her wonder if that was a gentlemanly maneuver, or because she had a hard time with the sticky latch. Or maybe, like her, he wanted to escape close confines. Lillie Jean climbed down the steps, her frozen feet stinging as they hit the hard ground.

"Does it ever warm up?"

He smiled a little. "Gets into the nineties in the summer."

"That hot?" she asked mildly.

"Ninety is pretty much sweltering to me."

She rolled her eyes, but said, "Yes. Ninety is hot. But you get used to it."

"I don't think so."

"You'd rather be cold than hot?"

"Without question."

"I can see why Grandpa moved to Texas." As soon as she said the words, she regretted them. An odd look crossed Gus's face, and she pushed aside her regret and forged on, facing the truth. "But he didn't leave because of the cold, did he?"

"No."

"His actions had far-reaching consequences."

Gus's face had gone stony, but his voice was surprisingly gentle as he said, "Probably farther-reaching than he ever imagined."

LILLIE JEAN WENT quiet after mentioning her grandfather and his reasons for leaving Montana for Texas. Except for a few duty questions about feeding, she remained quiet as they finished the chores, and he couldn't help but feel for her. In a distant, partnership kind of way, of course. He jammed the hay hooks he'd used to move the smaller bales into the stack and turned to find Lillie Jean staring at the hooks with a thoughtful expression.

"If I wrote murder mysteries, those would play a role."

"They do look kind of lethal," he admitted.

"Kind of?"

He smiled a little as they headed for the door. "When I was a kid, they were part of our pirate gear. We'd jam the handle up our sleeve to make a hook hand."

"You were a pirate?"

"And the barn was the ship." She gave him a sideways look, which he met with a sideways look of his own. Two cautious people connecting—even though one of them didn't want to. "It's not as much fun to play cowboy when you're living cowboy, but we did that, too."

"We?"

"There were some kids on the adjoining property." The property Carson Craig now owned.

"But you grew up in Oregon?"

"And spent a lot of time here with Thad when I wasn't in school. I liked being on the ranch because it was… stable." No parents yelling at one another, and after his mom had left, no sullen father ignoring him. He glanced sideways again. "But we're keeping things on a business level. Right?"

Color stained her cheeks as she was caught breaking her own rules. "Yes."

"Kind of hard in a closed environment like this."

"But not impossible."

"Nope. I can go to my house. You can go to yours. We'll live side by side, getting together to discuss business practices, treat each other politely. Coexist."

"Are you being sarcastic?"

"I am."

"Why?"

He stopped at the door. "Because I think friendship enhances a partnership as long as it's tempered with respect and a few ground rules."

"How many business partnerships have you been in?"

"One. With Thad. It's still working."

"Your experience is different from mine. I'm doing what I need to do."

He gave his head a small shake and stepped out of the barn just as the sun moved from behind a cloud spilling warm light onto the driveway. Lillie Jean closed the door and latched it, while he waited.

"*I'm* not your partner, you know," he said as soon as she joined him near the big rear tractor wheel.

She frowned at him. "Technicality."

"It's going to get kind of lonesome here if it's just you and Henry."

"I can live with lonesome."

"Good thing, because there can be a lot of that."

"Why do you want to be friends with me?" The words came blurting out.

He turned toward her. "I didn't say I wanted to be friends. I'm saying I don't believe in building fences where there doesn't need to be one. I'm not your cheating fiancé. I'm not going to take advantage of you."

"No offense intended, but I don't know that," she said stonily. Her cheeks were even pinker than before. "And my fiancé didn't cheat. Not in the romantic sense."

"I wasn't talking in a romantic sense. He cheated you out of your business—right?"

"In a very legal way. Once he decided he didn't want to marry me, he and Taia, the third partner, joined forces to ease me out."

"You don't have to worry about that happening here. It isn't like Thad and I can gang up on you."

"There are other ways to gang up on a person. I want things kept on a professional level."

"Lillie Jean…you're stubborn."

"No, Gus. First I was foolish. Now I'm a survivor."

SHE *WAS* A SURVIVOR. Her mother had been a survivor, too. Janice Ann Hardaway might have gotten pregnant young, and her man may have disappeared before her baby was born, but she'd not only made a life for herself, she'd given her daughter a picture-perfect childhood. Lillie Jean had grown up knowing the facts about her dad, but had never been encouraged to be bitter about them. Her father hadn't been up to being a father, and that was that.

Instead, Lillie Jean was taught to focus on the positives in life, to set goals and achieve, regardless of circumstances. Her granddad had provided the fatherly stuff, and her mom and grandmother had been her biggest cheerleaders. She'd done well in almost every endeavor she embarked upon. She had to do well—otherwise she would have disappointed her family.

Now she no longer had a family to disappoint, and was still working on fully accepting that fact. No family. No business. Just a big empty future laying ahead of her…and a guy, who wasn't really her business partner, standing a few feet away from her, watching her through narrowed eyes.

She had a feeling that Gus Hawkins was as stubborn as he accused her of being. That it wasn't so much that he wanted to be friends, but that he *didn't* want to be told they couldn't be friends. And it did sound kind of unnecessarily strict, and made her seem like a tight ass, which she wasn't. She was just watching her back, yet the way she was doing it felt wrong.

"Okay," she said softly. "Maybe I'm being overzealous." She perched a hip on the cold metal steps of the tractor, wrapping her arms around herself. "But I messed up by trusting when there were clear signs that I shouldn't have been trusting, and look where I am now."

"In some of the most beautiful country around? Half owner of a ranch?"

"An emotional wreck." She moistened her lips, barely believing she'd allowed those words to slip out, then looked past him to the field where they'd fed the cattle that morning. "Maybe not a wreck, but I was blindsided. Lost two things that I loved."

"Do you still love him?"

She slowly shook her head, her jaw muscles tightening. "I don't think I knew him. Not all of him. That bothers me. If you'd asked me a couple months ago, I would have sworn that I knew Andrew Landers better than anyone on the planet. But I didn't. So what does that say about my judgment?" She looked down at her feet as tears filled her eyes.

"Lillie Jean?"

She frowned furiously at the gravel, willing herself to get it together before she looked up at him. Wasn't happening. All these weeks of holding it together and now she was losing it. In front of an audience. Why?

"I need to keep things on a business level." She spoke to the gravel in front of her feet, the words coming out from between gritted teeth.

She heard Gus move and glanced up, startled to find him closer than he was before. He reached out and his hand hovered near her shoulder for a split second before he settled it on her shoulder, then slowly drew her into a loose embrace. Lillie Jean held herself stiffly before she let out a shaky breath against the rough canvas of his coat and closed her eyes. But she didn't move away. Didn't create the distance that she told herself she needed.

His hand started rubbing slow circles over her back and despite everything—the cold, the circumstances, the insanity of the moment—she felt herself relax. Human contact felt good. And she hadn't had enough of it lately. Finally, even though she could have stayed exactly where she was for a long, long time, she drew back and looked up at Gus, her heart doing a triple beat as she realized she wanted nothing more than to kiss the gorgeous mouth that wasn't all that far from her own.

Instead she put her palms against his chest and slowly

extricated herself from his embrace. "I…uh…guess I needed a hug. Thanks."

The expression that crossed his face told her that he wasn't a bit fooled. He was more than aware that she'd been teetering on the edge of breaking her own edict. But his tone was matter-of-fact as he said, "Anytime." He took a casual step back and Lillie Jean told herself to get a grip. A hug. Big deal. A near kiss. Nothing she couldn't handle.

What about the fact that, in spite of all your big talk and good intentions, you wanted to kiss him? What about the fact that you still do?

Lillie Jean's jaw muscles tightened as she told her little voice to hush. So she had some challenges ahead of her. Tall, rangy, cowboy challenges. Again, nothing she couldn't handle.

"If we're done with chores, I have some cleaning to do in the old house." She didn't quite meet his eyes as she spoke. Despite her internal pep talk, she felt raw, emotionally naked. What had started as a simple back-and-forth about what their relationship would or would not be had somehow managed to tip her over.

"And I have a bed to get. Do you need anything from town?"

"I think I'll drive in later. Alone." He didn't argue with her. Lillie Jean scuffed the toe of her running shoe through the gravel. "I also think we have more talking to do. About this partnership, I mean."

He pushed up the brim of his hat with his forefinger like she'd seen cowboys do in the movies. The gesture looked totally natural. "Given our circumstances? Yeah. I think we do have more talking to do."

CHAPTER EIGHT

GUS PARKED HIS truck in the graveled lot behind the Shamrock Pub. He was proud of what he and Thad had built over the past three years, but he didn't miss bartending. There had been times when he felt more like a playground monitor than the proprietor of an establishment, and it grated on him. He wasn't really a people person, whereas Thad loved dealing with the public, and he was good at it. His rules were not to be broken. Those who did, found themselves escorted from the establishment, or banned—sometimes for days, sometimes forever. But since the Shamrock was one of the more popular watering holes in Gavin, very few people allowed to return held a grudge, and those that did were not the type of clientele that the Shamrock was looking for.

Mimi was behind the bar when he walked in through the back door, setting up for opening. She looked up, then grinned at the remains of the lip print.

"Honest, I didn't know it was indelible ink."

Gus gave her a dark look. "Honest, you should have checked."

She laughed. "I would have done it anyway. Looks good on you."

"Thanks."

"You know I love you."

"What do you do to people you don't love?"

She smiled wickedly and flipped her long red braid over her shoulder. "You don't want to know."

No. He did not.

Mimi focused on slicing lemons, keeping her gaze down as she casually said, "You might have escaped the pub in the nick of time, you know."

Gus stopped. "Why's that?"

"I heard that Madison is coming back to town."

Excellent. "Thanks for the heads-up."

"She's going to look you up. I know she is."

So did he, because the woman didn't like losing. Gus's biggest mistake had been in dumping her before she dumped him. Now he was a challenge.

"Is Thad around?"

"He went to the bank." Mimi started cutting lemons again. "You can pull up a stool and tell me about life on the ranch while you wait."

Gus leaned his forearms on the smooth mahogany bar. "It's about what you'd expect."

"Boring and labor intensive?" Mimi had grown up on a hardscrabble operation that her family had ultimately lost. She was not a big ranch fan.

"It suits me." He just hoped he'd still be working the ranch for a while, and not be behind the bar, cutting lemons. "Keeps me out of trouble."

Mimi put down the knife and leaned her elbows on the bar. "Thad said you had big plans."

His gut twisted at the mention of his big plans, but Gus did his best to speak as if there was nothing standing in the way of seeing them through. "I have a lot of buildings to re-side and reroof. I want to get the fields back into production. Improve the fences. Start working on a breeding program. Nothing against Sal, but we have calves coming between February and June."

"Ouch."

"Yeah. I've only got six left to calve out. I'm selling them all once they're bred again."

"Let someone else have the headaches."

"Some people like to calve late." He wasn't one of them. He wanted the calves on the ground within a thirty-day period. So much easier to manage the herd. Make improvements.

"I hear you have a roommate." Mimi arched an eyebrow at him.

"Yeah?" Thad had told Mimi about Lillie Jean? Which was akin to telling the world.

"Thad said his partner's granddaughter was visiting."

"Yeah. She is."

"I didn't know Thad had a partner."

Join the club. "Kind of a silent partner. He and Thad started the ranch together years ago, then the partner moved to Texas, where it's warm."

"Ah." Mimi went back to her lemons. "I guess everyone has some surprises in their backgrounds."

Yes. A point that had recently been hammered home to both him and Lillie Jean.

The sound of keys in the front door brought Gus's head around. Thad let himself in and locked the door again. "Hey," he said with an easy smile when he saw Gus sitting at the bar. "Grocery run?" His smile might have been easy, but his eyes told a different story. He wanted to know how things were faring on the ranch with Lillie Jean.

"Yep. And there's a couple of ranch things I wanted to discuss with you before I move forward."

Thad looked at his watch. "Forty minutes to opening."

"I got this," Mimi said easily. "Ginny's supposed to clock in soon."

Thad nodded and silently headed to the door leading to the rear entrance of the building and the stairs to the upper story. At the top of the stairs was a narrow hallway with a storeroom at the end and a door leading to two apartments on opposite sides halfway down. Thad opened the door on the left and stepped into his apartment. It was a cozy place. Well kept with shelves and shelves of books.

Gus waited until the door was closed before saying, "I need a bed."

"Why?"

"Lillie Jean is moving into Sal's house while she's here."

Thad wrinkled his nose. "That musty old place?"

"She says she's fine with it."

"So she's staying longer than a day or two?"

"Yeah. I think she is."

"That's a good thing, right?"

"I hope," Gus said. He wasn't convinced of anything at the moment. "She's talking about keeping things on a business-level, so I guess she's going to be a partner until she sells. The question is whether she'll be a partner on the ranch, or in Texas."

Thad went to the fridge and pulled out a cola and popped the top, took a slug, then set the can on the table. "I'd buy her out if I could."

"So would I." Unfortunately, the value of land in their area had skyrocketed over the years. "Maybe we could both sell and settle elsewhere." Even as the words came out of his mouth, Gus was aware that he didn't mean them. The H/H had gotten under his skin. He loved the ranch, had dreamed of improving it for years. He was finally in a position to do so and—no, he didn't want to start again elsewhere. Not unless he had to.

"The sensible side of me agrees with you," Thad said. "But I lost my wife to Lyle. I don't want to lose my land, too."

No matter how this played out, he was going to lose something. Gus just hoped that Thad didn't find himself partnered with some know-it-all rich guy who wanted things done his way. There were lots of nonranchers with money who wanted to live the life and give the orders. Watch other people jump when they spoke. Their neighbor Carson came instantly to mind.

"You need to make friends with Lillie Jean. Convince her to keep you in the loop. Once we know what she's going to do, we can figure out what we're going to do."

Gus decided not to tell Thad that Lillie Jean had decreed that they would not be friends. There was only so much an old guy should have to take.

"I'd like to talk to Hal Warden and get some advice," Thad continued, "but you know how the real estate people are in this town. Everyone and their grandma will know that the H/H might be up for grabs if I do that."

"Yeah," Gus agreed. "Don't talk to Hal yet. Let's wait on Lillie Jean and I'll do what I can to stay in her good graces."

"It'd be best if you were in her confidence," Thad said helpfully.

"No doubt." *Isn't gonna happen.* "Can you give me a hand getting the bed down the stairs? She'll like us better if she's not sleeping on the carpet."

"What'll you sleep in if you stay in town?"

"I'll use the blow-up." Which he didn't see happening in the near future. Too much to do on the ranch.

Ten minutes later, Thad and Gus had the box spring and mattress wrapped up in his old sheets and loaded into the back of the truck. After sliding the frame in on top, Thad closed the tailgate and leaned an arm on it. "Sheets?"

"We have extra at the ranch."

"I probably won't be out for a day or two, seeing as you have help."

"Give a yell if you need someone to cover a shift." Although he hoped that didn't happen. He wanted to stay on the ranch, do what he could while he could, because his days there might be numbered.

"Will do." Thad gave Gus a nod and headed toward the back entrance of the Shamrock. He was walking slower, favoring the leg that had been smashed during his accident on the trail so many years ago. Thad was showing his age, and Gus couldn't help but blame the circumstances. And, fair or not, maybe Lillie Jean, too, for showing up out of the blue and giving the old man a shock he didn't need. He didn't blame her for showing up—he would have done the same, but he liked to think that he would have given some notice.

She's dealing with grief. Give her a break.

Thad was dealing with grief, too. Grief she'd stirred up.

Gus was about to open the truck door when someone hailed him, and he instantly tensed at the sound of the authoritarian voice. Crap.

Forcing his features into a bland expression, Gus turned. "Carson."

Carson Craig strode toward him from where he'd just parked his gleaming black Ford F350—the one with too many bells and whistles to be a respectable ranch rig. But it did its job in the impress-people department, as did the man's showy western outfit. Ostrich skin boots, leather vest, dark denim jeans with a crease down the center. Gus didn't know anybody who creased their jeans—except for Carson Craig. In his late thirties and too rich and smug for his own good, the guy made Gus's annoyance meter redline.

"Hawkins." Carson was a last name kind of guy, which was why Gus made it a point to always use the man's first name. "About that fence."

Gus hooked his thumbs in his pockets and rocked back on his heels. Yes. About that fence.

Carson waited and when he finally realized that Gus wasn't going to respond, he said with a touch of annoyance, "Have you had a chance to fix it?"

Just say yes.

"The hole was on your half. Therefore, it was your responsibility." Shortly after Carson had taken over management of his property, after having driven out yet another competent foreman, Gus had taken him to the midpoint of the boundary fence and explained that everything to the right was Gus's responsibility and everything to left was Carson's.

Carson remained unconvinced. In his mind, Montana fence law didn't matter. What mattered was whose animals broke the fence, and as he saw things, those animals always wore the H/H brand and he reiterated his belief for the umpteenth time. "The hole was created by your cattle, which ended up on my property."

"We don't know that my cattle created anything. We only know that my cattle wandered through and mingled with your cattle." Carson's cattle could have easily broken down the fence. "But I fixed it, so you can breathe easy."

Carson's features didn't relax, even though he'd just gotten the answer he'd wanted.

"It's the last time I fix your half," Gus said.

"We're neighbors."

Gus really hoped the guy didn't go on to say something stupid like, "Good fences make good neighbors." He didn't.

"Neighbors shouldn't become embroiled in legal hassles." Carson tipped back his expensive beaver cowboy hat and gave Gus a long, hard look.

Gus let out a weary breath. "Are you threatening me?"

"I'm saying we need to come to an agreement. If my cattle end up on your property, I'll fix the fence and vice versa."

"So...you're rewriting Montana boundary law."

"I'm taking a common-sense approach."

Gus shook his head and reached for his door handle. "Carson, you do what you got to do. I'm not fixing your fence again."

Ironically, Gus would have maintained the boundary fence in the name of being a good neighbor if Carson had been a good neighbor. The crazy thing was that the guy could be totally charming when he needed to be. He served on local committees and donated hefty sums of money to good causes—the new library fund, the senior center, the afterschool program. Because of that, the locals either liked him or tolerated him. But with Gus and Thad and every guy who'd been hired to manage his ranch, Carson was autocratic. The boss, who was never to be questioned.

Gus didn't play that game well.

He got into his truck without another word to Carson Craig, closed the door, started the engine. It was only when he'd put the truck in gear that he glanced toward his jerk of a neighbor, who was staring at him with a deep frown, as if debating disciplinary action for insubordination.

Good luck with that.

Gus lifted his forefinger to his hat in a mock salute

and put his foot to the gas. It wasn't until he was on the road home that he realized he was still holding his jaw so tightly that the muscles ached.

LILLIE JEAN DROVE to town shortly after Gus left, carefully maneuvering her grandfather's car around the remaining mud holes in the long road leading to the highway. She hadn't noticed the mailboxes when she'd driven into the property, but as she slowed to a stop where gravel met pavement, she caught sight of the lone metal box with bullet holes in the side. Welcome to rural Montana. Rural anywhere, for that matter. Texas mailboxes had their share of bullet holes, too.

Once in Gavin, she stopped at the first grocery store she came upon and stocked up on cleaning supplies and staples—bread, two jars of peanut butter, crackers, fruit, milk, eggs. The stuff she'd subsisted on while growing the business. She might have a right to stay on the ranch, but she didn't have a right to eat Gus's food, even if she was helping with chores—although if today was anything to judge by, the word *help* was a stretch to describe her part of the operation. Opening a gate, then shutting it barely qualified.

Maybe this was the learning phase. Maybe she'd drive the tractor soon and he'd open the gates.

Right.

In her experience, men didn't give up control of the gas pedal and steering wheel easily. He was keeping her on the ranch for one reason only—to stay in the loop as she made decisions. And she was okay with that, because staying on the ranch felt right. For now.

She arrived home ahead of Gus, took the bags of groceries to the old house, then returned to the main house with the second jar of peanut butter. She'd just walked into the kitchen when her phone buzzed and she dug it out of her pocket. She didn't recognize the number, but the text said it all.

This is Andrew. There's serious stuff we need to discuss.

Speak of the devil. Lillie Jean set the peanut butter on the counter and texted back.

Contact my attorney.

A heartbeat later she hit the phone icon next to the text. She wasn't going to wear out her thumbs. Andrew answered immediately.

"Lillie Jean. Where are you?"

"None of your business."

"We're missing some designs."

"Excuse me?"

"The Moon over Texas dress and the Morning Ride jacket among others."

"Have Taia draft them."

"You know she doesn't draft and, besides that, we no longer have the samples."

That was because she had the samples. And the patterns. Because she'd designed that intricate dress and jacket, two of their mainstays, prior to setting up the business. Those designs were her property. Her last official act before surrendering her keys to the store had been to go to the storage area and remove the items she'd brought to the company. She'd left behind plenty of designs, the ones she'd created after A Thread in Time was born.

"What I took were mine. It's well documented."

"Everything you brought to the company became a company asset."

And that was a flat-out lie, because in a heart-pounding moment after discovering that Taia and Andrew no longer wanted to share the business, she checked the contract and then did a thorough internet search.

"Nice try, Andrew."

"You know that Taia's dad is a lawyer, right?"

Of course, she knew that, just as she knew that Andrew was trying to intimidate her.

"Bite me."

There was silence at the other end of the phone. "Send the patterns back and we'll leave you alone." This from the man she'd planned to marry. The man she'd sat up late with planning their store. Their future.

"You have photos. Hire someone to draft it." She couldn't stop them from copying her dresses, but she wasn't going to make it easy on them.

"We're on a tight deadline for an event."

"Not my problem."

"It's for Isabella," Andrew said in a strangled voice. Their up-and-coming country music star client. Having Isabella wearing A Thread in Time designs had been huge. "The dresses she ordered for her big tour."

Just before Andrew and Taia pushed Lillie Jean out of the business. He probably thought that nice contract would be the beginning of something big.

"Again. Not my problem. Goodbye, Andrew. Give my best to Taia."

Lillie Jean turned off the phone, then tilted her chin up to stare at the ceiling. She'd never been a fan of drama and here she was in a full-fledged soap opera. She'd almost kissed Gus that morning, and now her blood pressure was redlining thanks to her ex-fiancé.

Enough.

She headed back to the old house, where Henry met

her at the door, as did the musty smell that permeated the place.

"There will be changes," she told the dog. She didn't know exactly what those changes would be, but she was going to take charge of her life. Leave Andrew and his issues far behind.

She glanced down at Henry. "We're painting." That should take care of some of the smell as well as the sad beige color.

The dog cocked his head and her phone rang. Kate.

"I just heard from Andrew. He wanted to know if you'd stored your designs with me. He made it sound like you stole them."

"Jerk."

"You know about this?"

"We talked. He texted me from an unblocked number. I answered."

"L.J.—"

"It was fine. I'm fine."

"Are the things he's looking for in the boxes in my attic?"

Lillie Jean had stored the boxes there because Kate's attic was little more than a crawl space—not an obvious place to store bulky boxes.

"They are. But you don't know that."

"No. I do not."

Lillie Jean let out a breath. "Sorry to get you into this."

"I'm glad to help."

"If you see Andrew skulking about, alert the authorities."

"You don't really think he'd skulk, do you?"

"I didn't think he'd dump me and steal my business. I'm taking no chances."

A cry went up in the background and Kate sighed. "One of the babies. Keep me in the loop."

"Will do. And if Andrew bugs you again, let me know."

She set the phone down, then jumped a mile when the front door rattled, and Henry let out a menacing bark. Gus had returned. When he saw her through the window in the door, he pushed the door open and stepped inside, carrying the jar of peanut butter.

"You forgot this."

Lillie Jean shook her head. The last time she'd seen him, she'd been on the brink of losing it, had come close to blowing everything by kissing him, so it was doubly important that she regain lost ground. "No. I left that on purpose."

"Payback?" he asked in a disbelieving tone.

"You have a problem with that?"

"You ate two sandwiches. One for dinner and one for breakfast."

"I figured the extra PB would help offset the bread."

"You're kidding."

Lillie Jean folded her arms over her chest. "I'm a payer-backer."

"Hope you don't plan to pay me back for the Band-Aid on your forehead."

She felt like smiling. She didn't. "I guess that remains to be seen."

"Is that a threat, Lillie Jean?"

Lillie Jean coolly raised her eyebrows before saying, "This place needs painting. It'll help with the smell."

"We have paint in the basement of the other house."

"Beige?"

"Maybe?"

"I was thinking color." She didn't see how Gus could object to painting the depressing walls.

He set down the jar on the rickety end table next to the recliner. "Do what you need to do."

"Do you want me to wait until everything is official with Thad?"

Gus shook his head. "Like you said, the place needs to be painted."

She picked up the jar of peanut butter and handed it back to him. Gus scowled, but she held his gaze, silently daring him to put the jar down again. He tucked the small jar into his coat pocket.

"I have a bed in my truck if you'll give me a hand."

He'd gotten her a bed and she was giving him a hard time.

No—you're keeping your distance.

"Happy to."

With Lillie Jean's help, Gus brought the mattress and box spring into the house, leaning them against the wall in the bedroom. He started to set up the frame, but Lillie Jean stopped him.

"I'll do that later." She stood back and slipped her fingers into her back pockets. "I guess I'll see you at six tomorrow morning?"

"You'll see me in about half an hour. We have a heifer about to calve and then you're going to learn to stretch wire."

Lillie Jean smiled a little as he let himself out the door. The guy was smart. The guy was playing it right. Acting as if nothing had happened this morning, getting things back on an even keel. She bit her lip as she watched his cowboy hat disappear when he descended the porch steps.

Of all the guys in the world, why did this one fascinate her so?

GUS DUCKED HIS head against the wind as he started to the barn. Life had been a heck of a lot easier when he hadn't known that Thad had a partner; when he'd thought he'd had his future figured out—when his biggest problems were coming up with money to fix the ranch and contending with Carson Craig's unreasonable attitude. There was so much to do on the ranch and here he was, dealing with peanut butter and painting. A woman who he wanted to know more about…a woman who'd felt so totally right in his arms that morning. He had a feeling that she wasn't immune to him, either—not judging from the way she'd studied his mouth before easing herself out of his embrace.

Not going to be friendly. Right.

It would be interesting to see how long the professional-distance thing lasted as he and Lillie Jean worked together—if they continued to work together. She could pack up at any time and head back to Texas, but if she did, he hoped she didn't leave Sal's house half-painted. He dove into most jobs with a willing attitude. Except painting. He hated that chore. And he didn't want Lillie Jean to leave before the ranch issue was settled, which left them in something of a conundrum. He couldn't think of one instance where he'd worked shoulder to shoulder with someone and didn't develop a level of intimacy…except for Geoff Mahoney. They'd put in fences on the H/H his first summer there. What a rich-boy jerk old Geoff had been, put to work by his father so that he'd know how it felt to be a common man. He'd treated Thad, his boss, like dirt, and hadn't lasted more than a couple weeks. Gus had been happy to do twice the amount of work if it meant no more Geoff.

Cool. He'd think of Lillie Jean as a female version of Geoff.

Except she wasn't.

She was a woman who'd been burned by her partner and didn't intend to be burned again. A woman who was going to screw up his life. Had already started making inroads.

He wasn't getting anything done.

He checked the heifer, who was down, but not looking too distressed, then went to the other side of the barn to load the four-wheeler with the fencing gear. When he was done, he grabbed the peanut butter jar from the top of a grain barrel and carried it into the kitchen and stowed it in the cupboard. Lillie Jean was a payer-backer. That was so…businesslike. But she'd also been tense when they spoke—like she wasn't any more immune to him, than he was to her.

Would that work for or against him? He had a bad feeling that it was the latter. Lillie Jean was self-protective and he had to be careful not to send her running back to Texas.

The wind hit him hard as he left the house again. The forecasted snow was on its way. So much for fencing. He just hoped that the heifer got her calf safely on the ground before the weather hit.

He went to Sal's house and knocked on the door. Henry let out a ferocious warning bark a few seconds before Lillie Jean pulled the door open. A blast of warmth hit him.

"The furnace works."

"Good to know." One less thing he'd have to deal with. She pulled on her coat, then frowned up at the sky.

"Is the cow in the barn?"

"Not yet. But she will be."

"Then what do we do?"

"Hope that nature takes an uneventful course." Which was about a sixty-forty proposition with the heifers.

Despite being a heifer and clueless as to the process, the cow allowed herself to be herded into one of the three straw-filled pens in the barn. She didn't like the looks of Lillie Jean, and eyed the new human suspiciously until she suddenly lay on her side, stretched her neck out and groaned. Gus stepped back to join Lillie Jean where she stood near a stack of small bales.

"First calf birth?"

"You have to ask?" she said, tucking a few strands of dark hair behind her ear. "But I did help deliver a baby once."

"Kitten or puppy?"

"Human."

The expression on his face must have been something, because for the first time since they'd met, Lillie Jean laughed. A light, infectious sound that stirred something in him he didn't want stirred, and made him feel like smiling. "How'd that come about?"

Her expression sobered, as if she'd just realized that she was breaking her rules again, getting too friendly. But her tone was matter-of-fact as she said, "My friend Kate was expecting twins. Her first kids. When the contractions started, she realized that things were *not* going slowly and called me. I beat the ambulance."

"And delivered the baby."

"Baby number one. The paramedics delivered number two."

"I'm impressed."

"It was pretty much a lot of reassuring talk followed by catching a very slippery little bundle. I was terrified."

"What other impressive secrets do you have, Lillie Jean?"

"That's pretty much it. Other than that, ho-hum life."

He made a noise in his throat. "Kate have a husband?"

She shot him a sidelong look. "Neither of us were lucky in love."

"Ah."

Lillie Jean started to move closer to the pen and without thinking Gus reached out and took her wrist, felt her give a start at the contact.

"Don't want to distract her," he murmured. "She doesn't like you." Lillie Jean eased back a step and he let go of her wrist. "Cows are like that. They don't take to strangers."

"She doesn't seem to be doing much." Lillie Jean lightly rubbed the wrist he'd grabbed.

"Heifers can take time."

But this one didn't. He'd barely gotten the words out when the birthing process started and less than fifteen minutes later the young mother was nuzzling her calf. Lillie Jean stayed a careful distance away, watching wordlessly until the newborn bull latched on to his mama and had his first meal.

"All is well," Gus said as the bull calf slurped away and the mother showed no signs of being anything but motherly.

"Now we fence?" Lillie Jean asked faintly. The snow was blowing sideways past the open bay door.

Gus scowled at the uncooperative weather. "Maybe we'll put that off for a while."

"Fine by me."

"Did you really think we'd work in these conditions?"

Lillie Jean gave him a considering look. "I didn't know if this was a case of following common sense or cowboying up."

"What's that supposed to mean?"

"I think it's fairly self-explanatory," she said. "Where

I come from guys do a lot of unnecessary stuff in the name of being a cowboy."

"I thought you came from suburbia."

"Doesn't keep guys who didn't know which end of a horse to feed from professing to be cowboys."

He couldn't help smiling.

"What?"

"Nothing." He'd wanted to say that he liked her take on life, that he liked *her*, but according to Lillie Jean, he wasn't allowed to like her. According to his own common sense it wasn't *good* to like her. So maybe he'd just focus on the reason Lillie Jean was there on the ranch, instead of wondering over and over again what would have happened if she'd gone with her instincts and kissed him that morning.

THE OLD FURNACE had done its job and the house was wonderfully warm by the time Lillie Jean ducked inside and started brushing snow out of her hair. But despite the warmth, and the vague odor of hot dust, the house was musty.

"We need to paint," she repeated to Henry, who whined and lifted one stubby front paw. Lillie Jean looked at him, then sighed. When you gotta go, you gotta go. She picked up the reindeer sweater and buttoned it under his belly, then put her coat back on and pulled up the hood, tightening the string so it wouldn't blow off this time.

"Make it snappy, okay?"

Henry rolled a brown eye at her as if to say, "What else would I do in the middle of a blizzard?"

But Henry had never seen snow and he liked it a whole lot more than she did. He ran and rolled and turned circles in the white stuff while Lillie Jean stood on the porch, her hands shoved deep into her pockets as the wind whipped at her. Finally Henry had enough and raced to the house, his tongue hanging out.

"Are you done?" she asked wryly.

Henry answered her by scratching on the door, as if she needed a reminder as to what her next step was. Like she was going to stay in the weather a minute longer than she had to.

But she had to admit once the door was closed, and her coat was laid out over the back of the old orange-and-brown-plaid recliner to dry, that she felt kind of invigorated. And really happy to be inside.

She stood at the window, watching the snow blow by. There were no swirling, drifting flakes, like in the movies. These were snow pellets moving at warp speed, creating a blur across the window, disorienting her. Or maybe it was the blur of her life doing that. A lot had happened in a short period of time and she was still adjusting to things that would have sounded crazy to her six months ago.

Lillie Jean closed her eyes, shutting out the dizzying white swirl, in an attempt to center herself. Acknowledge the strange circumstances in which she found herself.

You are in Montana.

You own half a ranch.

She opened her eyes to stare into the white again.

Your partner's nephew is one attractive guy and you have no idea how to handle that attraction, because it's going against everything your very logical brain is telling you. Do not get involved with your business partner.

He's not a real partner.

Once bitten, twice shy, remember? This is where the shy part comes in.

It was…kind of. This morning in the tractor cab, she'd been so aware of how near Gus had been that she'd focused on her breathing to keep from focusing on him. She'd been nervous and jumpy, and if the ground hadn't tried to freeze her from the bottom up, she might have chosen to walk back to the barn rather than to ride in the tractor. Although a lot of good that would have done, considering what had happened after the tractor ride.

She'd be in that darned cab every morning they fed the cows if she lived up to her word and pulled her own weight, which only seemed fair since she was living there and was essentially a joint owner. Which meant she was going to have to get a grip. Focus on other things—things that didn't have high cheekbones, great lips and scruff on their jawline that begged to be touched. Because she wasn't running again. Not just yet. She'd have problems no matter where she went, so for the time being she was going to dig in and confront the challenges before her.

She turned her back to the window, faced the bland beige walls. Thought about how much she did not want a bland beige life. She wanted color and excitement. She wanted to take charge, move forward. Stop running.

Lillie Jean crossed to the kitchen and leaned her shoulder on the doorjamb as she studied the small room. It could be cute. Really cute. Those white midcentury appliances cried out to be surrounded by warm colors and a fun motif. Cherries or lemons or chickens, maybe. No. No chickens. She'd stick with flowers or fruit.

You will? As in, you're redoing the kitchen?

Why not?

She could start taking charge of her life by working on her creativity. Yes, she was having trouble sketching clothing, but she could design a kitchen. Make curtains, towels. Surely Gavin or some town close by had a place where she could purchase supplies and maybe a kitchen revamp would spur her forward, get her creative brain bubbling again. She'd start by giving herself a more colorful environment in which to create.

Lillie Jean bent down and scooped up Henry and turned in a circle. "What do you say, bud? Shall we take advantage of this place while we're here? Lay a foundation, then transfer it to Texas? Show Andrew and anyone else who sticks their nose into our business that we're on the comeback trail?"

It seemed like a perfect idea and would solve the problem of Kate's insistence upon volunteering space in her small house until Lillie Jean got a job and settled elsewhere. Plus, she'd have all the peace and quiet she needed to get her creative juices flowing again.

Henry licked her nose and Lillie Jean laughed and turned another slow circle, waltzing her dog around the room.

"You're right. It's an excellent idea."

She wasn't about to commit to a life of freezing Montana cold—and obsessing over the guy next door—but the idea of staying until she got her mojo back was solid. She'd stay until it was time to go.

Or she sold her part of the ranch.

Whichever came first.

LILLIE JEAN WAS RIGHT—it was dumb to mix business and friendship. At least in their case, because even though they weren't yet friends, he felt a crazy attraction to the woman. It only made sense that as a friendship grew, so would the attraction, unless he found out something heinous about Lillie Jean. Or unless she was like Madison, a secret control freak who sought to manipulate everyone around her into doing her bidding. It had taken Gus a while to figure out Madison. A couple wasted months of his life. He really hoped the woman stayed in Missoula.

Gus didn't get anything close to a manipulative vibe from Lillie Jean. She was forthright in her answers. Told him straight-out that she planned to sell the ranch. Told him that she knew he'd asked her to stay so he could keep an eye on her. Had called him out on his jerky behavior when she'd first arrived, and when he'd suggested she was there to scam Thad, she'd been openly insulted and went on the offensive instead of trying to cajole him into believing her.

He was starting to like Lillie Jean. And he liked being around Lillie Jean, but he couldn't let that get in the way of his objective, which was getting her to work with him in regard to the ranch, so he didn't end up with some jerk of a rich partner. Carson Craig sprang to mind. How could he not after their recent run in? Carson had bought his way into ranching and was trying to manage a huge spread without a lick of experience. According to him, his experience in business better prepared him for running a ranch than actually living on, and working, the land.

Carson Craig was a tool.

The lights were on in Sal's house and every now and again he saw a shadow move past the kitchen window, looking almost as if it was dancing. Was Lillie Jean cooking or trying to get rid of the musty smell with the cleaning supplies he'd seen lined up on the kitchen counter earlier? What else was she going to do all alone in that house, with only her dog for company, except clean?

And here he was, thinking about her again.

Gus turned away from the window.

One thing he'd learned in life was that it was difficult to regulate emotions. You couldn't stop them, but you could manage them—that was the lesson Thad had taught him when he'd shown up on the ranch, angry at his father for dying and leaving him alone, angry at his mother for having a new family and not wanting to reclaim him. Yes, he was angry. No, he wasn't allowed to rail against the world and be self-destructive. He was to take his anger out in a productive way—which turned out to be bull riding—while looking to the future.

In retrospect, it seemed that Thad's knowledge of anger management came from firsthand experience. Lessons learned, and love lost.

Sad.

But Thad's hard lessons were the reason they were in the position they were in today and, bottom line, Gus needed to come up with a way to give Lillie Jean what she needed without losing control of the ranch.

He poured a cup of coffee and headed to his office to fire up the computer. It was slow but steady, and he sipped from the mug as he waited for the screens to load. At this rate it might take a good part of the night to research various means to his ends, but the sooner he discovered his options—other than relying on Lillie Jean to not sell out to a jerk—the better off both he and Thad would be.

CHAPTER NINE

"Do you get package delivery here on the ranch?"

Lillie Jean had waited until they were on their way back from fixing a long stretch of sagging fence before asking the question.

Gus had been giving her sidelong glances all day, as if suspicious of her sudden good mood, but she hadn't felt like sharing the reason for her uplifted spirits. It was such a simple thing, really. She was redoing the kitchen. She'd even run the idea past him in the most casual of ways— *Hey, I'm thinking of making curtains for the kitchen and painting*—had received a *That sounds good*, and considered the matter settled.

"Of course we get package delivery." He spoke in a tone that made her feel like a clueless suburbanite. Which, essentially, she was.

"Well, you're kind of isolated," she pointed out.

"Not that isolated. Are you ordering something?"

"I might order fabric for the curtains." And she was going to have Kate ship her sewing machine, but telling him about the machine might make him think she planned to stay longer than she was going to. No sense giving him false hope about her possibly keeping the ranch. As soon as she was back on her feet emotionally and creatively, she was heading to Texas.

"There's a quilting place in Gavin."

Lillie Jean perked up. "Yeah?"

He smiled at her reaction, almost as if he couldn't help himself.

"On Main Street, a block down from the Shamrock. Annie Get Your Gun."

He gave her a look from behind the steering wheel and she instantly gestured for him to turn his attention forward. It might have been her imagination, but it looked like his cheeks went red at her less than subtle hint to watch the road. She'd gently peeled off the adhesive suture the day before and, while she was certain she'd have a faint mark above her eyebrow for the rest of her life, the cut had healed well.

"I could take you to town," he offered.

"Or I could go by myself." The snow had melted off the road, so there was no reason she couldn't go alone.

"Just stay out of mud puddles."

"Ha. Ha."

Lillie Jean grabbed the plastic hand loop above the door as they headed to a bumpy part of the field. After two days of fencing, she was becoming an old hand at keeping her balance in the truck when it hit ruts and rough patches.

She wasn't doing so well convincing herself that Gus wasn't all that attractive. He was, and she had to take care around him. A couple of times she'd been studying him as he worked—in an attempt to learn proper wire-stretching or hole-digging technique, of course—and he'd casually glanced up, caught her mid-stare. Both times she'd continued looking right through him, as if daydreaming, because to suddenly drop her gaze would be too much of a tell.

Why, when she was still recovering from the emotional wounds caused by Andrew's betrayal, was she so drawn to this man?

She told herself that part of it had to do with him being a cowboy. Who wouldn't be fascinated by a cowboy? Despite growing up in Texas, she'd never met a real one before—only the drugstore kind. The kind who bought straw hats that were already distressed. Gus's hat was made of wool felt and every mark and scar on it told a tale of a long day doing some kind of manual labor. He had another hat hanging in the mudroom. A pristine chocolate-brown hat. Lillie Jean figured it was his dress hat, but she never asked because she was trying hard to keep things from getting too personal.

"I guess I better ask whether I should do my laundry in town, or if I can borrow your washing machine."

"Will you pay me back?" he asked, keeping his eyes straight ahead as he spoke.

Smart aleck.

"I'll give you a jar of peanut butter." Even though she told herself not to engage in repartee, she kept doing it. And she also kept feeling that warm sensation when he smiled, as he was doing now, with his gaze glued to the track in front of him.

Oh yeah. He was good looking *and* fun to banter with. Deadly combination for someone doing her best to stay aloof.

Gus had not asked about her plans for the ranch once over the past two days. They'd worked together on the fence, then she'd gone back to an ecstatic Henry, who thought she really needed to spend her days with him, as she had when she'd been an owner of A Thread in Time. Henry had gone to work with her and had been quite popular with the customers. She imagined Henry missed his old life, too.

"Do you need me to get anything for you while I'm in

town?" she asked as Gus parked near the barn. A polite offer to her ranch mate and nothing more.

The ranch mate pulled the keys out of the ignition and half turned toward her. She already knew what her reaction would be when he shifted his attention her way. She would look into his eyes, note that they were an amazing color. Then she would let her gaze slide over his long cheeks, try not to stare at his mouth and then fix back on his eyes—which were an amazing color.

"I'm good. I'm going to town myself. Tomorrow."

"Ah." Lillie Jean let herself out of the truck and started toward her house.

"Lillie Jean?" She stopped and turned. "Shoot me a text when you get there. I don't know what condition the driveway is in after the weather."

Good looking, fun to banter with, concerned about her safety. Lillie Jean gave a mental *argh* before saying, "Will do."

The drive to town was long and thankfully uneventful. Lillie Jean skirted the puddles and the big car only slipped in the mud a few times, and other than that, all was well. She drove into Gavin and stopped at one of the two lights on the main street, picked up her phone and sent the text to Gus.

Duty completed, she set the phone back on her purse as the light turned green and drove on. It wasn't hard to find the store Gus had told her about. Annie Get Your Gun had a funky retro storefront with a lot of glitz and color. Her kind of place.

Lillie Jean was greeted by the warm smell of potpourri and the equally warm smile of the dark-haired woman standing behind the counter arranging a vase of fresh flowers.

"Welcome to Annie Get Your Gun. Are you looking for anything in particular?"

"Fabric?"

"This way." The woman came out from behind the antique counter and led the way to a side room. Lillie Jean followed, taking a quick survey of the store as she walked. Jewelry, pottery, books, handiwork. Some of the antique furniture had price tags, and the artwork hung in every available space was original and unique. On the wall above the antique cash register was a glittered and bedazzled framed poster of Annie Oakley with her rifle across her knees.

Annie Get Your Gun.

Lillie Jean smiled to herself. The contents of this store were very different from those of A Thread in Time, but the two stores had a similar vibe, making her feel instantly at home.

"We have a lot of quilting cotton, a few bolts of batiste and lawn, some rayons and jersey knits. But mostly quilting stuff because our clientele are quilters."

"I understand." Lillie Jean stepped inside the room and turned a slow circle. There were antique dressers with quilts draped over the mirrors and patchwork aprons and other small items spilling out of the drawers. One entire wall was filled with bolts of fabric and a second had a decent collection of sewing supplies.

"My boss makes artisan quilts," the woman said from behind Lillie Jean. "We started this room to show off her designs, but there was a local demand for fabric and classes, so we're doing our best to meet the fabric demand. If we can manage to rent the second floor of this building, we'll start classes."

"How fun." Lillie Jean started perusing the long row of fabrics, running her hand over each piece that caught her eye. This was high-end cotton, some crisp and bright, ready to add pop to a quilt design, and some soft and silky, more suitable for apparel.

Lillie Jean pulled out a slender bolt, medium blue with lemons and tiny white dots. Perfect for a fifties inspired dress—or better yet, kitchen curtains. And once she got curtains up, maybe then she'd stop staring out the window at Gus's house and wondering what he was doing.

One could always hope.

"Do you have any more of this?" Lillie Jean asked.

"We only have the end of that bolt, but we can special order for you. Are you local?" The woman drew out the end of the question, not wanting to look as if she was prying, but curious about Lillie Jean, an obvious stranger in town.

"I'm staying on the H/H."

The woman's eyes lit up. "You must be the new partner."

"I am the new partner." Lillie Jean wondered what else the woman knew—or thought she knew—about her. "Lillie Jean Hardaway."

"I'm Annie Delaney. You have a great accent. Texas, right?"

"Right."

"Are you staying in the area long?"

"My plans are open-ended. After my grandfather died, I didn't have much keeping me in Texas, so I decided to travel north and see the ranch firsthand. Gus and Thad invited me to stay awhile and—" she shrugged "—here I am."

"Here you are," the woman agreed. "You used to work in clothing design, right?"

Well, she'd certainly been the topic of conversation—

probably in Thad's pub. "I did. I'm between enterprises now."

"We handle consignments if you have anything you'd like to display."

"I have nothing at the moment." And she wasn't certain her work would fit in this cute little store. She made Western-inspired outfits for entertainers and Austin free spirits. The store vibe was right, but there wasn't room for a clothing section, and Lillie Jean wasn't interested in making small things to sell. "I tend to make statement garments. Things I can't see the locals or tourists wearing."

Annie gave an understanding nod. "If you do make something, we'd love to see your work, just to see it, you know."

Lillie Jean smiled. "I'll remember that. And I won't be a stranger, because I'm going to need fabric for future projects and I like to touch it first."

"Don't we all," Annie said on a laugh. "I have catalogs with actual samples. You can touch those and order."

"Excellent. Right now, I'd like to order this lemon fabric and I'll buy what's left on the bolt."

Annie took the fabric from Lillie Jean and headed for the measuring table. "I'll give you twenty percent off since it's the end of the bolt."

Ten minutes later, Lillie Jean left Annie Get Your Gun with the blue lemony fabric in a glittery bag and a smile on her face. Community was an important thing in the art world and she felt as if she'd just found her Montana people. Henry turned a little circle on the front seat when she opened the car door, then put a paw on her lap.

"Yes. All is well," she told the little dog. Better than well. For the first time since Andrew dropped his bombshell, breaking their engagement, she felt as if she was regaining control of her life. Moving forward under her own steam rather than being chased.

"Hey, I HEAR THAT'S some new roommate you got."

Gus dropped the bag of grain he'd been carrying into the barn when Jess Hayward, one of his bull riding buddies, called. "Yeah. She's a nice lady. Is that why you called?"

Jess laughed. "No. But I thought it might spice up the conversation."

"I like things bland," Gus replied as he walked into the barn and opened the grain bin with one hand. He eyed the grain bag and decided he couldn't dump it in until the call was over. No sense pouring grain on his boots if the bag got away from him.

"Yeah, I remember that about you from the bar. How you blandly kicked Shelly out of the place. Blandly broke up that fight between the—"

"Hey, Jess?"

"Yeah?"

"Did you call for a reason?"

"Tyler and I are looking for a couple bulls. We've heard good things about yours."

"Bulls for breeding, right?"

Jess laughed. "We're not going to ride them."

"Hey, with you guys that's always a possibility." The Hayward brothers both had awesome bull riding careers and only recently retired.

"Not this time. Tyler is putting his wife's ranch back into production. We have the cows. Need a bull."

"I have some decent prospects if you want to take a look."

"We would. I got a couple wedding things I have to do,

and Tyler's got some commitments… How about next—" Gus could hear pages flipping "—Thursday?"

"Works for me. I'm fencing, so give me a call before you come."

"Will do. Looking forward to meeting your partner."

"Thad's partner. See you then."

Gus hung up the phone, retrieved the bag of grain and dumped it into the bin, then dialed Thad. They'd only spoken a handful of times since Lillie Jean had decided to stay a while and the conversations had been guarded. They were both dealing with the fallout of Thad's secret. Gus in a more direct way than Thad, who had his pub to distract him.

"Is everything all right?" Thad's voice sounded older than it had before Lillie Jean had showed up, and it may have been Gus's imagination, but he seemed to be moving slower, too.

"Yeah. Got the north side of the fence stretched between snow flurries. Only three cows left to calve, and the Hayward twins might buy a bull."

"And Lillie Jean?"

"She's doing okay."

Thad cleared his throat. "Any idea how long she's staying?"

"We haven't talked about that."

"You probably got to at some time."

"Agreed." Gus cleared his throat and studied the rafters again. "Last night I did research into Ag loans."

"Yeah?"

"Problem is that I don't have a down payment." And his only income, now that he'd quit the pub, was his manager's salary, which wasn't all that much.

"Maybe I could apply."

"You already have a small business loan, but yeah, we

could give that a shot. Or maybe I could sell my interest in the bar to someone you'd want to work with. That would at least give me part of a down payment."

He heard his uncle pull in a breath. "Yeah. It would." Thad didn't sound thrilled about the idea, but they weren't in a position to wait for the perfect solution. Lillie Jean was only waiting for a few documents to be finalized and then she could do whatever she pleased with her half of the H/H.

"I'm not trying to mess up the bar. I'm trying to save the ranch."

"Oh, I understand," his uncle said quickly, in a voice that said he was well aware that they were in a mess that he'd made. "I'll see what I can do on this end. I can meet with the Farm Service Agency guy when I go to Dillon for my dental appointment next week."

"Okay. You talk to FSA. I'll talk to Lillie Jean."

Who would hopefully be receptive to the half-baked plan of a desperate former bull rider with no job history to speak of.

Gus was nowhere to be seen when Lillie Jean returned from town with four gallons of paint she'd got at bargain prices because they were on the clearance shelf of the Gavin hardware store. She'd already found paintbrushes in the utility closet of the old house and had decided to forgo a roller. Rolling was faster, but brushing conserved paint and her money would go farther.

She made two trips to the car to bring in her purchases, stopping on the last one to see if she could spot Gus. There was no smoke coming out of the chimney of his house, but his truck was there. He was working around the place somewhere. The guy never stopped working and Lillie Jean felt a twinge of guilt at not doing her part today, although honestly, her part wasn't much.

After several days of morning chores, Lillie Jean's role was still that of gatekeeper. She opened. She stood and waited. She closed. She wore two pairs of socks to help fight the cold. After feeding, she and Gus walked among the pregnant cows so that they could get used to her, then attended to some daily chore, which usually involved her standing and watching and learning as he changed the oil on the tractor or reset a fence post or tightened wire. She'd seen the extent of her property when they'd once again driven the perimeter, dropping off fence posts to replace the rotted ones. She'd even managed to return home from that trip without a head injury. She was, however, failing miserably in her quest to ride in the tractor cab without being aware of every move the man made, of how he smelled and how fascinating his hands were as they moved the gearshifts. And when his thigh bumped hers…well, that was good and bad. Part of her loved it. The rest of her was terrified at her reaction.

But maybe being aware of Gus as an attractive man was a good thing. A sign of healing and recovery, instead of the threat she perceived it to be. She'd been hit with so many things, so rapidly, that she'd been in full-time defensive mode. Maybe it was time to loosen up a bit. Stop expecting the direst of consequences. Acknowledging Gus's hot factor didn't mean she was going to blindly allow him to manipulate her into doing something she didn't want to do. She was making a big deal out of something she didn't need to.

After closing the trunk of the Cadillac, Lillie Jean went back into the house and, instead of doing her laundry as planned, spread newspapers, pried the lid off the paint can and stirred. It felt good to be doing something creative. Something with color.

Henry ambled up as she stirred.

"Oh, no. Not this time." Lillie Jean had cleaned up doggy paint prints on her floors a number of times, and once had to use a washcloth to scrub dry lime-green paint off all four feet and the tip of his nose. She buttoned on Henry's sweater and after making certain the front gate was closed, let him out to experience fresh Montana air. Then she went back inside to battle dank musty walls.

Lillie Jean gave the paint one last swirl with the wooden stick, then dipped her brush and stroked a broad swatch of color across the wall. The perfect shade of aqua. A cheerful, inspiring color. One of her favorites. It would look great with the sunny yellow and apricot she'd gotten for the kitchen. The old house would be awash with color when she was done. Bargain shelf color. She hoped she could find something fun for the overly white bathroom next.

Lillie Jean laid out another stroke of color. Two sweeps of the brush and the old house already felt better.

A knock on the door gave her a start and she set down the brush.

When she opened the door, Gus made no move to step inside, didn't appear to notice the painting apparatus behind her. "I need some help."

"Sure."

He looked past her to the stripes of paint on the wall. "Nice color," he said before heading back out the door.

"Thanks," Lillie Jean called to empty air as he disappeared. She quickly wrapped the brush in a thin plastic grocery bag, stuck it in the fridge, then grabbed her coat.

She caught up with him where he waited near the gate. "What's going on?"

"One of the heifers calved while I was gone, but another heifer stole her calf. We need to get the calf back with her mother, so she can eat."

"Ah."

"Unfortunately, the thief is pretty adamant about keeping the calf." Gus stopped at the gate to the large pen where the remaining pregnant heifers were housed. Sure enough, there was a defensive-looking cow standing guard over a newborn who tottered around behind her, while the real mother, who was still dealing with afterbirth, stood a good distance away.

"Does the real mama know that's her calf?"

"First-time mothers get confused, and heifers sometimes don't produce as much of the bonding hormone as mature cows."

The calf stealer snorted loudly and tossed some dirt over her back. Gus shook his head. "That's a warning."

"And here I thought cows were placid creatures."

Now Gus snorted. "Right."

"What's the plan?" she asked as he reached for the gate. And more important, what was her role? Her heart was beating faster, even as she told herself that there was no way that Gus would put her into any kind of danger. Not unless he wanted to get the ranch the easy way.

"Not funny," she muttered to herself through gritted teeth.

"I'm going to try to herd fake mama and the baby into that pen. Hopefully I can get the cow in the pen and the gate closed before the baby gets in. If not, then we come up with a different plan."

"Kind of a 'think on your feet' operation?"

Gus smiled, his cheeks creasing. She was beginning to really love his smile. "Welcome to cattle ranching."

"I think I'm only a landowner. What's my job?"

"To telephone for help if that cow takes me out."

"Excuse me?" Lillie Jean's heart all but stopped.

"It won't happen. You're here as a precaution." He picked up a sturdy round pole leaning against the rail fence. "Always have one of these if you go into a cow pen. If you ever get attacked, hit them between the eyes. Hard."

He wasn't kidding. So much for the placid cow myth.

"Do you really have to do this?"

He gave her a curious look which told her, yes, he had to do this. The real mother cow wandered toward the barn, where the gate to a straw-filled birthing pen was open, as he let himself into the pasture. The calf-stealing cow shook her head and tossed more dirt.

Lillie Jean watched, half fascinated, half afraid as Gus approached the cow with the baby, gently circling the pair. Once behind them, he raised his arms, gave a couple low whistles. "Come on, mama. Into the pen." The cow shook her head at him, then made a noise at the calf and started walking along the edge of the fence. The calf trotted along, tripping a little, but keeping up. The fake mama automatically turned into the next open pen as a means to escape the man behind her and, slick as can be, Gus stepped between her and the calf and swung the gate shut. The cow spun around and shook her head, letting out a gusty snort as she realized that her kidnapped baby was on the other side of the rails. Gus gave Lillie Jean a quick thumbs-up, then took hold of the new calf and started guiding it forward toward the birthing pen where its real mom awaited.

"I need you to close the gate to the barn pen," he called to Lillie Jean as he pushed the calf along. Lillie Jean let herself into the corral and followed Gus as he pushed the calf the last several yards. Meanwhile the calf stealer paced the fence, growing more agitated by the moment.

"You'll have your own baby soon," Gus muttered as he gave the calf one final push into the barn. He stepped back, and Lillie Jean closed the gate to the birthing pen.

"That went well." Surprisingly well. "Now what?"

"Now we see if these two bond."

"If not?"

"Bottle baby."

"That sounds like a lot of—" The sound of rattling metal cut Lillie Jean off midsentence. She whirled to see the calf stealer hit the fence with her chest a second time before rising up on her hind legs and heaving herself over the gate, metal squealing as she landed with grunting thud on the other side. Their side. Gus grabbed Lillie Jean's arm and pulled her to the barn gate, and then he half pushed, half tossed her over the metal rails, before scrambling over it himself, landing in a heap next to her in the straw.

The mother cow standing at the far side of the indoor pen gave a start, then turned and blinked at them. The baby slowly approached, sticking his wet little nose on Lillie Jean's arm. The contrast between the unconcerned mother on one side of the gate and the rampaging cow from hell on the other was startling.

Lillie Jean scrambled to her feet, looking for an escape. "Please tell me she can't jump this gate, too."

"Too tall." Gus took Lillie Jean's hand and led her to the far side of the pen where he opened a smaller gate, allowing them into the barn proper. A shudder went through Lillie Jean as he let go of her hand. "This is not normal behavior," he added.

"Cows don't normally jump fences?" Watching that cow heave herself over that gate, which now had a healthy bow in the top rail from where she'd hit it going over, bordered on the surreal.

"No. That part is normal. I'm talking about the calf stealing. It happens, but not that frequently."

Lillie Jean's jaw muscles tightened as she considered the ramifications. "Are you telling me that every time I closed that gate while we were feeding and felt safe on the other side, that a cow could have come sailing over and...got me?"

"They don't care about you unless they think you're some kind of threat to them or their babies. During calving season, cows are a little more sensitive than the rest of the year."

"Good to know." Lillie Jean bit the words out as she scowled at him, but Gus didn't scowl back. If anything, his expression softened as he reached out to take hold of her coat sleeve and gently ease her a few steps closer to him. Outside the barn, the calf stealer paced back and forth, while in the pen next to them, the calf started tottering closer to its mother who studied her baby as if it were from another planet. Lillie Jean barely noticed. The man standing in front of her, his hand still on her sleeve, commanded her full attention.

His voice was low, and utterly sincere as he said, "I wouldn't knowingly put you in a dangerous situation. I didn't expect the heifer to jump the fence."

Lillie Jean gave a mute nod, unable to find her voice. Her heart still hammered, but it was no longer because of their near miss.

Gus's grip briefly tightened and then he let go of her coat and brought his hand up to slide around the back of her neck and thread up through her hair. A shiver went through Lillie Jean that had nothing to do with renegade cows, and then Gus brought his lips down to meet hers.

Finally.

The thought rocked her and Lillie Jean stilled for a split second, stunned by how right it felt to be kissing the man. How perfect his lips felt on hers. All thoughts of her attraction to Gus *not* being a big deal disintegrated under the warm pressure of his mouth. This was a big deal. This was…incredible.

Her fingers clutched his shoulders, even though she didn't remember moving her hands, and she found herself wanting to press closer instead of stepping back as sanity decreed.

When Gus lifted his head, he gently caressed her cheek with the pad of his thumb.

"I guess we both saw that one coming."

Lillie Jean wanted to believe that she hadn't see it coming, but as she stared into his clear green eyes, she found she couldn't lie. To him. To herself.

"Yes. It had been coming." And it was going to really mess up her plans if she didn't get hold of herself. She pulled in a breath that was shakier than she wanted, but her voice was firm as she said, "It's not happening again. Right?"

Gus's eyebrows pulled together, as if she'd just said the sun wouldn't be coming up tomorrow. "Business partners and all that?"

"Yes."

He stepped back, his fingers lingering on her cheek for a brief second before he dropped his hand back to his side. Lillie Jean felt an unexpected stab at the loss of contact, then gave herself a mental shake.

Distance is good. Proximity leads to unpredictable outcomes.

"I don't want things to get weird." There was a touch of irony in his voice.

"Then why did you kiss me?"

His eyebrows lifted. "Why did you kiss me back?"

"I—"

She wanted to protest, but he cocked an eyebrow at her, telling her she might as well save her breath if she was going to deny kissing him back. She had.

"Shall we call this a draw?" he asked.

"Yes." Lillie Jean dusted her hands off in a "get back to business" gesture. "I have a room to paint."

"I guess you'd better get to it."

She gave a jerky nod, only then noticing that the calf had figured out what a mama was for, and the mama was licking and nosing her baby as it nursed.

"Now that she's tasted him, things will be okay," Gus said.

"Good. I would have hated to risk our lives for nothing."

Gus didn't have an answer for that, although Lillie Jean would have paid a goodly sum to know what was going on in his head.

CHAPTER TEN

THE CALF STEALER gave birth two days after jumping the gate and scaring the heck out of Lillie Jean. As Gus watched her gently clean her baby, talking to it in that special tone mother cows used when communicating with their young, it was hard to believe that forty-eight hours ago she'd been ready to kill anything that stood between herself and the calf she'd decided was her own.

Heifers.

The cow raised her head almost as if she'd heard his thought, giving him a baleful look. Gus pushed off the fence just as his phone rang.

"It's a done deal," Thad said.

"Lillie Jean?"

"Is my official partner. She must have just found out herself."

Gus ambled toward the barn's open bay door, studying the ground as he walked. "I haven't seen her today, except for when we fed." They'd talked about working on the fence, but it had started to rain. "She's holed up in her house."

"Maybe you could see her. Kind of, you know, feel her out?"

"Find out what she plans to do now that she can do something?" Gus had a pretty clear idea of her plans, but his butt was on the line as much as Thad's, so yeah. He'd feel things out.

"I'll call you back when I know something. It may not be today."

"All right. But I want your take on things before I talk to her."

"Sounds good. Hey," Gus said before his uncle could hang up. "How are you doing?"

"What do you mean?" Thad sounded surprisingly cagey.

"I guess I mean, how are you doing?"

Thad snorted. "Mimi is trying to fix me up with Ginny. Fortunately, Ginny figured it out and filled me in."

Gus gave a mental sigh. So much for Ginny dragging Thad out of self-imposed bachelorhood.

"Did you know about this?" Thad asked.

"I had nothing to do with it." He might have thought it would be nice if the two of them got together, but he hadn't done anything to work in that direction—especially after finding out about Thad's former wife. If Thad had wanted a woman in his life, he'd had plenty of time to find one. But he hadn't, because Nita Hardaway's memory still haunted him.

"Good thing."

"I'll do what I can to call Mimi off."

"Both Ginny and I appreciate it."

"And I'll let you know what I find out from Lillie Jean."

"Thanks."

After his uncle hung up, Gus leaned back against the straw stack and studied Lillie Jean's house through the bay door. They'd barely exchanged more than a sentence or two over the past two days. Gus figured it was because of the kiss. He also figured it wasn't because Lillie Jean hadn't liked it. She had. So had he.

She was afraid that growing close would mess up their business arrangement, and she had a point, so he'd take his cue from her and pretend it never happened. If she sold her part of the ranch and left, there was a better than average possibility that he'd never see her again. If she stayed...well, a lot of random kissing would be distracting.

Gus shook his head as he stepped out into the rain.

Despite everything, he couldn't help but feel that a little distraction wouldn't be all bad.

TRANSFERRING OWNERSHIP OF the ranch from her grandfather to Lillie Jean turned out to be ridiculously simple. Lyle had left no debt; his bank accounts, tiny as they were, had transferred upon death, and, essentially, so had his interest in the ranch. Even the legal fees had been taken out of the estate, so as Lillie Jean stood on a stool, painting the upper part of the kitchen wall, she owned her half of the ranch, free and clear. She had no debt, but she also had no capital to start a business.

She looked down at Henry, who was staring up at her, one stubby paw raised in the air. "We're official ranchers, Henry."

Henry seemed unimpressed. He wanted to go back where it was warm, and Lillie Jean understood, even if the thought of leaving gave her a slight pang. Try as she might, she couldn't get Gus Hawkins out of her head.

How long would it take to sell a place like this? Or an interest in it? As Gus had pointed out after she first arrived, they could be partners for a long, long time.

Or she might have a hit of amazing luck and sell instantly.

Her amazing luck—the good variety—hadn't made much of a showing lately, but hey...the ranch had transferred without an asteroid falling from the sky and destroying the place, so maybe the extreme-luck phase of her life, good *and* bad, was winding down. The best thing to do would be to contact a real estate agent who specialized in ranch properties, discover her options. Which she would do as soon as she called Thad. They needed to have a meeting. Come to an understanding. Start their business dealings off on the right foot.

She hated to cause Thad grief, but as she'd told Gus more than once, this was not a situation of her making. While she'd love to simply walk away and leave the old man—and his nephew—to their ranching, she couldn't afford to. She had a future to build, a business to develop.

Lillie Jean climbed down off the stool and stood back to admire her work. The yellow transformed the dingy kitchen, and the apricot trim she planned to add around the windows and doors would only add to the sunny appeal. She'd just started hammering the lid back onto the paint can when a knock sounded.

Gus.

A bubble of anticipation began to rise, and she brutally popped it. The man was off-limits.

She stepped out of the kitchen and waved him into the house. He immediately took off his hat, shaking water droplets onto the rug. This carpet would have to come up. She could only imagine what it had encountered over years of ranching life.

"You heard?" She guessed from the solemn look on his face.

"Yeah," he said without asking what she was talking about. "I did. So I came to talk."

He took a moment then to survey the living room with its soothing aqua walls, then crossed to the kitchen and blinked at the muted lemon yellow. "Colorful."

"Better than beige."

So much better than beige. The appliances looked downright happy in their new environment.

"I'm making curtains out of that fabric." She pointed to the swatch of lemon fabric she'd purchased from Annie Get Your Gun. "I'm waiting for my order to come in. My sewing machine should be here any day now."

"Does that mean you're staying awhile?"

"It means that I plan to stay busy while I'm here."

He gave a silent nod and transferred his gaze back to the kitchen. "Looks better."

"High praise."

That teased a half smile out of him, which Lillie Jean found gratifying, even though she told herself to knock it off.

"You want to talk?" she asked, gesturing to the recliner and the hard-back chair in the living room.

"Maybe we could go to the main house."

Now Lillie Jean smiled a little. "And have some coffee?"

Gus shrugged a shoulder under his heavy canvas coat. "Well...you know."

"Right. I'll grab my laundry and meet you over there."

Where they would have a business discussion. Business. Nothing but.

Gus was making a new pot of coffee when she arrived with her laundry basket under one arm, her small bottle of detergent and dryer sheets balanced on top. Her grandmother would have had a fit if she'd seen Lillie Jean stuffing everything into one load, but it reduced her time in the main house, so that was how she was doing her laundry. She'd put her underwear in the mesh bag she stored them in when she traveled, but other than that, it was every garment for itself.

She stopped inside the door and studied the kitchen walls, which were a utilitarian wedding veil white.

"You're not painting the kitchen yellow," Gus murmured, and she gave a small laugh, surprised that he'd so easily read her thoughts.

"It'd perk you up in the morning."

"No doubt, but I like my white." His tone was wry, but he held his body tensely. And as he waited for the coffee to finish dripping he shifted uncomfortably, focusing on the machine until it gave its gasping gurgle.

After filling two mugs and putting one in front of Lillie Jean, he took his seat on the opposite side of the table. "I've been looking at some options," he said abruptly.

Lillie Jean cupped her hands around the steaming mug and waited for him to continue. They'd had more than one serious conversation at this table and they were about to have another. "What kind of options?"

"Ways to buy you out. *If* you want to sell," he added.

"I do." She wanted to sell and then decide what she wanted to do next. Texas or someplace on the West Coast? It all depended on how much she got and how long it took to sell. And she wanted to help out Kate—the only problem was how. Kate could be one stubborn woman.

"I've started looking into Ag loans. Between Thad and I, we should qualify, but I have to find a buyer for my half of the pub. Then the farm appraisal takes some time." One corner of his mouth tightened ruefully. "A lot of time. Like six months sometimes."

"I see," Lillie Jean said slowly. Six months? It seemed like a long time considering everything that had happened to her recently. Six months ago, she had a business, an engagement ring, a grandfather who, as far as she knew, owned no property other than a few personal belongings and an old Cadillac. Her life had been so different six months ago.

"Can you guarantee a purchase?"

"No. But I'll do whatever I can to buy this place."

Points for honesty. Gus didn't hedge, so neither would she, even though it was uncomfortable to say, "I don't know if I want to wait that long before putting the ranch on the market if it's not a sure thing." That's what she got for giving in and kissing the man. "It might take forever to sell this place—"

"Or it may happen tomorrow."

"Yes." She laced her fingers together, so she could hold her hands still. This was not an easy conversation, and it was made more difficult by the fact that she liked Gus, and she felt for his circumstances—which was why she'd wanted to keep her distance from the get-go. That hadn't worked out as planned, but she had to do what she had to do. She mentally steeled herself as she said, "I have to do what's best for my future plans. I'll try to accommodate you and Thad, but you have to understand that I can't wait forever." Especially when she didn't have a job.

Gus's expression went stony—or rather stonier. This conversation was as hard on him as it was on her. "I essentially grew up here, Lillie Jean. I love this place. I'd like a chance to make it my own without having to take on a partner."

"I understand that." She hated being the bad guy, especially when she couldn't help but recall how much she'd enjoyed kissing the guy. And acknowledged how much she didn't want to hurt him. "I'm not going to make any hard-and-fast decisions right now. What I *am* going to do is to see a real estate agent, discover my options."

"Could you do whatever it is you do here? Run your business from the ranch?"

"Makes it a little difficult to have a storefront," she murmured. And she wanted that. The contact with her customers energized her. And she wanted the possibility of hiring Kate to work with her again. They could build a decent business together if she had the capital to begin.

"Could you work on preliminary stuff here, while Thad and I discover what we can and cannot swing? After all, it's rent free."

He had a point. Other than the cold, the ranch wasn't a bad place to be. She was enjoying working on the house, transforming it from drab to fab, as Kate's mother would say. She wouldn't have to worry about finding a stopgap job and a stopgap apartment so that Kate wouldn't insist upon housing her. And her grandfather's small savings account would see her through a few months, so she wouldn't have to touch the insulting amount of money she'd received from Andrew and Taia.

"You might find out that you enjoy being part of the H/H."

Lillie Jean's gaze came up. Now he was grasping for straws. "Oh yeah. The next time I have a near miss with a mama cow, that's exactly what I'll be thinking."

Gus was smart enough to keep his mouth shut and let her work things through. "I will visit real estate offices, but I won't make any decisions until I have more information," she said again. "And maybe I will stay for a while as things play out."

"You'll give me some time?"

He wanted a commitment, which she refused to make until she had more information, but Lillie Jean found herself saying, "I can't guarantee *how much* time."

He reached across the table to lightly cover her hand with his; the contact was brief and warm and she felt it to her toes. "Thank you."

She had to admit that his cautious smile almost made the promise she hadn't wanted to make worthwhile.

"You're welcome."

Lillie Jean made her escape a few minutes later, taking a deep gulp of crisp Montana air as soon as the mudroom door closed behind her. She'd come back for her laundry later, hopefully when Gus was out working. She felt unsettled, edgy. Disappointed in herself for feeling that way. This should have been nothing but business, but it felt like more. It felt as if she was setting herself up for a fall.

All you did was promise a little time. Nothing more.

Yeah—but you did it because you want to stay on the ranch a while longer. And that, my girl, could spell trouble.

"SHE'LL GIVE US TIME?" Thad asked before letting out a hacking cough.

"No guarantees, but she's willing to listen."

Thad cleared his throat, then gave another small cough. "Good."

"Are you okay?"

"I'm coming down with some kind of a bug."

"Can you get someone to cover for you at the bar?"

"I caught it from Mimi. That leaves Ginny all alone. Callie is out of town."

"I'll cover." The fact that Thad didn't fight him, meant he was feeling low. "Maybe I can meet with Jess and Ty about those bulls—if wedding plans permit, of course." They'd had to cancel the Thursday meeting due to some kind of emergency perpetrated by Jess's future mother-in-law.

Thad laughed, ending with another small cough. "Well, you know Selena."

Jess's future mother-in-law was a force to be reckoned

with. "Oh yeah. I'll be there in a few hours. I can cover tomorrow, too."

"Callie will be back tomorrow. And, just so you know, Madison came in yesterday. She seemed disappointed that you weren't there."

"Well, if she knows I quit, then maybe she won't be back." Not that he was afraid to see her. It was just that Madison loved a crowd, and one never knew what she might do in front of that crowd.

"One can hope."

"Yeah." Gus said goodbye and hung up. He had more important issues to deal with than Madison. If she showed up tonight, he'd deal. He called Jess Hayward, arranged an evening meeting, then grabbed his hat and shrugged into his canvas jacket. He wanted to check the new mothers one more time before heading to town. He'd planned to tag and vaccinate the new calves tomorrow, with Thad's help, but that was out the window now that his uncle was under the weather.

The rain had let up, and when he left the house, Henry was outside in his sweater pacing back and forth in front of the gap in the porch skirting where Clancy's food dish sat. The cat was probably there, taunting the little dog, who was too smart to go under the porch, but too manly to let a taunt go unchallenged.

Kind of reminded him of Carson Craig. Except for the smart part.

After checking the mother cows and babies, who were doing well and could be released into the main herd as soon as the last three calves were tagged and vaccinated, Gus once again headed to Lillie Jean's place. Henry met him at the gate, and Gus smiled down at the muddy little dog.

"You ruined your sweater," he said. Henry gave him

a wide canine grin, and then his head jerked around as Clancy sauntered out from under the porch. The dog charged and Clancy shot across the yard, gracefully bounding up and over the picket fence.

"Maybe next time." Henry seemed to agree. With the cat vanquished, he trotted beside Gus to the porch, where Lillie Jean opened the door before Gus had a chance to knock.

"I was just heading over to get my laundry." Her eyes rounded in horror when she saw the mess Henry had made of the reindeer sweater. "Guess I'll be washing that in the sink."

"I just wanted to let you know that you'll be on your own here tonight. Thad's not feeling well, so I'm covering his shift at the bar."

"Thanks for letting me know."

"I could come home after my shift."

She tilted her head, her expression perplexed. "Why would you do that?"

"I didn't know how you felt about being alone on the ranch all night."

"As long as I have a door between me and the wilderness, I'm fine."

"You're sure."

She gave him a curious look. "I'll be fine. I appreciate you checking."

"Not a problem, Lillie Jean. I'll see you tomorrow."

LILLIE JEAN WAITED until Gus drove away in his good pickup, not to be confused with the bad pickup—the one with the rock-hard dashboard and the badly sprung seats that she rode in when they did fence work—before heading over to his house to put her laundry in the dryer. She tossed in a dryer sheet and started the machine, then wandered into Gus's kitchen to see if there was any leftover coffee. She'd yet to buy a machine of her own, and was essentially caffeine-free because of it, but that didn't mean she didn't appreciate the occasional hit.

The pot was still warm, so she poured a cup and leaned back against the counter as she drank, enjoying the sound of her clothing tumbling in the dryer.

Life wasn't bad on the ranch—she was getting used to the cold and, even though she was wary of cattle now that she knew they could jump fences, she got a certain satisfaction from feeding every morning. Henry enjoyed his life running in the yard and chasing the gray cat who lived under the porch. And the house…she was falling in love with her house project. Color everywhere! Staying another month or two didn't seem like a bad alternative to heading home immediately. As Gus had said, it was hard to beat free housing. All she would pay was her part of the utilities and food.

Lillie Jean finished her coffee, washed the mug and put it back on the shelf before dumping the rest of the coffee and rinsing the pot. There. Duty done. Payback complete.

She pulled out her phone and dialed Kate to give her an update. Kate's mom answered almost immediately.

"Hi, Julie. Is Kate around?"

"She's in the examining room with Caleb."

"You're at the doctor's office?"

"Urgent care. Caleb put a bean in his ear."

"Oh, dear heavens."

"On the plus side, Kate's hours have been increased at the market and she qualifies for insurance coverage. It starts next month."

Which meant that she'd be covering the cost of today's bean removal.

"How about you? Are you doing all right?"

"My hours haven't increased, but that means I'm available to babysit while Kate's at work."

"Still no help from Dennis."

A growling sound answered that question. Lillie Jean had never really liked Dennis. She'd tolerated him for Kate's sake, but Dennis was self-centered, and Kate was a natural born helpmate. All fine and dandy, except that Dennis took advantage. Constantly.

"By the way, Lillie Jean." Julie's voice lowered, as if she was afraid of being overheard. "Kate was going to call you this morning, except this bean thing happened. Andrew came by last night."

"What?"

"He wanted to know if you left anything with us. He was pretty pushy with Kate until he realized that I was there."

"I'm so sorry," Lillie Jean said, pressing her hand to her forehead. The last thing she wanted was to bring trouble down on her friends.

"Oh, don't worry. I put a scare in him."

"You shouldn't have had to do that."

"I never liked Andrew. I kind of enjoyed it." And there it was. Both she and Kate had chosen poorly.

"Look," Lillie Jean said, taking a couple of paces across Gus's kitchen, "I'm sending you money today and I want you to ship me the two boxes in the attic. I'll send the money as soon as I hang up." She probably shouldn't have left them with Kate in the first place, but she'd never dreamed she'd be in Montana for so long.

"I don't think Andrew will be coming back."

"All the same... I want the boxes here with me. I'll send enough money so that you can ship them using a priority method."

"Understood."

"As to the other stuff." Meaning her clothing, her books, her cookware. "I—"

"Will leave them in the garage, right where they are."

Julie used her no-arguments mom voice, so Lillie Jean didn't argue. "If you will send me a text when the boxes are on their way, I'll make sure that Andrew knows where they are." She gritted her teeth together. "That way he'll leave you alone, and I don't think he'll be coming to Montana to get them."

"How long are *you* going to stay there?"

Lillie Jean face flushed as she said, "For a little while. I'm still working out how to handle the sale." And again, the thought of leaving kind of ate at her.

"We look forward to you coming back. Your bedroom is still available."

Her bedroom being the other half of Julie's bedroom.

"Thank you. I appreciate that. I hope that once I get back to Texas, I can hit the ground running. Start over quickly and give Andrew a run for his money."

"Me, too, darling. Let's us just show that man."

Lillie Jean would like nothing better.

CHAPTER ELEVEN

THE BAR WAS BUSY, which meant more revenue, and less time to think. Gus couldn't say he was unhappy about it. The only problem was that he'd expected it to be slow, so he could discuss bulls with Jess and Tyler Hayward.

The twins came into the pub a little after 7:00 p.m., pausing just inside the door. One of them—Gus never could tell the guys apart from a distance—tipped back his cowboy hat and surveyed the room with a shake of his head.

"Mad rush," he said as he approached the bar, and Gus nodded. Now that the twins were closer, he could identify Tyler by the scar on his chin.

"I don't know how long this will last." He poured two beers and set them on the bar in front of the twins. "But it looks like some of them are digging in for the night."

"We can talk between pours," Jess said before he and his brother lifted their beers at the exact same time.

"Back in a sec," Gus said before heading to the end of the bar to take Ginny's drink order. A few minutes later he was back in front of the twins, a bar towel slung over his shoulder. "Tell me what you're looking for."

Jess leaned his elbows on the bar. "Ty and I bought a small herd of registered Angus—"

"Hey, Gus."

Somehow Gus managed to keep from reacting when Madison, the one person he hoped to not see that evening, appeared out of nowhere and squeezed her way in between Jess and Tyler. She gave each twin a sparkling smile. The woman was drop-dead gorgeous, but neither Jess nor Ty did more than nod and ease sideways in opposite directions, giving her more room at the crowded bar.

"I thought you were in Missoula for good," Gus said. Starting her new life as a property manager there. She'd made it very clear that she was never returning to Gavin, and he saw no reason to let her know that he'd known she was back.

"Guess I changed my mind. Can I have the usual?"

"Which is?" When he and Madison dated, the usual had changed along with her mood.

She gave him a playful look. "Surprise me."

Gus poured her a glass of water and set it in front of her. Madison's eyebrows lifted. "Surprise," he said. "Would you like something else?"

"You know what I want."

Gus's stomach tightened. They were not good for each other. Madison disagreed.

"This isn't the time."

Madison cocked one eyebrow at him, took the glass of water and joined a table nearby.

Jess cupped his beer glass with both hands and pointedly brought the subject back to bulls. "Skye and Tyler invested in additional property, so we can graze in the summer."

"We're just looking for a decent bull." Tyler shrugged. "We'd be pretty steady customers if you have bloodlines that work for us."

"Behind you," Ginny said as she squeezed by, a full beer glass in each hand. She exited out the end of the bar and disappeared into the crowd.

"Yeah. About that." Gus leaned in. "I don't know what

our breeding program looks like in the future, because I don't know where we'll be in the future."

"What does that mean?"

"Thad's silent partner's granddaughter—" whom everyone in town knew about by now "—wants to sell her interest. If she sells to someone I can't work with, then I don't know what'll happen."

The twins did one of those silent communication things they did every now and again, then focused back on Gus who held up a finger before moving down the bar, taking orders and filling glasses. When he got back, Tyler leaned an elbow on the bar. "Is there any way to convince her not to sell?" he asked.

"You can follow my ex-husband's example and use sweet talk and manipulation," Ginny said as she slipped behind him again. Gus made a face at her and she patted his arm. "Kidding."

He barely had time to acknowledge her comment before one of the guys sitting at Madison's table pushed up to the bar and ordered two whiskeys neat. Gus poured, then turned back to the twins.

"I'm hoping she doesn't put the place on the market until I have a chance to come up with the money to buy her out." He left out the part about her wanting the money to start over ASAP. That was Lillie Jean's business and he wasn't spreading it through a pub, even with guys he trusted. The selling part would be common knowledge after she visited with the real estate brokers.

A shout went up from the far end of the bar and Gus headed that way. When he came back, Tyler asked, "Is she going to give you some time to come up with the funds?"

"I hope so. I'm looking into Ag loans."

"Prepare for a wait," Jess said. "We just got one and it took close to a year."

"Thanks," Gus said drily. The crowd was growing, and Jess and Ty were being shoved closer together. The time for conversation was over. "I have bulls to show you," he told the twins. "You want to see them?"

"Day after tomorrow," Jess said, before saying, "No. Wait. Emma has some wedding thing I need to okay. The day after the day after tomorrow."

"That would be Saturday?" Gus asked, wanting to make certain he had the right day-after-the-day-after.

Jess frowned as he consulted his phone calendar. "Yes. Saturday looks clear."

"Midday," Ty added.

"Works for me," Gus said as he moved down the bar. "See you then."

The rest of the shift sped by as they tended to do when it was busy. Madison hung in there, moving from table to table. To his surprise, she stuck with water, which meant that, unless she'd been pilfering drinks, she was stone-cold sober as she approached the bar around midnight.

The place was still full, but with Ginny working shoulder to shoulder with him they were holding their own. Madison leaned her elbows on the bar and gave him a soulful look. "I heard you might lose your ranch."

"Don't believe everything you hear in a drinking establishment," he said lightly. "More water?"

She smiled a little. Shook her head. "I didn't realize you had a partner."

Gus somehow kept himself from saying that was because it was none of her business.

The smile widened. She knew him fairly well. Knew he was purposely not talking, so he talked. "What brings you back to town, Madison?"

"I like being a big fish in a small pond." Gus couldn't help smiling at the very truthful reply. The smile faded as she said, "And this woman, your partner? She's living on the ranch?"

Gus set his forearms on the bar and leaned closer. "Madison…let's keep the conversation on less personal matters."

She regarded him silently for one long moment, then wrapped her elegant fingers around the glass and gave him a knowing half smile. "Fine. I guess I'll see you around?"

Probably not, since he didn't plan on taking a lot of shifts.

"Yeah. Sure. Good night, Madison."

"Night, Gus." She sauntered away, leaving him staring after her.

He didn't mind helping out his uncle at the pub, but he couldn't wait to get back to the ranch. Now, as Tyler said, he needed to figure out how to hold on to it.

LILLIE JEAN'S PATTERN boxes and sewing machine arrived three days after she'd spoken to Julie. As the delivery truck drove away, she carried the boxes into the house one at a time and stacked them on the kitchen table. At least Andrew wouldn't get his hands on them now. Isabella was going to have to settle for whatever Taia managed to design for her, and Lillie Jean had a strong feeling that the musician was not going to be happy. Taia's aesthetic was heavily influenced by ultramodern minimalism, whereas Isabella liked Western-inspired pieces that spoke of 1940s and 1950s. In other words, she preferred Lillie Jean's specialty.

Even though there was no chance of anything happening to the boxes in her absence, Lillie Jean stowed them in her bedroom, beside her bed, and set her laundry basket on top. They represented the beginning of her new business, and she wasn't going to leave them chilling on the kitchen table while she went to town to pick up her lemon fabric from Annie Get Your Gun and visit one of the local real estate offices.

Her first stop upon reaching Gavin was the ranch supply store she'd read about on her phone, where she bought two pairs of jeans and four T-shirts in unattractive colors on deep discount. Who cared if a shirt was the color of mud if it would eventually be covered in mud? Henry was waiting with his nose pressed against the window when she returned to the car.

"New sweater for you, Bud." Lillie Jean pulled the fleece doggie vest with decorative buttons down the back out of the bag. "And look. I have a shirt the color of muck, one the color of dust, and two the color of creek slime."

Henry lifted his front paw as she tried on his vest. It fit well, but she was going to sew a piece of orange ribbon to it, so she could see him when he chased bunnies, and sometimes Clancy the cat, on their evening walks.

After the ranch store, Lillie Jean drove on to Annie Get Your Gun where she parked in front of the real estate office on the opposite side of the street. She hesitated before going in, then bit her lip and turned to cross the street. Property went for a lot of money in Montana. A lot more than it did in her part of Texas. The value of her interest in the ranch wasn't going to drop if she gave Gus a little time before putting the place on the market. She'd eventually get her money, and, in the meantime, she'd work on new designs. And—finally—she *was* working on new designs. Designs she liked.

Painting the house seemed to have shaken loose something in her brain. She'd spent a couple of evenings searching through retro photos on the internet and debating as to how she could reimagine them. She'd even reached for her sketchbook a time or two. It felt good to be moving on, and, in a way, she had the isolation of the ranch to thank for that. She could see why Gus loved the place, and maybe that was what had kept her from walking into the real estate office. Gus and his love of the place.

Her stomach tightened. She couldn't let feelings for Gus trump common sense. If she sold the ranch, her future was secure.

You promised him time.

Exactly. She'd go to the real estate office another day. There was no hurry.

The bell atop the door rang as Lillie Jean entered Annie Get Your Gun. A small group of women was gathered around the jewelry display case and two more ladies stood in the doorway of the quilt room, where Annie was holding up a crib-size quilt. Annie glanced at the door as Lillie Jean came in, then smiled broadly.

"Hi, Lillie Jean. Welcome back."

"Hi, Annie." Lillie Jean edged past a woman at the display case, pretending she didn't notice the way the blond was staring at her.

Annie handed the crib quilt to one of the ladies she'd been speaking to, and then crossed to the counter and reached beneath it. "Your fabric." She set a box on the counter. "You should have a lot of fun with this."

"Oh, I'm going to," Lillie Jean said. She was going to disappear into the project ASAP, keeping her mind on her sewing and not on Gus. "I'm probably going to put in another order soon. I'm making a bathroom ensemble next."

"Then you'll be staying in the area?"

Lillie Jean turned toward the woman who'd spoken,

a tall willowy blonde with a short geometric haircut. Pretty much the antithesis of herself. "I…uh…" *Don't know how to answer a direct question about my personal business to a stranger.* So she held out a hand. "I'm Lillie Jean Hardaway."

The woman took her hand, gave it a warm squeeze. "I'm Madison Jones. A friend of Gus's."

"Oh." A hollow pit seemed to open inside of her. This was quite an attractive friend. "Nice to meet you."

"Likewise." She stepped away from the jewelry case and Lillie Jean automatically moved with her. "Gus is kind of torn up about the future of his ranch." Lillie Jean's lips parted, but she had no idea what to say. She didn't have to say anything because Madison continued on with a gesture that made the single stone on her elegant silver bracelet catch the light. "He and his friends were having a war council about it at the bar a few nights ago."

Lillie Jean's cheeks started to feel warm. "Oh?" she asked politely.

"Not that Gus would want that to get out, of course—"

"Then why mention it?"

Lillie Jean's blunt question brought Madison to a stuttering stop. She pressed her palm against the front of her tasteful linen dress. "I want you to understand how much Gus's ranch means to him."

"It's Thad's ranch. And mine."

"Yes. Of course."

Lillie Jean narrowed her eyes, aware that everyone in the shop was trying to appear engaged in other matters while listening to her conversation. "I'm sure Gus appreciates your concern. I'll pass it along to him."

"You don't—"

"It's not a problem." She reached for her package, which, thankfully, she'd paid for upon ordering. All she wanted was to get out of the shop, back to her car and her little dog. Madison Jones had an agenda and Lillie Jean didn't want to be part of it.

"Thank you," she said to Annie. "I'll be back when I have more time." She gave Madison a cool look then headed for the door, well aware that many pairs of eyes were following her exit.

She somehow crossed the street without being hit by traffic, which was a feat, since she'd walked blindly to her car and forgot to unlock it before trying to open the door. If she'd been certain no one was looking, she'd have brought her forehead down to rest on the steering wheel after sliding inside. But people probably were watching, and discussing, and she wasn't about to show weakness. So she put the key in the ignition and started the car, surprised to find that her hands were shaking.

Lillie Jean had never been a fan of confrontation. She'd listened to her mother's advice about finding peaceful solutions and rolling with the punches, but in this case, it felt too personal. The crazy thing was that she didn't know if she was more upset about the confrontation with an aggressive stranger in front of an audience, or the fact that Gus had been discussing her.

Or maybe it was the fact that she'd almost choked at the thought of that woman being with Gus. Was she jealous?

It certainly felt like it.

And that was a red flag of the highest order.

TYLER AND JESS were still at the ranch when Lillie Jean returned from her morning errands. She got out of her big sedan and opened the back door, allowing Henry to jump out before she reached in to pull out a large bag and a good-size package.

"Need help?" Gus called.

She barely glanced at him before shaking her head. "I've got it."

Gus started toward her and the twins fell into step. "Couple guys I'd like you to meet," he said when they got closer. "Jess and Tyler Hayward. They're here looking at bulls."

Lillie Jean looked from one twin to the other with surprise, then juggled her packages so that she could extend a hand. Gus automatically caught a box as it started to tumble.

Tyler touched his hat. "I'm Ty. He's Jess."

Lillie Jean smiled a little. "You should wear different colored hats."

"Oh, we've been through that," Jess said with a laugh. "And different colored shirts—anything so Mom and Dad could tell us apart at a glance." He looked over at Gus. "We need to get going. Maybe you could tell Lillie Jean about the spaghetti feed."

"I'll tell her," Tyler volunteered. "My wife is the chairman. All proceeds go to the drug-free graduation party."

"Good cause," Jess added. "Gus always goes."

"I'll try to be there," Lillie Jean said.

Tyler shook his head. "Don't try. Just show up. It'll be fun."

With a wink and a smile, he nudged his brother, who touched his hat, and then the two of them beat a retreat to the shiny blue pickup parked next to the tractor. Lillie Jean met Gus's gaze briefly as she held out her hands for the box he still held, and there was something in her expression that he didn't understand.

He thought about saying they'd talk later, but instead relinquished the box and followed the twins. They arranged for the brothers to pick up the bull on Sunday, and when he looked back to the car, Lillie Jean was gone, leaving him with a sense of unfinished business. He had a feeling that something had happened in town.

What were the chances that she'd cut loose with the information?

Things had been strained between them since they'd negotiated at the kitchen table. Gus figured it had to do with Lillie Jean's problem with mixing business with friendship, but since she'd agreed to give him some time, he followed her lead. Polite mornings in the tractor followed by Lillie Jean disappearing into her house for the day. But he had his guarantee of time, and that was all he wanted. Right?

Of course.

But he still found himself opening her gate after the twins left and heading up the walk to the manager's house. It took two knocks before Lillie Jean opened the door. She lifted her eyebrows, waiting for him to state his business—which wasn't exactly tripping off the end of his tongue. So Lillie Jean surprised him by taking the lead.

"I met one of your friends today."

There was something in her tone that told him exactly who. "Madison?"

"Got it in one."

He had a nasty feeling about this—especially when Lillie Jean was looking at him as if he'd purposely sicced Madison on her. "What did she do?"

"She pled your case."

"What case?"

"The 'Gus needs his ranch' case."

Gus rolled his eyes skyward before saying, "She hated the ranch." It was one of the reasons they'd broken up.

She'd wanted him to expand the bar into a bar-restaurant and focus his energies in that direction.

"She might hate the ranch, but she likes you."

Gus brought one hand up to rest on the doorjamb. "What'd she do to make you think that?"

Lillie Jean took a step closer. "She was marking territory." She wrinkled her nose, a note of distaste in her voice as she asked, "Did you *date* that woman?"

"We worked together. And...yeah. We went out for a while."

"And then?"

"I broke it off and she quit the bar. Moved to Missoula." He could see that Lillie Jean was drawing a parallel between her situation with her fiancé and his situation with Madison, but they were not alike in the least—except for the fact that Madison quit because she didn't want to work with him any longer.

Okay. Small parallel.

"Good choice on your part," Lillie Jean said darkly. Despite her carefully distant attitude, he could tell that Madison had upset her.

"Agreed." The look on her face was killing him. No one deserved a public Madison attack. He reached out to run his hand over her upper arm, squeezing lightly as he said, "Madison likes to stir up trouble."

Lillie Jean dropped her gaze, but she didn't move away from his touch. When she looked up at him again, her expression was both troubled and determined. "It sounds like our business dealings are common knowledge."

"They're not."

A touch of heat sparked in the depths of her blue-green eyes. "Then why did Madison say that you had a war council in the bar to brainstorm ideas to keep me from selling?"

Gus abruptly dropped his hand.

"The matter came up when I was discussing the bulls with the twins."

"Must have been some discussion if she called it a war council."

"No." Which sounded blatantly untrue, but as he remembered it, they'd discussed things as he'd moved between patrons, and he hadn't said anything that Lillie Jean wouldn't have told the real estate agent today.

"Then why did…" Her voice trailed off and she made a gesture of frustration. "Never mind."

"No," he repeated as he reached out, almost as if he couldn't help himself, and gently lifted her chin with his thumb and forefinger so that she had to meet his eyes. She looked angry, hurt, conflicted. She also looked as if she'd very much like to shut the door in his face. "I wasn't complaining or making you out to be the bad guy. I was discussing the situation with my friends. Maybe I shouldn't have."

"I don't care about that," she said stiffly.

"Yeah." His voice was gentle. "I think you do."

She took a step back and he let his hand fall back to his side. "I care about not screwing things up," she said in a low voice. "And I care about being called out in public by your girlfriend—"

"Ex-girlfriend."

"Which wouldn't have happened if you hadn't been discussing me in a bar. I don't like kamikaze attacks."

"Like showing up on a ranch unannounced?" he asked mildly. Lillie Jean blushed, but before she could respond, he said, "That was a low blow."

"No. Maybe it was a necessary blow."

"How so?"

"It helps remind me to keep my distance."

"Why do you need to be reminded, Lillie Jean?"

Her eyes went wide as his meaning hit home. "This is why I don't mix business with friendship. Things get out of hand."

He shifted his weight onto one hip, crossing his arms over his chest, wanting very much to ask what "things" she was referring to, but instead saying, "Madison called my discussion with the twins a war council because she's possessive and she wants to stir up trouble. I didn't discuss anything at the Shamrock that isn't common knowledge now that you've spoken to the people in the real estate office."

Lillie Jean's gaze shifted in an odd way.

"*Did* you talk to the real estate people?" Because if she hadn't…well, that would be a good sign, if he hadn't mucked things up too badly.

"I told you I'd give you time. And I will."

"So that's a no."

Her eyes flashed again, as if she was drawing strength from anger. "That's a none of your business. Giving you time is not the same as giving you a blow by blow of what I'm doing and what I found out."

Of all the women to get under his skin, why did it have to be her? "Fine. But remember one thing… I'm not your enemy. And I'm not your jerky fiancé."

"Then what are you, Gus?"

He let out a shaky breath, surprised at the question, which, if answered truthfully, might get him into a boatload of trouble. "Damned if I know, Lillie Jean. But apparently I'm nothing close to what you need."

LILLIE JEAN CLOSED her eyes and leaned a palm against the front door, letting her head drop as Gus headed down the path from her house. She heard the gate creak open then closed and then…nothing.

That was what she wanted from him. Nothing.

She could not afford to get involved with this man. First, she didn't want to get involved with anyone. She was still licking her wounds from Andrew, still not fully convinced that she could trust her own judgment. Then this guy shows up in her life.

No—you showed up in his life.

Details.

Second, she was starting to think with her heart instead of her head. She worried about Thad. Her grandparents had caused him a lot of pain all those years ago, and now she might hurt him all over again. And, heaven help her, she hated stomping on Gus's dreams of managing the H/H.

But if it came down to his dreams or hers, she had to choose hers. Right?

Or come up with a compromise, and right now, giving him time to secure a loan was her compromise. Admitting that she'd felt downright possessive about him today when Madison had done her number in the gift shop, or admitting how much it stung to think about him discussing her in a bar—not part of the deal.

Admitting to herself that she had a problem where Gus was involved…yeah, she did need to do that. She grabbed her coat and let herself out of the house. There were noises coming from the barn and she followed them to where Gus was ripping into the engine of the four-wheeler.

Confront the issue. Burying your head in the sand won't solve anything. You need to create some real distance.

Lillie Jean squared her shoulders and stepped into the barn. "Problem?"

His head jerked around at the sound of her voice. He slowly straightened, a wrench in one hand. "Yeah. I'd say we have a problem."

"I meant with the four-wheeler."

"And I meant with us."

Now that was the way to address an issue. Lillie Jean swallowed her self-conscious reaction to his blunt words and said, "I owe you an apology."

He gave her a wary look as he cupped the wrench in his free hand. "For…"

"Blaming you for my own insecurities."

Please don't make me explain what I mean. Because she didn't know if she could.

He gave a silent nod, frowning down at the ground near her feet. "You know," he said slowly, "there's nothing wrong with feeling, and there's nothing wrong with trusting. Just because you got it wrong once, it doesn't mean you'll get it wrong every time."

"There's no guarantee I won't, either."

"That what's scaring you." It was a statement rather than a question. And it was totally true.

"I guess that with everything that's happened lately, maybe I do need a guarantee." Lillie Jean's voice was a little too low. A little too husky. But she was afraid if she spoke louder, it might crack with emotions that she did not want to show. "Since that isn't going to happen, maybe it'd be best if I keep to my own space."

"No more morning chores?"

That hadn't occurred to her, but now that he'd said it…

"If you can manage alone, then yes." If she didn't share that small cab with him every single morning, making a show of earning her keep, then perhaps she could get a handle on this thing.

One corner of his mouth tilted into a humorless half smile. "I'll try to muddle through."

"That wasn't how I meant it," she said.

"Yeah. I know. You were being polite." He dropped the hand holding the wrench to his side. "Whatever works for you, Lillie Jean. I guess all I want is for us to live in peace until this ranch deal is settled."

"Then I think it's best if we keep to ourselves."

CHAPTER TWELVE

GUS MADE A conscious effort to relax his jaw muscles as he headed back to the four-wheeler. He worked until dinner figuring out the issue with engine, glad to have something to focus on other than the situation with Lillie Jean. He was more than capable of feeding the cattle on his own, but he'd liked having her along in the morning. Had kind of looked forward to it—the way she'd climb up into the cab and shoot him that sleepy-eyed, half-smiling look that said she was out of bed way too early. And how sometimes he'd catch her studying him only to have her pretend she wasn't. She was. And he spent his fair share of time studying her. Wishing. Wanting. Wondering.

They had a problem, all right, and Lillie Jean wasn't interested in finding a solution. Her solution was to sell and go back to Texas. Except she could go back to Texas now, and she wasn't. Why? Finances? Jerky ex-fiancé? A combination of factors?

He could take solace in the fact that staying at the ranch was the lesser of the evils in her life.

Chores the next morning were…chore-like. He not only missed the convenience of having the gates opened and the cows shooed away—he missed Lillie Jean.

Man up. This is your reality.

If she wanted space, she was getting space. The best way to avoid a ranch mate was to leave the ranch proper, so Gus decided to use the four-wheeler to check the remainder of the boundary fences. Once those were mended, he'd check the fences in the high country—the federal allotment where he turned the cows out after calving—on horseback. The snow line was receding, and he wanted to get a start on the repairs as soon as he could.

It was sobering to think that if he and Thad didn't get their loan, this might be the last year he'd make these kinds of decisions on his own. Depending on how things turned out, it might be the last time he made repairs at all. The thought was downright depressing and when he arrived at the last brace that needed work, he slammed the posthole diggers into the ground so hard that he was winded afterward. Maybe the Ag loan guy was wrong. Maybe the process wouldn't move at a snail's pace.

And maybe Henry would grow some legs.

Gus smiled a little as he took off his hat and wiped his forehead with his jacket sleeve. He liked the low-rider dog.

When he'd driven by Lillie Jean's house that morning, Henry was furiously digging at the fence while the cat taunted him from the other side. Henry would be well off to stay on the safe side, but as near as Gus could tell, the dog had no idea that the cat was nearly twice his size and could outrun him, outfight him.

Gus picked up the post he'd dropped off a couple days ago as he and Lillie Jean had driven the perimeter and plunked it into the hole. He'd do well to focus on what he was doing, rather than what-ifs. But the what-ifs were hard to push aside.

Once the brace was rebuilt, Gus got on the four-wheeler and continued along the fence line for one final check. Good thing, too, because Carson Craig's cattle had punched another hole through the boundary fence and there was fresh poop on his side. Great.

When he found the cattle, if they hadn't crossed back over, he'd call Carson to come get them—although he was fairly certain that his neighbor would demand that Gus drive them to the Craig spread. The ironic thing was that the hole was on Gus's half of the boundary fence. If he went by Craig law instead of Montana law, then Carson would be fixing the fence, since his cows had busted through.

Although he'd probably argue that Gus's cows had made the hole and his cows had simply taken advantage. There really was no winning with the guy.

The sun was low and the temperatures dipping by the time Gus finished patching the fence. He shrugged into his heavy coat, climbed on the four-wheeler and headed back to the ranch without seeing any Craig cattle, which meant he wasn't going to call the guy. The less contact the better.

As he approached the ranch, he saw Lillie Jean come out of the barn and then circle around behind one of the sheds. Huh. Maybe she needed to scrounge something for her painting project, although he couldn't imagine what. She came around the shed when he approached the barn and he could see from the way she held herself that something was wrong. Way wrong.

Instead of driving into the barn, he pulled up next to her and cut the engine.

"Henry's gone."

"He was in the yard when I left."

"Yeah." Her face was pale, her eyes wide. "That's where I left him. When I came out to call him in, I found the place where he'd burrowed under the fence." She hunched her shoulders as a gust of wind hit her from behind. "He's never dug out before and he's never ever not come when I called." She blinked rapidly. "What if…"

She couldn't finish the sentence, but Gus did, mentally. What if something had got Henry? He was a little guy and there were predators that weren't afraid to sneak close to a ranch in search of prey.

Gus got off the four-wheeler, his gaze sweeping over the ranch yard. "How long have you been looking?"

"Not long. Maybe five minutes." Her mouth trembled slightly as she said, "He always comes when I call."

It took everything Gus had not to reach out and pull her into his arms, hold her, tell her he'd find her dog. Instead he dropped his chin so he could look Lillie Jean in the eye. "He might be holed up somewhere, scared. You look in and under the buildings, I'll check out the orchard and the area around where the equipment is parked."

"Right." Lillie Jean started back toward the barn.

"There's a hole in the barn foundation near the rear door," Gus called after her.

She raised her hand without looking back and he started toward the equipment.

Henry's name echoed through the growing darkness as he and Lillie Jean called and called. Gus had a very bad feeling as he searched around the old combines, balers and grain trucks. The air was too still. No whines. No yips.

In the distance Lillie Jean was calling, an increasingly desperate note to her voice. He wasn't going to give up the search, but soon they'd have to get flashlights. He started back toward the driveway, when a movement caught his eye.

Only Clancy, sitting on top of a post near the pole pile.

Gus shifted course. "What'd you do to him?" he asked the cat, glad that no one was around to hear this bit of madness.

Clancy stretched himself up higher and then Gus heard it. The faintest of whines.

He turned toward the pole pile. There wasn't much space beneath it. But had Henry managed to push his way under it? He crouched down low.

"Henry?"

He was answered with another faint whine. Gus jumped to his feet and yelled Lillie Jean's name. She came running.

"You found him?"

"Listen."

Lillie Jean crouched beside him. "Henry?"

The whimper was louder this time and Lillie Jean's gaze flashed up to Gus's face. "How do we get him out?"

"Carefully."

She reached out to grip his forearm, looking as if she was about to cry. "Thank you, Gus. Thank you for finding him."

He brought a hand up to cup her cheek. Her skin was cold beneath his touch, and again he felt the urge to draw her close, warm her. Henry made another noise and he tore his gaze away from hers, dropped his hand.

"We need to proceed carefully so we don't shift the pile onto him…"

It took nearly fifteen minutes of careful moving and shifting of poles until they made a space big enough for Gus to lean into and touch the little dog's warm body. He snagged a couple fingers into the sweater and tugged. Nothing.

"The sweater is hung up," he muttered.

"Oh no."

"I can get it, if I can just reach the buttons…" Gus worked first one button through the hole, then the second. When he pulled his hand back, Henry followed, wiggling his way out and then turning small joyful circles, yipping at Lillie Jean as she tried to get hold of him. Finally she managed to scoop him into her arms and he continued whining as he gave her doggy kisses.

"Your next sweater will have quick-release fastening," she promised the little dog before looking up at Gus, a joyful smile on her face. Without pausing to think, Gus wrapped his arms around Henry and Lillie Jean, pulling them close, getting a few canine kisses of his own.

Lillie Jean leaned into him, her cheek resting against his chest as she cuddled the dog, and then he felt her go still. Gus casually dropped his arms, stepping back and doing his best to pretend he felt nothing but reunion joy. That he hadn't been one bit affected by Lillie Jean's hair brushing his jaw, or the satisfying feeling of having her in his arms.

"Happy ending," he said gruffly.

"Yes." Lillie Jean sounded breathless and he had the feeling that she, too, was pretending. "Look," she lifted the dog so he could see Henry's face. "He's bleeding."

"Cat scratches," Gus guessed. He looked over his shoulder, but Clancy was no longer sitting atop the post. Well, at least the gnarly old feline had pointed Gus in the right direction.

"I'd better see to them," she said without looking at him.

"I have ointments."

"Great." Lillie Jean started toward the houses and Gus fell into step, keeping a healthy distance between himself and the woman who was driving him just a little crazy.

GUS PERCHED ON the plaid recliner in Lillie Jean's living room, holding Henry steady while she crouched in front of him, dabbing antibiotic ointment on the little dog's nose. Henry rolled his eyes and did his best to pull away, but Gus gently held him in place until Lillie Jean sat back on her heels.

While she'd been focused on treating the deep scratches, she'd been fine. Or close to fine. Now…she was too close to Gus for comfort. She could feel the warmth radiating off his body, smell hay and earth and guy—a surprisingly heady mixture for someone trying to keep herself from going into sensory overload.

"He should have a tetanus shot." Gus ran a hand over Henry's little domed head, stroking his ears.

"Yes," Lillie Jean agreed.

"I'll get one."

"Excuse me?" She stood and reached for Henry, who wiggled until she set him on the floor. Gus got to his feet.

"I'll be back with the syringe."

"You have tetanus vaccine just hanging around?"

"This is a ranch," he said. "I also have penicillin and tetracycline. I've just got to check expiration dates."

"Okay."

As soon as he was gone, Lillie Jean sat on the floor and called Henry. He climbed into her lap and she stroked his ears. "You are never going outside without being monitored again." Even though Gus had promised to fill in the hole, there was nothing stopping her intrepid little dog from digging another.

"It was that cat, right?" Lillie Jean murmured to the dog. "He led you astray."

Henry whined as if to say, "Exactly. It was the cat."

"Now you need a new sweater and—" the door rattled "—it looks like you're about to get a poke."

She scooped up Henry as Gus came back inside and sat in the recliner. Gus popped the top off the syringe and knelt down to expertly administer the shot. He was good, because Henry didn't move. When he was done, he ruffled the dog's ears.

"Thank you," she said, hoping Gus didn't notice how husky and uncertain her voice was.

She was still upset over the Henry scare, but she was also still working her way through the group hug next to the pole pile, and how secure she'd felt in his arms.

Secure. Yeah. Right. Good one, Lillie Jean.

Lillie Jean and her little voice were going to have to have a serious talk one of these days. She was getting tired of small whispered truths ruining her justifications.

She cleared her throat. He was still kneeling in front of her, petting Henry, his fingers occasionally brushing against hers, when he raised his gaze and it was all she could do to keep from swallowing. Oh yeah. He was feeling it, too.

Stop lying to yourself. You like him. You want him.

Lying was better than messing things up.

Yeah? Well, they're pretty messed up now, so...

"Lillie Jean—"

An odd calm came over her when Gus said her name. Without thinking or wondering or rationalizing, she leaned forward to slide a hand around the back of his neck and pull him toward her, tilted her head, and met his lips in a soft, sweet kiss.

Soft and sweet quickly turned to fiery and hot. She pulled back, while she still could, bringing her back firmly against the recliner cushion. Henry twisted his head to look up at her with a confused canine expression, as if asking why he'd just been squeezed between his two rescuers.

"That was in the name of honesty," she said.

He gave her a crooked half smile, but his gaze was serious as he said, "I like it when you're honest."

"It's hard."

He rested his hands on her knees, one on either side of Henry. "I know," he said softly. "But I'm a fair guy. I don't believe in taking advantage and I don't believe in manipulation."

"You're not Andrew," she said with a wry twist to her lips.

His grip tightened on her knees. "Lillie Jean, I have no idea where this is going, but I think we should stop denying feelings."

"I'm only staying for so long." Which was, again, honest. She was going home.

"I know. And if everything works out, I'll be married to the ranch."

"So what are you saying?"

He smiled for real, a genuine smile that crinkled the corners of his eyes and creased his cheeks. "I'm not really sure. But I'd like to keep being honest with each other. And that means communication. With each other," he clarified.

"Point taken." She reached out to touch his cheek. "Maybe I'd like to continue doing morning chores again."

"Maybe I'd enjoy the company." He got to his feet. "We'll play this by ear, Lillie Jean. Communication and trust."

"Sounds good," she said. It also sounded scary. But she was going to give it her best shot—in the name of honesty.

GUS HAD THE tractor running when Lillie Jean came into her living room, putting on her coat as she walked. She was a little late, but it was actually for a good reason— she'd had a decent night's sleep for the first time in over a week. Something about everything being out in the open, where it was easier to deal with, rather than wondering what Gus was thinking, or what her next move would be to keep Gus from knowing she was spending too much time thinking about him. Yes, she might be signing up for trouble, but honesty was better than feeling shifty and uncertain.

She'd just grabbed her gloves off the kitchen table when her phone rang. She looked at the phone, then at the idling tractor. No one called that early unless it was important. Lillie Jean reversed course and grabbed the phone off the table, her heart rate bumping up when she saw that it was Kate.

"Is something wrong?" she asked.

"What? Why?"

"It's 6:00? In the morning?" A time when she'd normally be out feeding, but Kate didn't know how ridiculously early she got out of bed.

"Oh." Kate gave a small laugh. "Time difference and I've been up for hours. I would have called last night but I fell asleep when the kids went down. Anyway," she said, her voice growing serious, "I think you should call Andrew."

"The guy you told me to block?"

"I ran into him in the hardware store. He's going to pieces. Taia pulled out of the business. Isabella only wants your designs and is threatening to cancel the order. It sounds like the place is bleeding money."

"He's had it for four months."

"Couldn't happen to a nicer guy." But Kate's tone lacked conviction. If Kate felt sorry for Andrew, then he had to be in rough shape. "I think he'd sell the place back to you."

"I wonder how bad it is? If it can be salvaged?"

"I don't know. The direction Taia wanted to go was a big flop, which was why she bailed."

Leaving Andrew holding the bag.

"I thought both she and Andrew wanted to go in the same direction."

"Not to hear Andrew tell it. Now he's wishing they'd left things as they were with your aesthetic, instead of going ultramodern minimalistic." Kate gave a small sniff. "Apparently that didn't go over well with the established clientele and they haven't yet managed to attract new customers."

"Bleeding money. Just the kind of business I want to invest in."

But the truth was that she wanted her business back— if it could be salvaged. The workroom and the storefront…she wanted it.

"If you did decide to give it a go," Kate said tentatively, "I'd help you."

Which was code for "please buy back the business, and let me build it with you."

"You know none of this may work out," Lillie Jean felt compelled to point out. "Andrew may prefer to let the business die rather than sell it back to me."

"If it works out that way, I understand. But at the very least, call Andrew and find out what's going on."

"All right. I will." Lillie Jean ended the call and headed out the door, walking quickly across the gravel driveway to the tractor, her mind going about a hundred miles an hour. Andrew was in trouble. He might want to sell. Yes, she had to look into this.

Gus leaned across the cab to pop the door open as Lillie Jean climbed the stairs. She eased into the jump seat and shot him a quick smile. She'd kissed this man. Twice.

She wanted to kiss him again, and it probably showed. "I feel self-conscious," she said.

Honesty.

He smiled a little and put the tractor in gear. "Me, too. We'll work through it."

Lillie Jean let out a breath and felt herself start to relax. And this morning, as she watched his hands on the levers and occasionally glanced at his profile, she didn't worry about being caught, because when their gazes connected, he gave her that sexy half smile she loved so much.

She opened gates, cut strings on the giant hay bales, then stood near the gate that was holding back the cattle as Gus loaded the hay into the feeders. The calf-stealing cow was now totally mellow and barely noticed as her calf came up to give Lillie Jean a curious once-over. A few more calves approached, scattering when Gus turned the tractor and headed back to pick her up. Lillie Jean waited until he was close by, then swung open the gate and the cattle poured through, some walking, some loping toward the feed. Once again, she climbed the steps and got into her seat.

"Hey," Gus said as he put the tractor into gear. "Do you want to go to the community spaghetti feed tonight?"

Like a date?

"To tell you the truth, I'd forgotten." Put it right out of her head. "But...why not?" It'd give her a chance to meet more people. Being totally isolated on the ranch was good for her creativity, but she missed being around people. There had to be a happy medium in one's life and she hadn't achieved that in Montana.

"We'd be home by eleven."

"Are you telling me I'll need to sleep fast to be up in time for chores?"

He cocked an eyebrow at her. "Maybe."

"Do you need help today?" she asked.

"No. I have a little more fencing to do from the four-wheeler, then I'm going to town to get feed."

"I have calls to make."

"Real estate?"

She had to give him points for sounding matter-of-fact about a subject that had to twist his gut. "My ex. About the business."

"Ah."

He didn't ask for more information and she didn't offer any. After he parked the tractor, they went their separate ways, Lillie Jean to her house, Gus to his. She did not want to make this call. Did not want to hear Andrew's voice again.

Tough.

Lillie Jean pulled off her gloves and hat after closing the front door behind her. She stripped out of her feeding jeans, slipped into her painting pants, then settled on the recliner, phone in hand. Henry jumped onto her lap as she dialed the number to A Thread in Time. Andrew answered, probably because there was no one else around now that Taia had left.

"Hi, Andrew."

"Lillie Jean." He sounded stunned.

"Kate thought you wanted to talk to me."

"I didn't tell her that."

"I know." Lillie Jean waited, allowed Andrew time to get his thoughts together. This wasn't a call she particularly wanted to make, but if, on the off chance Andrew did want to sell instead of going bankrupt, she needed to know.

After several silent seconds ticked by, Andrew said, "Taia left."

"I heard."

"Isabella hasn't canceled her order yet, but she will if I don't come up with what she wants." He cleared his throat. "Would you consider coming back?"

"I would consider buying the business back—if you haven't ruined the reputation yet."

"I haven't been raking in the orders." Because he didn't have Kate out there actively marketing when she wasn't busy with the bookkeeping. Her friend had a gift that she hadn't been aware of until she'd gone to work for A Thread in Time. "But I haven't reneged on any. Yet."

"Andrew…" Lillie Jean planted a palm on her forehead. Funny how she felt absolutely nothing for this guy other than impatience. Had she ever really loved him? Or had she just been very comfortable?

"Taia's dad is a lawyer."

"I know." What did that have to do with anything?

"He wrote her a pretty decent contract. I…uh…owe her a bunch of money. I also owe the vendors. I'm more than sixty days behind."

"How…?"

"We went to some trade shows in California and Arizona, thinking we'd rake in the orders. Didn't happen."

"You used the vendor money to finance trips to the trade shows?"

"It was a gamble."

No. It was stupid.

"Andrew, we had a nice little business. It was growing. It had a great reputation." They were making key contacts in the music world.

"It still has a great reputation." His tone shifted. Hardened. "If you can buy me out, pay the vendors, A Thread in Time won't have the stigma of a bankruptcy."

"Or I could start over with a new name."

"Your name will still be associated with a bankrupt business."

"How? I'm no longer part of the business."

"You were, and you haven't been gone that long."

Lillie Jean scowled at the phone. "Are you threatening me?"

"No. I'm offering to let you buy back the business. It shouldn't be a problem since you've come into some money."

"Have you ever heard the phrase 'land rich, cash poor'?"

"You're breaking my heart, Lillie Jean."

Yeah. What would that feel like? He'd stomped all over her heart.

"Put some numbers together," she said. "Email me."

"I'm not blocked?"

"I'll unblock you. And, Andrew, don't try to play me. Your name will take more of a hit than mine will if the business goes south."

CHAPTER THIRTEEN

WHEN LILLIE JEAN walked into the high school gymnasium, all eyes turned her way as people scoped out Thad's new partner—at least that was how it felt to Gus. Lillie Jean didn't seem to notice, but he had a feeling it was an act. He touched the small of her back, guiding her toward the classroom where the coats were stored. After five consecutive spaghetti feeds, he knew the drill.

People smiled and nodded, their gazes openly curious as he and Lillie Jean passed by. He'd give proper introductions after she'd had a chance to get her bearings. Annie Delaney raised a hand and when he started to wave back, he realized that she was waving at Lillie Jean. Cool. She had a friend.

"There's one of the twins," she said, leaning close so he could hear her.

"Tyler."

"How can you tell?"

"Up close he has a scar on his chin. Far away he's standing next to his wife. Jess—" he pointed out the other Hayward brother, who was setting up chairs with the help of a pretty redhead "—is with his fiancée, Emma."

"I guess that's easy enough." She scanned the crowd, taking in the kids playing around the edges of the gym, the generations of single families sharing tables. "This is nice."

"Surely they do stuff like this in your town."

"But the difference is that I know everyone there. The good, the bad, the ugly. Everyone here has a clean slate for me."

They spotted Madison at the same moment, standing near the end of the long serving line, talking to a small group of overdressed women.

"Most everyone," Lillie Jean muttered. Gus gave a low laugh, and then she turned to look over her shoulder as someone said her name. Annie.

"Hi, Gus. I wanted to introduce Lillie Jean to my family if I can steal her away."

"I'm here to meet people," Lillie Jean said to Annie with an answering smile.

"I see Thad." His uncle was sitting at a table near the back corner with a couple of his buddies. Either Mimi or Ginny were running the pub.

Lillie Jean followed his gaze. "I'll head over and say hello when I'm done."

"Have fun," he said as she and Annie started through the crowd. He didn't think she'd heard him, but she shot him a look over her shoulder that told him she had. He pushed his thumbs into his back pockets, suddenly at loose ends. He looked around, then headed over to join Thad.

"Hey," Thad said as Gus approached. "Thanks for covering for me."

"Feeling better?"

"Yeah. I am." He glanced at his watch. "I have a little over an hour before I go on shift. Tyler said I could go to the front of the line."

"Nice of him."

"Yeah." The old man cleared his throat. "I'm a little surprised to see you escorting Lillie Jean."

"Well, you know, she wanted to get out and I always come to this thing, so…"

"Here you are."

"Yes."

"Heard that she and Madison had a bit of a dustup."

Not much happened in Gavin that wasn't reported in the Shamrock, and probably every other bar in town.

"I'm not sure exactly what happened."

"Heard Lillie Jean took her down a notch." Thad fixed his gaze on his nephew as if suspecting him of harboring secrets. He wasn't, except for the fact that he was watching all the guys who were watching Lillie Jean.

"That's what I heard, too." He gave his uncle a quick humorless smile. "Let's just hope they stay on opposite sides of the gym tonight."

"Yeah. Nita looked delicate, too, but she could hold her own." Thad fell into silence, then gave Gus a look. "There's no chance that you two…" He let his voice trail.

Gus refused to take the hint. "What do you mean?"

Thad frowned deeply. "I watched you two come in," he said as if that explained everything.

Gus shot a look at the three guys sitting a couple chairs over. They were arguing about the future of cattle prices and didn't seem at all interested in Gus or Thad, so Gus turned back to his uncle. "What are you getting at?"

"I guess all I'm saying is that if Lillie Jean is anything like Nita, then I understand why you would fall for her. I'd hate to see you end up like me."

Gus blinked at his uncle's quantum leap. "You're moving kind of fast. We're at a community spaghetti feed."

"And your head is about to swivel off your neck watching her."

Gus found himself struggling for a reply when he was saved by Thad's phone buzzing in his pocket. His uncle dug out the flip phone and opened it. "Yeah?" He let out a frustrated breath. "All right. Yeah. I'll get there as soon as I can."

He closed the phone and looked around the room.

"Problem?"

"Ginny's coming down with that bug Mimi and I had. I have to head to the bar. Hector's my ride."

Gus scanned the room. No sign of Hector. He leaned sideways to pull his keys out of his pocket. "I'll run you over there. I can drop a plate of food by later."

"No need. I'll order a pizza."

Lillie Jean was sitting with Annie and her family at a table far from the door, so Gus simply led the way out of the gymnasium, thinking that maybe it was better than checking in with her, so Thad didn't get any more ideas about saving Gus from himself. He wouldn't be gone that long, and he could easily find her when he got back. After all, she was the most striking woman in the room.

LILLIE JEAN HAD missed the feeling of community, and it appeared that she had to travel no farther than Gavin to recapture it. She sat at a table with Annie and her family, doing her best to tell yet another set of twins apart—Annie's daughters—and making small talk with the extended family sitting around the table. They seemed fascinated by the fact that she designed clothing for a real country-western musician, even though only one person at the table had heard of Isabella. As they talked, Gus's table filled up and it took her a while to realize that Gus and Thad were no longer sitting there. Well, they had to be somewhere, and until she found them, Lillie Jean was staying right where she was. She felt safe from Madison who was giving her looks across the room that reminded her of the calf-stealing cow.

There was still no sign of Gus when the people started lining up for dinner, so she joined the line with Annie's family. After filling her plate, she turned to see if Gus's table had opened up, only to be startled by a light touch on her elbow.

She glanced up to see a darkly handsome man smiling politely at her. Even though she was a suburbanite, she *was* from Texas, and she recognized a super expensive beaver cowboy hat when she saw one.

"There's room at our table if you need a place to sit," the man said pleasantly.

He had a little bit of Texas in his voice, so Lillie smiled back. "Thank you." She was there to meet people, after all.

"Carson Craig," he said as he handed her a napkin before getting one for himself.

"Lillie Jean Hardaway."

He led her to the table and made introductions and it soon became apparent that she was not sitting at a table of locals, with the exception of Carson, but rather with a table of his guests, up visiting from Oklahoma.

So much for meeting the neighbors, but Lillie Jean settled in and ate as she made small talk with people who were much, much wealthier and well traveled than herself, but they all seemed to be nice down-to-earth people who just happened to have money. They, too, were fascinated by the fact that she was a designer and she answered questions until she saw Gus come in the door and then head for what was left of the spaghetti buffet.

"I appreciate the conversation," she said to the table in general. "I need to check in with my...friend." Yes. A much better word than *date*, although calling Gus a friend felt odd, primarily because she'd made such a big deal about them not becoming friends. She felt as if they had the potential to become much more than friends, and it kind of scared her. But she wasn't backing off, and that right there told her that maybe she was on the right track this time.

"It's been nice talking to you, Lillie Jean." Carson got to his feet, dug in his pocket and pulled out a card. "If you wouldn't mind calling me sometime in the near future, I have a matter I'd like to discuss."

"A matter?" Lillie Jean repeated dumbly. She hadn't even gotten a chance to discover what part of Texas he was from and he had something to discuss with her?

"Don't look so alarmed," he said with an easy smile. "It's all business and can be handled over the phone."

"Is it about the ranch?"

He gave her a charming smile. "Talk to you soon, Lillie Jean. I'm looking forward to it."

And she was mystified.

THE LONG FOOD tables were almost deserted by the time Gus got back to the gymnasium. He loaded a plate and found a seat at an empty table. A second after he sat down, Lillie Jean sat on the opposite side of the table. "You disappeared."

"Sorry about that. I ran Thad back to the bar. The plan was to get back before you knew I was gone, but kegs had to be moved to access a faulty line, and… I'm sorry. I hope you got to talk to some people."

"I did. I had a great time."

"Glad to hear it."

"Madison kept a respectful distance."

"Another plus."

"She has her sights set elsewhere," Lillie Jean said matter-of-factly. "She was trolling for this good-looking blond guy. He seemed interested, too." Gus gave her a "better him than me" look and she laughed. "I don't think she and I are ever going to be friends, though."

"She's not a good friend," Gus replied before biting into the garlic bread. "It took me a bit to figure out that it's all about her, but I eventually got the picture. She's good," he added when Lillie Jean cocked an eyebrow. "She had Thad fooled, too, and Thad doesn't fool easily."

"I guess my first impression kind of colored my view of her."

"First impressions can be tricky," he agreed. "I suspected you of being a scam artist."

"No kidding." She kept a straight face, but her blue-green eyes were lit with amusement. Thad was right. Gus's feelings for Lillie Jean were growing. He'd liked her before, but now that she'd dropped her guard, accepted that the draw they felt for one another wasn't going away anytime soon, things felt different.

Annie and Trace Delaney and their girls drifted over to say goodbye.

"Maybe you can come to my class and talk about your job," one of Annie's twins said to Lillie Jean.

"My class, too," the other chimed in.

Lillie Jean smiled. "I'll see what I can do."

After the family left, she said, "Annie told me that Career Day happened about a month ago, and I doubt I'll be here for next year's."

Gus didn't answer. He finished the last of his spaghetti, then gathered up his plate and gestured toward the door. "What do you think about eating and running? Unless you want to stay for the raffles?"

"The two I signed up for are 'need not be present to win.'" She tilted her head, her dark hair sliding over one shoulder. "I've had fun, but I wouldn't mind getting home." She gave him a pert smile. "I have early morning chores, you know."

He smiled back, then got to his feet. After dumping their plates, they walked to the classroom where the coats were stored. "I honestly am sorry about missing most of this thing."

"Yeah?" she said as he handed her jacket to her.

"I'll make it up to you."

"How?"

"I'll give you a tour of the park."

"I thought we were going home."

He turned after they exited the school and put his hands on her shoulders. "When we get back home, we'll fall back into our roles. But here…here we're just Gus and Lillie Jean."

"Kind of like two different people?"

"Nope. Kind of like the same people in a different place. What if I'd met you elsewhere, Lillie Jean? And you were through dealing with your ex and his thieving ways. What would you have thought about me?"

She bit her full lower lip as she looked up at him. "Honestly? I probably would have been very interested and not worried about hiding it."

"Likewise." He pushed his hands into her hair and slowly lowered his head to kiss her, keeping it soft when he wanted to make it so much more. "But we have a situation that makes things trickier."

She rose up on her toes and kissed him back, then wrapped her arms around him and leaned into him. "I'm not going to think about that tonight."

Gus eased back and then tucked Lillie Jean's hand over his arm. "Then I am in no hurry to get home."

LILLIE JEAN AND Gus never made it to the park proper. They stopped at the playground just inside the entrance and sat in the swings, talking about their childhoods. Gus's was markedly different from Lillie Jean's. Until moving in with Thad, he'd had essentially no support system. His mom had actually walked away from him and his dad, married another man, started a new family Gus had never met. He'd been justifiably angry, but then Thad, as he told it, slapped him into shape with some tough love.

"Thad is a good man," Lillie Jean said. "But try as I might, I can't see him married to my grandmother."

"I don't think he'll ever get over her."

Nor did Lillie Jean, despite not knowing him that well. It was the way he looked at her with that hint of sadness, as if mourning what had been and never was. She liked Thad, and she could see where her grandmother would have found him attractive back in the day. Maybe it was just because she'd only seen her grandparents with one another and their bond had been so strong that the idea of her grandmother with another man boggled her mind.

"Has he had other women in his life?"

Gus shook his head. "Mimi was trying to fix him up with Ginny, but he's having none of it."

"Sad." Lillie Jean nudged the swing and got it moving, shifting as she felt the stiff card she'd gotten from Carson Craig in her front pocket. "Do you know a man named Craig?"

"Carson Craig?" Gus's body tensed as he said the man's name.

"Yes."

"Was he at the spaghetti feed?"

"I sat with him at dinner."

"He's my neighbor."

"He wants me to call him."

"Don't."

Gus didn't add anything, so Lillie Jean finally said, "I assume there's a reason?"

"He would be impossible to work with."

"I see." She hadn't gotten that vibe from him. He'd seemed very affable.

Gus let out a breath and then rubbed the back of his neck before twisting the swing to face Lillie Jean dead on. "I appreciate you giving me time to nail down a loan, but if it doesn't work out, and you sell to Carson, Thad and I will have to sell ourselves."

"That bad."

"I can't begin to tell you."

Lillie Jean nudged the swing a little higher. Her good mood was fading fast. Once again, she'd broken her friendship-business rule and once again it was coming back to bite her.

"I'm going to hear what he has to say." For all she knew, it might not be about the ranch. Maybe he wanted to order one of her custom designs.

But in her heart of hearts, she knew that it was about the ranch.

"I can't stop you."

Now Lillie Jean turned to face Gus, feeling as if an invisible wall had risen out of nowhere to separate them. "I have a chance to buy back my business. I talked to Andrew tonight. I don't know the details. I don't know how long he can wait. He's sending me the numbers."

"The amount he cashed you out isn't enough?"

"Not even close. I have to buy out two partners. And there's some debt now. I need to act while I can still rescue it."

"This is better than starting fresh?"

"If you knew the number of hours Andrew and I put into our business to begin with, the amount of equipment I'll have to procure...yes. Definitely better. And my friend Kate could come back to work for me right away."

"That's important to you."

"She can bring her kids. Right now, child care eats almost her entire paycheck. Her mom lives with her, and babysits when she can, but she has to make a living, too. It's a rough situation."

"But not of your making."

Lillie Jean wondered if he was purposefully echoing her own words back at her, then decided not. His expression wasn't one bit ironic.

"I talked Kate into coming to work for us. She quit her job in Austin. Andrew fired her the same day he forced me out. She hasn't been able to find another job in her field." So yes, Lillie Jean did think it was a situation of her making.

"There's got to be an option besides Craig. Even if Thad and I can't come up with funding."

"I hope you're right, Gus. And I hope that Andrew can wait a while for cash and maybe we can work something out with the vendors. They might be willing if it means getting paid what they're owed instead of pennies on the dollar." She got up from the swing, leaving it swaying behind her. "Maybe we should head back to the ranch."

Gus got to his feet. He only stood a couple feet away from her, but it might as well have been a couple of miles. "Yeah. We should do that. Before it gets too late."

From the way Lillie Jean's stomach was knotting, she suspected that it was already too late.

When they reached the truck, Gus opened the door for her. After Lillie Jean got in, she reached for the handle, but Gus's hand was still on the frame.

"I like you, Lillie Jean. I want you to have what you need in life. But please, if there is any other way, do not sell out to Carson Craig."

LILLIE JEAN GAVE herself points for (a) showing up to feed

the cattle with Gus the next morning even though she'd gotten next to no sleep, and (b) acting as if they hadn't argued about Carson Craig the night before. Gus did the same. They behaved with perfect politeness toward each other, but Lillie Jean figured it was only a matter of time before Craig's name came up again. Mainly because she was going to see him, and she was going to give Gus a rundown on the results of the meeting. The first was in the name of not letting friendship sway her business decisions…and the second was because she'd promised Gus open communication.

But that communication was temporarily on hold, judging from their silent morning.

After Gus parked the tractor, he turned off the ignition, then waited until Lillie Jean had opened the door before saying, "I'll be riding the fence in the high country today and tomorrow."

"Do you want me to come?"

"I'm going on horseback. I'll be back in the late afternoon."

"Oh, okay. Thanks for letting me know."

Lillie Jean jumped to the ground, and then headed to her house, where Henry waited at the gate. Not only could she wash clothes while Gus was gone, she could do the other things she had on her agenda.

But before she did anything, she called Julie, Kate's mom.

"Were you not able to reach Kate on her phone?" Julie asked after saying hello.

"I wanted to talk to you," Lillie Jean said. "I want the straight story about Kate. How is she doing with the job hunt and all?"

"Not well."

Lillie Jean's heart sank. She'd half hoped for a miraculous "She's been called in for an interview!"

"I mean, she's hopeful, but…it's not a good market." Julie's voice grew suddenly stern. "And don't you go blaming yourself for this, Lillie Jean. Kate took a risk when she quit her job, just as you took a risk when you started your business. If we're going to blame anyone, it's Andrew, and it looks like karma has come back on him bad."

"Did Kate tell you that Andrew might sell?"

"She did. But he wants cashed out. I know, because I approached him."

"You did?"

"I watch out for my girls," Julie said primly. "And you know there's no way any of us, I mean those of us in Texas, will be able to cash him out."

"It won't be easy for me, either. Not unless the ranch sells instantly."

"I know, honey. You've got to wait for the right person to come along to buy that place. But if you leave it in the hands of the real estate agents and come home, then maybe the three of us can work something out. If nothing else, we can take turns babysitting and work in shifts at our minimum wage jobs." Julie laughed, but it was a little too close to home for Lillie Jean to find it funny.

"Thanks, Julie. I'll be in touch. Give Kate and the kids a hug for me."

"Will do, honey. And you take care."

Lillie Jean hung up the phone and went to her newly painted dusky blue bedroom and picked up her bag of laundry. Gus had ridden by the window on a big bay horse as she'd spoken to Julie, looking every inch the cowboy he was.

She wanted her business, and she wanted a chance

to find out what was meant to happen between herself and Gus.

The way things stood, she could have only one, short of some kind of miracle. But if she never talked with Carson Craig, she'd never know what her possibilities were.

She picked up the card from the kitchen table and dialed Carson Craig's number. He answered almost immediately and when she identified herself, he told her he'd hoped she'd call.

"You said this could be done over the phone," she reminded him when he suggested meeting in town for a nice lunch.

"The first part can."

"What is this first part?" Lillie Jean asked.

"I've heard you're in the market to sell your interest in the H/H Ranch."

"If I were?"

"I'd be interested." He cleared his throat. "But I know that there might be issues with your partners. We've had some run-ins in the past."

Lillie Jean frowned down at the table. This must be what Gus had been talking about.

Carson gave a self-conscious laugh. "My fault entirely. I didn't know as much as I thought I did. I…messed up, I guess you could say. Gus and Thad tried to point me in the right direction, but I was stubborn."

"I see." A lame response, but what else could she say as he poured out his soul?

"I've learned a few things. Like let cowboys handle the cowboying. The H/H abuts my property and it would be the perfect way to expand, however, I'm more interested in using it as a tax write-off. My plan is to lease it back to Thad and Gus, let them make a living on it. As I see it, their lease wouldn't be that much more than the property taxes they're currently paying. I'd get my tax break, they'd have control of the land. And if I sold, I'd give them first right of refusal."

Lillie Jean let out a breath, hardly daring to think that this sounded...well...perfect. A win-win. And the guy admitted he'd messed up in the past.

"I'll need a little time to think this through."

"And to talk to Thad and Gus. I understand." He gave another low laugh. "Try to look past their prejudices, because I promise you, I gave them cause. Thank goodness I learned a lot since those early days."

Lillie Jean hung up slowly, then picked up her basket and headed out the door to do her laundry. She couldn't help it—she felt compelled to trust Carson Craig. Maybe this was a case of getting off on the wrong foot. Of Carson being arrogant in the beginning, as he'd confessed, and Gus never seeing enough of the man to get a second read on the matter.

CHAPTER FOURTEEN

LILLIE JEAN DIDN'T see Gus that evening. He rode into the ranch in the very late afternoon, just before the sun set, and after turning his horse loose in the pasture, he got into his truck and headed down the long driveway. When he didn't return within a reasonable amount of time, she knew that he'd gone to town, rather than for the mail. Last time he'd told her when he'd gone to town and wouldn't be back until late. This time he must have assumed that if she was fine being alone then, she was still fine with it. And she was. It wasn't as if she was his keeper.

But she did want to talk to him, and she didn't get the chance until they fed the next morning. She'd fallen asleep early, which would have never happened in her old life, so she had no idea what time he'd returned to the ranch. He looked tired as he reached across the seat to pop open her door, and when she got inside she didn't give him her usual sleepy half-smiling glance. She had things to say, and she wanted to say them when he wasn't about to keel over from exhaustion.

"Did you cover a shift last night?"

"Yep." He put the tractor in gear and it lurched forward. "Should be the last one. Our sub, Callie, is back in town, so I can focus on the ranch."

Yes...about the ranch.

She'd talk after feeding, except that Gus had a phone call and headed to the house to get some tax numbers for

Thad. Lillie Jean watched him cross the gravel, phone to his ear, then headed to her own house. She made a cup of tea and sipped it at the window until she saw Gus head back into the barn. Moment of reckoning.

Lillie Jean found Gus saddling his horse. He looked over his shoulder as she approached, then back at the rigging he was fastening.

She settled a hand on the horse's neck. "He's got a lot of hair." The horse's coat was so thick that she could ruffle it backward.

"Which means we're not done with winter yet."

It was April, but in Montana, that didn't mean it wouldn't snow. Lillie Jean, who'd at one time essentially ignored the weather, except during storm season, now checked daily. And yes, there was rain in the valleys, snow in the mountains in the forecast.

"How long will you be gone?"

"I'll be home before dark. I'm starting on the west side of the allotment fence, where it joins our property today."

"Why not take the four-wheeler?"

"Too many problem areas when it's this muddy. Don't want to rip up the ground."

It made perfect sense and Lillie Jean was out of small talk, which meant she had to push on to the big issue.

"I talked to Carson Craig. On the phone. Yesterday."

Gus's hand stilled on the cinch strap, and then he started pulling again. "Told him to jump in the lake, I hope."

"He wants to make me an offer on the ranch."

Gus instantly turned toward her, a hard expression on his face. "And you said…?"

"I needed time to think."

He made a noise in his throat that sounded very much

like a low growl, then gave the cinch one last pull before fastening it. "'No' would have been a better answer."

"It's not what you think."

"Yeah? Well, how is it?"

"He said he would be strictly hands-off. That he would lease the ranch back to you and Thad for a little more than the cost of the property taxes. He wants the write-off. He said he'd made mistakes in the past and that you were right and he was wrong."

Gus lowered his chin, shook his head. "He's playing you."

"Are you sure?" she asked in a low voice. Because she hadn't read it that way.

"I'm only going to consider selling to him, if you can't buy me out." Her voice had risen defensively, and she took a breath before saying in a calmer tone, "This is business, Gus."

Gus set a hand on the seat of his saddle as he met her gaze. "Yeah. I get it. Business." He narrowed his eyes. "Do you honestly believe that Craig would lease this ranch back to me?"

"Why wouldn't I believe that?"

He rolled his eyes as if the answer was beyond obvious, which it wasn't. "Because he'll tell you whatever you want to hear to get this place."

"I'll have it written into the contract."

"You don't get it, Lillie Jean. Once you sign your half away, you have no say." Gus untied the horse and then expertly bridled him, leaving the halter on. He coiled the lead rope and tied it to the saddle, then led the horse out of the barn.

"I didn't make this situation."

He turned on her. "Yeah. You've pointed that out a time or two. And I agree. You didn't. But that doesn't mean you can put me in a bad situation and I have to take it with a smile on my face." He put a foot in the stirrup and swung up into the saddle, gathering the reins. "I'll take it, Lillie Jean. But no smile. You'll just have to live with whatever bad feelings that dredges up." He turned the horse toward the pasture, then looked back over his shoulder. "Nothing personal. Just business."

SHE'S DOING WHAT she has to do. She owes you nothing.

That didn't change the fact that life as he knew it was probably pretty much over. He loved his ranch, but having Carson Craig as a partner was unacceptable. He couldn't do it. Maybe Craig *would* lease his part of the place to Thad in the beginning, but the chances were good that when the lease came up for renewal, that the man would have other plans. Or he would sell.

Gus pointed Red up the mountain and the gelding put his head down and started climbing. He was a good horse and Gus hoped he'd land in a place where he needed a horse. There were no guarantees. Ranch jobs paid next to nothing and he didn't know that he'd pursue ranch work if they lost the H/H. Thad was married to his pub and chances were that if Gus sold his half, Thad would do exactly what Madison had suggested—expand into a restaurant, rather than sink his profits into another ranch. Gus wanted no part of a restaurant. He no longer wanted to be part of the bar.

What you want and what you get...

Yeah. Right.

Red continued to climb, zigzagging his way up the mountain, traveling down into brush-filled gullies where Gus could barely see the fence and back up the other side. The ground was muddy—too muddy for the four-wheeler, and the terrain they were on now was too steep and brushy. Red pushed his way through undergrowth and started climbing again. So far the fence was okay. It could use tightening, but there were no holes to put him in trespass when cows slipped through.

He'd hit the first corner brace and was traveling north along the western boundary fence when the flurry hit. It was a quick little storm that barely laid any snow on the ground; there, then gone. As the flakes stopped swirling, Gus found the first downed wires. Gus dismounted and assessed. Definitely possible to do a patch job. He got the fencing pliers, staples and wire out of the saddlebags and started to work. His gloves soaked through in short order, but he got the job done before his fingers went numb.

And so it went for the remainder of the morning. The long western boundary fence, which bore the brunt of the drifting during winter months, had a number of holes, and each one seemed to take a little longer to fix than the one before it.

After eating a sandwich, Gus considered options. The repairs had taken longer than he'd expected, and if he kept riding north, he'd hit the snowline soon. He could turn around and go home or ride cross-country to the eastern boundary fence and check it out on the ride home. He should still get home before dark, and, truth be told, he wasn't that interested in heading back to the ranch just yet. Cross-country it was.

Swinging up into the saddle he turned east and started following a deer trail. The snow dipped lower in a few places and Red had to pick his way through the pristine white, his feet punching holes as he went. They entered a small meadow and a covey of Hungarian partridges hunkered down near a large boulder took to the sky. The horse bounded sideways as wings drummed and the birds rose around him, making it look like the boulder had come to life.

Gus sat deep in the saddle, did his best to help the horse keep his head up and get his feet back under him, but Red went down. Gus rolled into the snow as the horse struggled and then lunged back to his feet. The gelding took one limping step forward and Gus knew he was in trouble.

LILLIE JEAN SPENT a good part of her day pacing. First because of the unsettled business between herself and Gus, and then because it was getting dark and Gus hadn't yet returned to the ranch.

Gus was a capable individual. He knew what he was doing.

But even as she told herself Gus was an expert, Lillie Jean found herself flashing back on the cow incident. How they were both surprised by the calf stealer sailing over the fence. Accidents happened to experts as well as novices.

At what point did she stop worrying and act?

Exactly forty-five minutes after darkness fell.

Lillie Jean bundled up and headed outside, leaving Henry standing on his back feet and looking out the front window. She stood in the middle of the wide gravel drive and debated strategy. Did she start the four-wheeler and follow the fence? Did she call for help?

A gust of wind hit her and Lillie Jean tucked her chin into her coat as she headed back to the house and looked up the number for the Shamrock Pub. It took a few minutes to get hold of Thad.

"Lillie Jean. Is everything okay?"

"Gus rode the fence today and he's not back yet."

"Which fence?"

"The one where you put the cows out to graze this spring."

"The allotment."

"Yes." In her stress the word had escaped her.

"He was supposed to come back tonight, right?"

"Where would he spend the night if he didn't?"

"Cow camp."

Lillie Jean didn't bother asking for an explanation of what or where cow camp was. "He said nothing about a cow camp."

"Well, if he got into trouble, that's where he'd head."

If he was ambulatory after said trouble. Lillie Jean's stomach tightened to the point of nausea. "How do I get there?"

"You don't."

"But—"

"I'll be out shortly. It's snowing here, so it might take me a little extra time."

"It's not snowing here."

"Good. Hang tough, Lillie Jean. Gus knows what he's doing."

"Thank you." Lillie Jean ended the call and paced to the window where she peered out into the darkness. Where was Gus? Why did this have to happen after they'd had a fight?

Lillie Jean shoved the thought aside and put on her coat again. Henry tried to follow, but she closed the door before he could escape. The yard lights were dimmed by a low hanging fog moving in, chilling Lillie Jean, making her shudder uncontrollably. It would take Thad an hour to get there and then how long would it take to mount a search?

What if Gus was lying out there in the snow and cold, developing hypothermia?

Lillie Jean tried to believe he was at the cow camp, whatever it might be. That he was doing cowboy stuff, camped out near a fire out of the wind. Or perhaps in some rustic shack.

A choking sob caught in her throat, startling her.

She was losing it.

Wrapping her coat more tightly around herself, she strode through the halo of light under the yard lampposts and into the darkness, stopping at the pasture gate that Gus should have ridden through more than an hour ago. Closer to two hours, really.

"Gus!"

His name ripped out of her lungs, splitting the dark silence and then seeming to echo through the night. Lillie Jean pushed her hands deep into her pockets and dipped her chin, only to have it snap back up again when she heard a call in the distance.

Coyote?

Missing cowboy?

She was going with missing cowboy.

Lillie Jean opened the gate and slipped through, taking a few hurried steps before she stopped and called Gus's name again. This time she recognized his return call.

She headed on through the night, tripping over a clump of frozen grass and going down to her hands and knees. She jumped back up to her feet, brushing her stinging palms against her jeans, then instead of stumbling on, she waited where she stood, knowing Gus would be heading toward the lights of the ranch. But when she finally spotted him, she started moving.

"Gus—"

She barely got the word out when he reached out to pull her against him. Lillie Jean wrapped her arms around his neck, pressed her face against his cold cheeks, inhaled deeply.

"I was so worried," she muttered against his neck. His grip tightened, and then he leaned back, looking down at her through the darkness before his mouth came down to find hers. A homecoming of sorts, and when Lillie Jean pulled back, the tears that she'd been fighting were even closer than before.

She blinked a couple of times, thankful for the darkness.

"Are you okay?" he asked.

"Am *I* okay? What happened to you?"

"Red pulled a tendon. I had to lead him off the mountain."

Another shudder went through her and Gus held her more tightly against him, bringing his cheek down to rest against her hair. "It's okay," he murmured.

"No. It's not."

She felt him smile and eased herself out of his embrace. What did it mean that she didn't want to let go of him? Didn't want to step back?

Trouble was what it meant, but Lillie Jean would deal with that later. Right now, man and horse needed to get out of the weather.

They continued the slow walk to the barn. Lillie Jean held open the pasture gate and Gus and Red passed through. Once they were in the welcome shelter of the barn, Gus began unsaddling the horse. Lillie Jean took the saddle from him, carted it into the tack room and then returned for the damp blanket and the bridle. By the time she'd returned, Gus was kneeling, running his reddened hands over the horse's leg.

"Do we need to call a vet?"

Gus shook his head. "No. An injury like this takes

time to heal. Not much else we can do, except give him some analgesic to help with the pain and swelling."

Lillie Jean helped fork straw into the pen where the first heifer had calved, then filled the water barrel while Gus brushed down the horse and then forced some medicine into his mouth through a big plastic syringe. She was glad to be moving, because when she stopped moving, she might have to think about what had happened between her and Gus out in the pasture—and how very right it'd felt.

They stood side by side near Red's pen, watching as the horse nosed at his hay.

"You should get in out of the cold," Lillie Jean finally said.

"Yeah." He started to move, then stopped and reached out to take her hand, turning it over. The heels of her palms were skinned and darkened with imbedded grit.

"I fell." And had been so cold that she hadn't realized the extent of the damage she'd done.

"Where are your gloves?"

"My coat pocket. I was in such a hurry—"

Gus lightly ran his thumb over the wound, the sensation making the rest of the words stall out in her throat.

"Come on," he said, taking a light hold of her elbow and steering her toward the barn door.

"I can take care of it."

"No doubt. But I have the medical supplies."

Once in the house, they shed coats and hats. Gus unlaced his boots and pulled them off, taking his socks half with them. He reached down to pull the socks the rest of the way off and tossed them into the empty clothes basket next to the washer. Lillie Jean didn't say a word as he led her through the house to the small bathroom where he gently washed her palms, the water stinging as it hit the scrapes and warmed her numb skin.

Her left palm was raw and starting to seriously sting. The right wasn't so bad.

"Sit."

Lillie Jean sat and watched, her heart twisting with an emotion she did not want to feel as Gus knelt in front of her, dabbing ointment on the scrapes and then carefully applying a large bandage over her left palm. When he was done, he sat back on his heels and looked up at her without letting go of her hands.

"We have us a situation here, Lillie Jean."

He echoed Thad's words from what seemed like a long time ago—the day after she'd first showed up on the ranch, only this time they seemed truer than before. This was a situation.

And then, even though she knew she was only making a bad situation worse, she pulled her hands from his grip, gently framed his face and leaned in to kiss him. He kissed her back, gently, almost reverently, and then they jerked apart as the back door rattled.

"Are you here, Lillie Jean?"

"I phoned Thad when you didn't show up on time," she said before calling to the kitchen, "I'm here, Thad. So is Gus."

And she was both relieved and disappointed that Thad had chosen that moment to arrive. She wanted to talk to Gus—no...she needed to talk to him—but she had no idea what to say. What to do. Because she'd done exactly what she'd told herself she would not. She'd fallen hard for her business partner.

CHAPTER FIFTEEN

"LILLIE JEAN—YOU need to think about *you*. If you get an offer, take it. Buy back your business. Come home."

Kate's solution sounded simple. It should have been simple. Except for the part where it wasn't.

Lillie Jean wanted her business back. Then Kate could not only work for her, she could bring the kids with her and not have to pay day care, thus freeing up Julie to work more hours at her job. After leaving Gus's house the night before, Lillie Jean had bit the bullet and left a message for Isabella to contact her. The singer had a contract with Andrew, and Lillie Jean didn't want to look like she was trying to undermine that contract, but she was getting desperate. To her surprise, Isabella texted her back in short order, making it clear that if Andrew didn't deliver, she wanted to wear Lillie Jean's designs. That could get Lillie Jean and Kate through the first few months while they worked to regain their footing and rebuild their reputation. And hopefully Isabella would bring them clients to replace the ones Andrew and Taia had lost.

Just Lillie Jean and Kate. It could work. It could solve a lot of problems. All she had to do was to come up with the capital to take over ownership.

"Lillie Jean?"

"There is no offer yet, and even if there is, the guy has to agree to some things." And if he didn't, then Lillie Jean didn't know what her next step would be. If she couldn't buy the business from Andrew, then she had no real workspace, no machines except for her home sewing machine. She'd be working out of a rented apartment, trying to fill orders while saving enough money to acquire a real workspace, and then develop a storefront. And, of course, she'd have to get a day job.

Back to square one.

Lillie Jean hung up the phone and then checked her look in the mirror. Unlike the first time she'd met Carson Craig, Lillie Jean had taken pains to be as professional as possible. She'd sewn a simple sleeveless dress from some deep blue linen, twisted her hair up into a knot, put on some makeup. Her shoes—the black leather flats she'd worn while she drove north from Texas—had seen better days, but she'd rubbed some hand lotion into them to spiff them up, and all in all, she felt ready to talk business.

She drove to town on autopilot, going over scenarios in her head, very much as she had when she'd driven to Montana. But never in a thousand years had she thought that she'd be going back to Texas feeling like she'd left part of her heart in Montana.

Maybe she and Gus could work something out. Maybe she could stay a long-distance partner...thus letting down Kate and essentially sentencing herself to years of rebuilding.

Maybe you could stay on the ranch.

Then what? Have a wild fling which may well develop into a highly uncomfortable state of affairs?

Lillie Jean gave a grim snort. Yep. Definitely a situation.

The Evergreen Restaurant was an upscale establishment on the outskirts of Gavin, and Lillie Jean imagined that during the tourist seasons it was probably quite popular. But on a cold March day, there were only a half-dozen cars in the lot—most of them brand-new.

And then there was the old Cadillac.

Lillie Jean pulled in next to a shiny Land Rover and parked. Oh yeah. Her homemade linen shift and light cardigan were certainly going to fit in here. She wasn't even going to think about shoes shined with hand lotion. She grabbed her purse, a high-end gift to herself that would fit in, and got out of the car.

Carson Craig sat next to the picture window on the far side of the restaurant, a glass of wine at his elbow. He raised a hand and smiled as Lillie Jean entered the room and several heads turned her way. Lillie Jean didn't recognize a single face, perhaps because this wasn't the spaghetti-feed kind of crowd.

"Glad you could make it," he said after rising to his feet to pull out her chair. Once he was settled again, he signaled the waiter, who hurried over to take her drink order. "I took the liberty of ordering lunch."

"Thank you." Lillie Jean wasn't there for lunch. In fact, she didn't feel like eating at all.

"If you don't mind talking business before the food gets here, have you considered my offer?" Carson slowly swirled his wine, the ruby liquid coating the sides of the crystal glass.

"I have. Here's my situation—I promised Gus Hawkins time to procure a loan to buy me out."

Carson leaned back in his chair and, even though he was still smiling, the expression in his eyes had shifted, moving from warm to wary. "How much time?"

"As long as it takes to get an answer. If he's unable to procure financing, then I'd be happy to negotiate with you."

"I see."

The waiter set down the wine and Lillie Jean gave him a quick smile of thanks before once again meeting Carson's gaze. "If we come to an agreement, Gus will have final say in management issues."

"He will?"

"Yes. Because I'm only selling 45 percent interest in the ranch."

"You'll retain the other 5 percent?"

Lillie Jean smiled and reached for her wine.

Carson leaned his forearms on the table, bringing his face that much closer to hers. He was a handsome man with dark hair and striking blue eyes, but Lillie Jean felt like pulling back as he got closer. The affable veneer had evaporated.

"Here's my offer," he said smoothly. "I'll pay you cash for 50 percent. And I'll pay you as soon as I can cut a check."

"I told Gus he'd have the time—"

"This is a limited time offer."

"How limited?"

"Three days. Then the offer is officially off the table."

"I see."

Carson's handsome mouth curved up on one side, giving him a self-satisfied look that made Lillie Jean understand why Gus itched to smack him. The change in the man was remarkable.

"You might find that it's not that easy to find someone to buy half of a run-down property. It's different for me because my ranch is adjacent, and my offer would be quite generous given the circumstances."

"If I say no, your property is still adjacent," Lillie Jean said softly.

Carson Craig's eyebrows lifted.

"I'm not selling 50 percent." Lillie Jean's mama taught

her to roll with the punches, but her grandpa had taught her to throw a few of her own.

"Then we don't have a deal, and you may never be able to rebuild your clothing business."

Lillie Jean managed to keep her expression from shifting. Of course he'd researched her—and even if he hadn't, the Gavin grapevine would have taken care of the matter.

"A chance I'll have to take." She sounded so cool, but inside she was dying. She could take the money so easily—help Kate, help herself. But then there was Gus and Thad to consider, not to mention her dislike of the arrogant man sitting on the other side of the table, fully expecting her to cave under the pressure he was so expertly applying.

"I'm in a position to aid you in your endeavors. I have property in Texas. I know people. People who can have a great effect on one's business dealings."

Lillie Jean sensed he was speaking of both positive *and* negative effects.

She smiled at Carson. "And I know someone who might feel the need to build a nice big pig farm on the boundary fence of your property. I hear that the scent carries."

Carson gave her a frowning look. "Is that a threat?"

Yes. It was.

"I don't like threats," he said as if she'd answered him aloud.

"Neither do I, Mr. Craig." She rose to her feet, shouldering her purse in one smooth motion. "I'm done talking. We will not be doing business."

Again, heads turned as she left the restaurant, but not for the same reason as when she'd arrived. Perhaps she'd spoken that last bit too loudly.

Oh well.

She marched out to her car and started the engine with a blast of exhaust and swung the big car into reverse. Carson Craig was lucky the food hadn't arrived before she left, or he might have been wearing some of it.

No. She did not like threats.

Lillie Jean headed back through town, cruising slowly by Annie Get Your Gun and then pulling to the curb near the Shamrock Pub.

"We're closed." The red-haired woman behind the bar called when Lillie Jean cautiously stuck her head through the door. Lillie Jean couldn't help but wonder if she was the person who'd put the lip prints on Gus's forehead.

"I'm looking for Thad. I'm Lillie Jean." The woman gave a "so what?" shrug. "His ranch partner," Lillie Jean added.

The woman's mouth fell open. "Oh, sorry." She set down the glasses she held. "Upstairs. Just head through the back entrance and take a left. The stairs are right there."

"Thanks."

Lillie Jean crossed the bar and went through the rear doorway, pausing before she started up the stairs. One deep breath and up she went, the hard soles of her flats making an echo as she climbed. When she reached the top she realized that she didn't know which door to knock on, but that problem was solved when the door to her immediate left swung open.

"Lillie Jean." Thad blinked at her in surprise. "I thought Mimi needed something."

"No. It's just me."

Thad stood back and opened the door wider. "Would you like to come inside?"

Lillie Jean drew in another deep breath. "Yes. I would."

Thad's apartment was roomy with two large windows looking over Gavin's main street. Pleasant, but a far cry from his view at the ranch. Yet, he, a ranch guy, had chosen to live in town for most of his life, according to Gus. And her grandfather, who apparently had also been a ranch guy, had chosen to do the same.

"Do you have a housekeeper?" Lillie Jean asked with a gentle smile, hoping to break the tension that had started radiating between them the second Thad opened the door.

"No. I like puttering around."

Indeed he did. The apartment was spotless, the dishes rinsed, the counters wiped clean. The only sign of everyday life was the half-filled coffee cup next to his glasses and a folded back magazine on the end table next to a leather chair.

Thad waved her to the chair close to his and Lillie Jean perched on the edge of the dark brown upholstery while he took a seat. A few silent seconds ticked by and then Lillie Jean dove in.

"You are my business partner, and sometimes, working with Gus, I forget that." Thad gave a nod, and there was something about the shift in his expression when she mentioned Gus that alerted her to the fact that he may have been thinking about the two of them on the ranch. "I need funding to buy my business back. And if I can't buy my business back, then I need funding to start another. I have some money, but not nearly enough."

"Can you take out a loan, using the ranch as collateral?"

Something Lillie Jean had thought about long and hard. "If I have to make loan payments, then I can't hire my friend. Not unless the business takes off immediately." She went on to explain about Katie and talking her into quitting her corporate job and the issues with child care for her twins. "I feel responsible."

"I know that feeling," Thad said softly. Lillie Jean frowned at him, but he offered no explanation.

"I talked to Carson Craig a little while ago."

Thad's reaction was very much like Gus's, except his expression was even more deadly. Gray eyebrows crashed together, but before he could speak, Lillie Jean said, "I'm not doing business with the man. He tried to play me, just like Gus said he would. But, Thad… I'm going to have to start the ball rolling soon. I know I promised you guys time, but *I'm* running out of time."

"You want to go home."

Thad was studying her closely. "I need to go home. Pick up the pieces. I got a nice start here on the ranch. I made sketches, planned a collection of pieces that I think can sell well. But I can't operate from Montana when my clientele are Austin musicians."

"Do you *want* to go home?"

Lillie Jean frowned as Thad repeated the question. Then she understood. "My life would be easier if I went home."

"So would Gus's."

Lillie Jean should have been insulted, but she wasn't. Probably because Thad told the truth.

"I'm not my grandmother," she said softly, meeting Thad's blue gaze. Yes, she could see where her grandmother might have gotten lost in that gaze fifty years ago. "What happened between you and her is not going to happen between Gus and me."

"That's not what I'm seeing."

"You've barely seen us at all."

"I've seen enough to recognize someone who's getting in over his head."

An odd sensation curled through her midsection, part gratification, part red alert.

"Lillie Jean, I very much doubt that Gus is going to want to leave Montana and settle in a nice little Texas town. And by your own admission, you can't run your Texas business from Montana. So where does that leave the two of you?"

On the brink of a situation that could only go downhill.

"I like you, Lillie Jean, and despite what my grandnephew thinks, it's not because I'm…projecting, I think is the word…my feelings for Nita onto you. You're a nice girl. And Gus is my only relative. I don't want to see you hurting one another."

"You're telling me to go home before trouble starts."

"I can make you a loan. Unsecured. It may not be enough to buy back your business, but it'll be enough to get you started again."

Lillie Jean was clutching her hands together so tightly that one of them was going numb. "I—"

"Do the right thing. For both of you."

"Think I might love him," she said as if he hadn't spoken.

"Then don't set up a situation where one of you ends up like me." Thad let out breath that was close to a sigh. "After Lyle and Nita left for Texas—" he swallowed before continuing "—I could barely stand to be on the ranch. More than that, I could barely stand to be with myself." He met Lillie Jean's gaze. "It almost killed me in the beginning. It wasn't until I had a real chance to die out on the trail after a horse accident, that I decided to live. But I left the ranch. It was the only way I could turn my life around."

"I don't see Gus and me being at that point."

"Yet."

Now Lillie Jean sighed. His message was clear. Leave before it got to that point. And she was beginning to see how it could. Right now the thought of leaving ripped at her in such a way that it pretty much told her she had to leave. Before it was too late, as Thad had said.

"If you want to loan me money, I'm not going to argue with you. But if your agricultural loan doesn't pan out, I will sell my half of the ranch."

Thad gave a solemn nod. The situation was what it was, and he was accepting of that.

"However, to avoid Carson Craig–type situations, I'm giving you 5 percent of my share before I sell."

Thad's eyes widened in shock. "Why would you do that?"

"So you can maintain control no matter what." *And to make up for what my grandparents did.* She didn't— couldn't—say that part out loud, but she thought maybe Thad understood. "I made that offer to Carson. To sell 45 percent. He tried to threaten me, so no deal."

"I don't know what to say."

Lillie Jean got to her feet and held out a hand. Thad also rose and took her fingers in his warm, leathery grip. "I'll get with my accountant later today. Send the money to your grandfather's accountant in Texas?"

"Yes." Lillie Jean felt oddly numb as the finality of what she was arranging hit home. "That would perfect."

Gus GLANCED TOWARD Lillie Jean's house as he headed to the barn to rub liniment on Red's sore leg. Henry's face appeared in the window, then disappeared again. Gus didn't know where Lillie Jean had gone that day, but she'd been dressed nicely when she left the house and got into the Cadillac. His best guess was that she was visiting real estate agencies, getting ready in case his loan didn't go through.

Depressing thought.

Red nickered a low greeting as Gus approached with the liniment in one hand, rag in the other. Gus set down his supplies and patted the horse on the neck. Red was glad for the company, but he'd also figured out that a visit meant grain to eat while Gus worked on him.

It didn't take long to treat the leg. He was done before the gelding was even half done with his grain, but he was loath to leave the quiet of the barn. Not that the house wasn't quiet, but it was a different kind of quiet. A lonely quiet, which he'd never noticed before Lillie Jean had showed up on the ranch.

He was beginning to understand why Thad stopped living on the ranch shortly after Gus had graduated high school and headed to college in Vegas. Lonely was more of a state of mind than a set of circumstances. When he let himself back out of the barn, Henry's face once again appeared in the window and Gus decided to rescue the little guy—let him into the main house to spend time with him instead of the two of them rattling around in their respective dwellings. Tomorrow he was heading out again to tackle what was left of the boundary fence on his backup horse, Gabe. The snow was receding, and he'd probably have a shot of reaching the top fence.

Henry's head kept bobbing up in the window as Gus let himself in through the front gate. When he opened the front door of Lillie Jean's house, the little guy was all over him, yipping and giving doggy kisses.

"Yeah. We'll go do guy stuff, but I need to leave a

note." After seeing Lillie Jean when she'd thought she'd lost Henry, he wasn't taking any chances. There was a packet of sticky notes on top of her sketchbook, so Gus crossed the room and wrote a quick note, then peeled off the paper square. Yes, he was tempted to look at her sketchbook. No, he wouldn't do it without an invitation. He had to admit, though, that she'd made the sad old manager's house a lot more cheerful. He particularly liked the kitchen with the yellow walls and blue-and-yellow lemon-print curtains. The colors fit the place and made the old appliances take on a funky character they hadn't had before.

"Come on, Hank. Let's head next door."

He popped the sticky note on the door and headed toward his own house, Henry trotting beside him.

Less than an hour later, Henry raised his head from the bone he'd been gnawing on beneath the table and then Gus heard the Cadillac. Lillie Jean was home. Just knowing she was on the ranch made him feel better. He finished making the entries in his computer bookkeeping program, then closed the laptop lid just as Lillie Jean knocked on the door.

"I got your note." She held up the sticky on one finger.

"You look nice," Gus said, wondering how she'd come up with a dress—unless she'd packed one for her road trip.

She looked down. "This was supposed to be a bathroom shower curtain, but I decided to wear it instead."

"It looks better on you than it would on a shower."

"Thank you." Her expression went serious. "Gus... I'm going home."

The ground seemed to shift beneath him. Yeah, they had things to work out. A lot of things, really, but he wasn't ready to see her leave.

"Did you sell to Carson?" His voice sounded so very normal, when he felt anything but. And the stunning thing was that he was more concerned about Lillie Jean slipping away than having to deal with Carson Craig on a daily basis.

"You were right about him. He's a jerk. So, no."

The fact that he barely registered his near miss spoke volumes. "Lillie Jean—"

She started shaking her head before her name had left his lips. "I have a chance to kick-start my business. Isabella, one of our more famous clients, wants me to outfit her for a tour, and that will help me get started again. Andrew essentially reneged on his contract with her, so she's transferring her business to me."

"You have the means to buy your business back?"

"I'm going to try, but Andrew will file for bankruptcy before I can come up with what I need. He's peeved about Isabella—at least she thinks he is—which means he's not going to cut me any deals."

"Which means starting fresh?"

"With my Isabella contract. Yes." She smiled a little. "It was good being here, on the ranch. I'm stronger. I got a new perspective. I designed part of a new collection."

"And that's all?"

She slowly shook her head. "No," she said quietly. "That's not all. But I need to go, Gus. I need to resolve some issues in my old life before I can move into a new one."

"When?"

"Tomorrow. Early."

He had about a thousand things to say, but words refused to form on his lips. Lillie Jean was running again, but what was she running from this time?

"I'd kiss you goodbye," she said in a voice so low it was hard to hear, "but I don't think it's a good idea."

"Why?"

"Because I might never stop." She took a backward step, her gaze holding his. "Maybe there will be a better time in our lives, Gus. But this isn't it."

CHAPTER SIXTEEN

Gus hated walking by Lillie Jean's house, because every time he did so, he automatically checked to see if Henry's little nose was pressed to the front window. Henry wasn't looking out the window and Lillie Jean wasn't coming down the walk, pulling on her gloves as she got ready to help him with chores.

After she'd driven away two weeks ago, with a promise to text when she stopped for the night, wherever that might be, the ranch had taken on a whole new feel. One that Gus didn't like, one he was certain his uncle Thad understood all too well.

What was it with these Hardaway women?

Grandmother. Granddaughter. They'd both left the ranch feeling empty.

He was mixing fertilizer when he heard the distinctive roar of Thad's old truck. His uncle didn't normally drop by the ranch just because. Either there was a chore to attend to, or he had to pick up or drop off something one of them needed.

Gus pulled the brim of his cap back down and finished filling the tank. By the time he was done, Thad had parked next to Lillie Jean's house. He got out of the truck, wincing a little as his feet hit gravel.

"What?" Gus instantly asked from several yards away.

Thad waited until he got closer before saying, "Got a call from the Ag guy today."

Gus's stomach twisted, but then his uncle broke loose with a wide smile. "Our loan application got approved pending the appraisal, which might take a while, but one step forward."

Gus felt his cheeks creasing into a broad smile as he let out a long breath. "Good to hear."

"And we got to hope against hope that the appraisal matches the amount of money we need. If it doesn't, then we're back where we started."

Like Gus didn't know that. He shoved his thumbs into his front pockets. "Lillie Jean could still sell." She needed the cash and when she left there'd been no renewed promise of her giving them the time they needed to officially nail down the loan. "We could still be dealing with some kind of a jerk partner."

Thad's expression shifted, and again Gus asked, "What?" His uncle looked almost…guilty.

Thad cleared his throat the way he did when he felt self-conscious. "Even if she sells, we'll maintain control."

"Why's that?"

Thad looked over Gus's shoulder toward the house where Lillie Jean had lived until a few weeks ago. "Carson offered to buy her out and she told him she'd only sell 45 percent. The other 5 percent she's giving to me."

Gus's jaw dropped. "Giving?"

"Yeah. Giving. So we can control the decisions made on the property."

Gus sat on the bottom step of the tractor., then shot his uncle a hard look. He was getting tired of secrets. "Why is this the first I'm hearing about this?"

"I thought I'd wait until she was gone to tell you."

Gus tried to tamp down his flaring anger. It wasn't all that easy, but his voice was fairly even as he said, "It's been two weeks. Were you waiting until she was *good* and gone? And what did her being gone have to do with your telling me?"

"I saw you getting twisted up in knots over her. I recognized the symptoms." Thad sent him a speaking look. "She needed to go back home before it was too late. For both your sakes."

"Too late?" Gus gave his uncle an incredulous stare. "I'm a grown man, Thad. I can deal with knots."

"And I'm a protective uncle who's felt those knots." He cleared his throat. "Still kind of feel them."

Gus got back to his feet, clapped a hand on his forehead. "I don't... You..." He muttered a curse under his breath. "How?"

"She came to see me. I think she came to understand just how low I was after losing Nita. And I don't think she wanted to do that to you." Thad shifted his weight. "So I loaned her this year's cow money. It's not enough to do what she wanted to do, but it's seed to get her started."

"You paid her to leave?" Gus paced a couple of steps, then turned back, trying, really trying to keep himself under control.

"No. But she had things she needed to do and, Gus? You were tying her up in knots, too."

"Yeah?" Gus got to his feet. "Well, good. And you know what? I still have a few more knots to tie."

"Don't go doing anything stupid."

Gus rounded on his uncle. "Like avoiding a ranch for thirty years because it had bad feelings? Like never buying out the guy who ran off with your wife?"

"I loved her." Thad ground the words out, his face red.

"Then you'll understand why I'm going to do what I'm about to do."

LILLIE JEAN, KATE and Julie had accomplished a lot in four weeks. Thanks to the loan from Thad, and a healthy deposit from Isabella, she was able to buy what she needed to make the tour garments, colorful retro Western looks that perfectly complemented Isabella's songs and personality. She'd reverted to her old sleep cycle, staying awake long into the night, sewing garments in Kate's tiny basement under a tight schedule before falling asleep on a futon jammed between piles of storage boxes. Only now she also got up early to sew some more. She'd met the impossible deadline and already had a handful of orders and had been able to swing a lease on a workspace. Thank you, Isabella. And Thad.

If things continued as they were, she'd be able to pay back his cow money before he needed it. He'd taken a gamble on her and it'd paid off. The only part of the whole thing that wasn't so great was the part where she missed Gus so very much.

It'd been so hard not to contact him, but the last thing she wanted was to make this separation more difficult than it already was. Hearing his voice…no, she couldn't handle it.

Her new workspace wasn't as large as A Thread in Time, which was now officially defunct, but could eventually become a showroom/store, and there was a small living space upstairs—or there would be once she got it cleaned and painted. It was all rather cozy and Lillie Jean should have been enjoying it more than she was.

She should have been enjoying everything more than she was. But there was this empty space in her heart…

An empty space that Julie addressed one day while she and Lillie Jean watched the twins and Kate took a well-deserved nap.

"Lillie Jean, I know you've taken some hits," Julie said in her soft drawl, "but you're winning again."

Lillie Jean frowned at Julie, wondering what her

point was. Julie reached out and patted Lillie Jean's arm. "Honey, you're down. Further down than you should be after doing what you just did. My goodness. You've outfitted a tour from a dinky little basement sewing room."

Lillie Jean pressed her lips together, stunned to feel a rush of emotion at Julie's empathetic tone. She missed her mother. Missed her grandfather. And she missed Gus.

"I know it stings not to have your old business back. To see Andrew and Whatever-Her-Name-Was stomp the reputation into the ground, but you've got a good start on business number two. And you have us."

"I do. And thank you."

"I should be thanking you," Julie said. "I love what we're doing. Who knew all that sewing I'd done for Kate back in the day would serve me so well?"

Indeed, Julie had been a godsend when it came to the foundation work for the garments, cutting Lillie Jean's time at the machine by at least a third and making it possible for her to meet the deadlines.

Julie smiled a warm motherly smile that shifted toward no-nonsense as she lifted her eyebrows and said, "What's bothering you, Lillie Jean?"

Lillie Jean's eyes went wide. "I...uh..."

"Something to do with the ranch?"

Julie studied Lillie Jean like she was a little girl in trouble for something, making her feel as if she may as well stop hedging. Julie had her "get to the bottom of this" look on her face. "I'm guessing that maybe it's a guy up north. Am I right?"

Lillie Jean hadn't said one word to Kate about Gus except for telling her that he was her type shortly after arriving on the ranch, so she scowled at Julie as if she was speaking nonsense. "It wasn't that long ago that I was engaged to be married."

The scowl didn't work. Nor did her excuse.

"Then he must be something if you fell this hard this fast."

Lillie Jean started shaking her head. This was the last thing she wanted to talk about. She hadn't meant to fall in love with him. Had convinced herself that Thad was right and that they hadn't spent enough time together and that their worlds were two different to mesh effectively. She'd believed they were setting themselves up for a fall.

"Are you in contact?"

"That would be a mistake."

"Why?" Julie ran a comforting hand over Lillie Jean's shoulder, and Lillie Jean flashed back on her own mother doing the same thing. She opened her mouth, meaning to say that they needed to drop the subject, but instead she said, "We never even went on a date. We went to a spaghetti feed, but so did everyone else in town. We just rode in a tractor and talked and fixed fence." She looked down at her hands. Her fingernails were just starting to recover. Despite wearing gloves, ranch work had decimated them. She pointed to the scar on her forehead. "He did this to me."

Julie gasped and Lillie Jean quickly said, "Not on purpose. He was driving and the truck slipped and I wasn't wearing a shoulder harness."

She pressed her lips together tightly as she thought about Gus and how gently he'd dealt with her wound, even though he didn't like her all that much at the time. "He put the adhesive suture on. Did a good job, too."

Julie brushed Lillie Jean's hair away from the scar. "Yeah. I'd say he did. You'll hardly see the mark a year from now."

"There was so much about him I liked."

"But you left."

She let out a breath. "Every time I thought about selling, I'd think of him and how much it would hurt him and..." *It scared me.* "How can I make business decisions with that kind of a mentality?" She turned to Julie. "I want the capital from the ranch to build some security here at home. To grow my business and to buy a house and a car that isn't the size of two cars."

She brought her hands up to massage the back of her neck. "But I don't want to ruin his life. Which made me realize that I was probably in love with him." Just as she'd told Thad. "I'm not ready to be in love."

"So you came back to what's familiar."

"Rather successfully, too." Although her success wasn't making her particularly happy or keeping her warm at night.

"I think you should talk to him."

"To what end? Getting myself back into the same mess I was in with Andrew? Mixed up with another business partner?"

"The situation may be similar, but are the men the same?"

"No." *Not even close.* "But if things don't work out—"

"You sell the ranch."

"And stomp on his dreams."

Julie rubbed Lillie Jean's shoulder, then gave it one last squeeze before dropping her hand. One of the twins toddled closer and started patting Lillie Jean's bare leg with a sticky palm and Lillie Jean pulled the little girl up onto her lap, snuggling her close.

"I think I'll leave things as they are for the time being. Build my business. Focus on things I have half a chance of controlling."

"Whatever you think's best."

"It's best." She hadn't told Julie about Thad and her

grandmother, or the deep sadness in his voice when he'd spoken about Nita and Lyle and how empty the ranch had felt after they'd gone. He'd seemed to think that she was doing the same thing to Gus, even though he hadn't said so in so many words. And he'd seemed to think that it would be better if she'd left sooner rather than later. It'd made sense to leave, but the fact that Gus was no more out of her head than he'd been the day she'd left, feeling as if she was leaving a little part of her soul in Montana, made her wonder if she had done the best thing.

And if she hadn't, what was she going to do about it?

CLEANING THE NEW workplace was a job and a half, the "half" part coming from the mayhem the twins created while Lillie Jean, Kate and Julie scrubbed and washed and repainted. Julie had an evening job at a local drugstore, but she always helped during the day.

"We should strip this floor," Kate said, peeling off a loose flake of paint to show a solid wood plank below. "Whoever painted it should be beaten with a newspaper."

"There might be damage elsewhere you don't know about," Julie said as she measured the window casings.

The mother-daughter banter always made Lillie Jean feel like smiling—and made her even more aware of how much she missed her own mom. What would Janice Ann say about the direction her daughter had taken in her life?

She'd be proud of the business, but would she be proud of the way she'd run away from her feelings? Lillie Jean's mom had never really had a man in her life. She'd done just fine without one. Or so Lillie Jean had assumed.

Had her mom been lonely? Did she have regrets? She paused to lean on the broom she was using, watching Julie and Kate wrangle over whether the windows would look better with blinds or pull-down shades when her phone buzzed.

She took a look, then almost dropped it.

I'm in town.

Why was Gus in town? Lillie Jean shot Julie a suspicious look, then looked back at the phone. Julie didn't work that way. She was the sort who would have told her, "I'm contacting this man for your own good."

Instead of texting back, Lillie Jean stepped out onto the sunny sidewalk and pushed the call icon. A second later Gus answered.

"You're in Texas."

"Yeah. I am." His voice was rougher than she remembered. Or maybe he was as nervous as she was. "Long drive."

"You drove?"

"I needed thinking time."

That was not a good sign. "Did Julie have anything to do with this?" Lillie Jean asked suspiciously, just in case she'd read the woman wrong.

"Who's Julie?"

"Never mind." Lillie Jean's thoughts tumbled over themselves. Gus was in Texas. There could only be one reason for that. The reason she'd been trying to talk herself out of ever since she got back home.

There was a moment of utter silence before he said, "Can we meet?"

"You kind of set things up so that we have to meet, didn't you?"

"Yeah. I did." And he didn't sound one bit repentant about it.

She gave him the address of the shop, then sank down

on one of the wooden benches that flanked the door. Gus was in Texas. She needed to come up with a plan of action—fast—but her brain seemed stalled out on the fact that in a few minutes she was going to see the guy who'd been haunting her dreams. A guy who'd driven all the way to Texas to see her. A guy who—

The thought went unfinished as a dark pickup truck with Montana plates pulled to the curb. Lillie Jean felt a burst of nerves as Gus got out and started toward her like a guy on a mission. Lillie Jean rose to her feet, wondering why he looked more angry than happy to see her.

Instead of saying hello, Gus stopped a few feet away and said, "One person shouldn't make the decisions for two."

Lillie Jean's chin dropped and her eyebrows rose. "Excuse me?"

"I said, one person—" he pointed at her "—shouldn't make decisions for two." He moved his finger back and forth between them. "I'm excluding Thad from the equation, because this should be between just you and me."

"I didn't—"

"Yeah. You did. I know Thad was trying to save me from myself, but, what the hell, Lillie Jean? Did *you* think you were saving me, too?" His voice dropped to something close to a growl. "Because I don't need anyone doing my thinking for me."

It took Lillie Jean a moment to find her voice and say, "I thought I was saving both of us."

"What about communication?"

Good point. Excellent point. But once she'd made her decision to leave, she'd been afraid of being talked out of it, plain and simple. Afraid of the consequences—and that was what she needed to make clear.

She met his eyes, willing him to understand that she

hadn't been trying to hurt him. That she'd chosen the less of two evils. "I was scared, Gus. I wasn't ready to fall in love. I convinced myself that if I didn't see you every day, I'd move on."

"And did you?"

Lillie Jean swallowed. "No." The word hung in the air, but she couldn't think of anything to add.

Gus stared at her, his mouth hard, then he shoved a hand through his hair and shifted his gaze down the street toward the quiet intersection. He held himself so tautly, seemed so uncertain as to his next course of action that an unexpected sense of calm settled over Lillie Jean.

He was angry at being left out of the loop. Angry that she and Thad had made decisions without him. Rightly so. She'd thought she was saving them both. She'd been wrong. But now he was here. In Texas. With her. And it felt utterly right.

She folded her arms over her chest. "Why did you drive down here instead of calling?"

Gus brought his attention back to her, and there was something in his expression that made her breath catch. "Because some conversations need to take place in person."

"Without warning."

"Yeah," he said in a low voice. "Without warning. What would that be like?"

It wasn't hard to follow his meaning. "This is different than when I showed up at the ranch."

"How so?"

Lillie Jean didn't hesitate, even though saying the words aloud took courage. "I didn't go to the ranch because I cared about you."

Gus's eyes narrowed ever so slightly. "You think I came down here because I care?"

His words should have given her a heart attack, but instead they only made her more certain. "Yes. I think you did."

Gus went still, and then, after a long second he asked, "And how do you feel about me?" There was just enough of an edge to his voice to tell her how important her answer was to him.

"I love you."

And there it was. The thing that bound them together. The thing they'd have to work their lives around, because now that he was with her, Lillie Jean wasn't about to let him go. What she hadn't realized was a possibility that morning was now a certainty. She was going to figure out a way to be with this man.

"Lillie Jean…"

For one frozen moment, they faced off, then he reached for her and Lillie Jean went home, wrapping her arms around the man she loved, pressing herself against his solid chest. Beneath her cheek, his heart beat a steady rhythm. One she wanted to hear for the rest of her life.

"I missed you so much," he murmured against her hair. "The ranch wasn't the same after you left."

"That was one of Thad's worries."

Gus leaned back to look down at her. "It didn't matter about the ranch. It was me feeling empty that made me climb into the truck and drive." He gave her a serious look. "That and Thad confessing that he'd kind of eased you on your way."

"It wasn't all Thad. I was scared of my feelings, and it felt like the right thing to do. I thought I was stopping a situation that could hurt us both. And I really did have unfinished business down here."

"Are things settled now?"

"The important things."

Gus stepped back and let his hands slide down Lillie Jean's arms until they reached her fingers, which he laced with his own. "Are you still afraid of being in love?"

"I think this is the first time I've ever been in love, Gus. I've never felt anything like this before."

He brought his forehead down to lightly touch hers. "I love you, too, Lillie Jean. It happened fast. I wasn't expecting it, but I do."

She rose up on her toes to meet his lips in a kiss that seemed as much a healing of the past as it was a promise for the future. When she let her heels touch the ground again, she stroked the side of his face, loving the rough feel of the scruff beneath her palms, and said, "Come on inside. There are some people I want you to meet."

Six months later.

DUE TO THE WONDER of digital communication and overnight delivery, Lillie Jean Designs was taking off in a big way in little Serenity, Texas, while the designer lived sixteen hundred miles away on a cattle ranch that no longer felt as if its heart was missing. A heart Gus never knew existed until the night he'd come upon the old Cadillac stuck in the mud, and now couldn't imagine living without.

The beauty part was that he didn't have to. Lillie Jean Hardaway had agreed to become his wife in the spring. They'd chosen the date she'd arrived on the ranch for their wedding day, and Gus couldn't be happier.

Thad was getting used to the idea. It probably wasn't easy on him, having a full-time reminder of his lost wife, but Lillie Jean wasn't Nita, and Thad didn't live on the ranch. They'd be okay. And Thad had taken an interest in Lillie Jean's business partner, Julie, when she and

Kate and the twins had come to visit during the summer. He'd done the tour guide thing, and then he and Julie had slipped away for a quiet dinner the night before she was due to fly back to Texas.

Was a long-distance romance a-brewing?

He had no idea…but he was hopeful. And in the meantime, he had a romance of his own to maintain.

Lillie Jean came out of her house, pulling on her gloves, and Henry pressed his little nose against the window. She smiled as she saw him waiting for her near the gate.

"You're late."

"Finishing a sketch and I lost track of time." They walked to the idling tractor and Lillie Jean climbed the steps first because it was her turn to drive.

"Are you still going to help me cut the silk this afternoon?" she asked.

"I'm a man of my word." He was also a man who'd learned a great deal about fabric—like the fact that silk was hard to handle and cutting involved a labor-intensive process of laying out tissue paper and cutting a single piece at a time.

"Yeah, I know." She sent him a cheeky smile as she reached for the gearshift. "That's why I love you."

"Lillie Jean?"

She glanced his way, and he placed a gloved hand lightly on her cheek, holding her steady as he leaned in to kiss her lips. Then he smiled at her and settled back in his seat as Lillie Jean put the tractor in gear.

* * * * *

MILLS & BOON

Coming next month

THEIR CHRISTMAS MIRACLE
Barbara Wallace

'Can I get you lads something to drink?'

Thomas's breath caught. It happened every so often. He'd catch the hint of an inflection or the turn of the head, and his mind would trip up. This time, it was the waitress's sharp northern twang that sounded uncannily familiar. He looked up, expecting reality to slap him back to his senses the way it had with his cottage memories. Instead...

He dropped the phone.

What the...?

His eyes darted to Linus. His brother's pale expression mirrored how Thomas felt. Mouth agape, eyes wide. If Thomas had gone mad, then his brother had plunged down the rabbit hole with him. And, mad he had to be, he thought, looking back at the waitress.

How else to explain why he was staring at the face of his dead wife?

'Rosie?' The word came out a hoarse whisper; he could barely speak. Six months. Praying and searching. Mourning.

It couldn't be her.

Who else would have those brown eyes? Dark and rich, like liquid gemstones. Bee-stung lips. And there was the scar on the bridge of her nose. The one she always hated, and that he loved because it connected the smattering of freckles.

How….? When? A million questions swirled in his head, none of which mattered. Not when a miracle was standing in front of him.

'Rosie,' he said, wrapping her in his arms.

He moved to pull her closer, only for her to push him away.

He found himself staring into eyes full of confusion.

'Do I know you?' she asked.

Continue reading
THEIR CHRISTMAS MIRACLE
Barbara Wallace

Available next month
www.millsandboon.co.uk

COMING SOON!

We really hope you enjoyed reading this book. If you're looking for more romance, be sure to head to the shops when new books are available on

Thursday
1st November

To see which titles are coming soon, please visit
millsandboon.co.uk

MILLS & BOON

LET'S TALK
Romance

For exclusive extracts, competitions
and special offers, find us online:

f facebook.com/millsandboon

⟲ @millsandboonuk

🐦 @millsandboon

Or get in touch on 0844 844 1351*

For all the latest titles coming soon, visit
millsandboon.co.uk/nextmonth

Jeannie Watt lives in the Mason Valley on a seven-hundred-acre cattle ranch and hay farm, which she shares with her husband, her parents and many animals. Jeannie taught junior high school for about a hundred years and recently retired. When she's not writing or feeding animals, she enjoys sewing, knitting, running, making mosaic mirrors and reading.

Also by Jeannie Watt

Discover more at millsandboon.co.uk